Emily pressed herself even closer to him, wanting to be ever nearer and nearer. Wanting she knew not what. But her sudden movement sent him off balance, and he stumbled backward into the bank of potted palms.

She landed hard on top of him, and the impact, along with the crash of plants to the floor, shocked her awake. It was like a cold rain suddenly falling over her head.

"Your Grace?" someone said in a hushed, shocked voice.

Emily, still lying prone on Nicholas's chest, peered up through the loosened skein of her hair. At least ten people stared back.

This was a nightmare. It simply had to be. It couldn't be real, couldn't be happening to *her*. Not to the Ice Princess, the most proper lady in all London.

Nicholas lifted her off and rose to his feet in one smooth movement. He held on to her hand and kept her firmly by his side.

"I am sorry to disrupt the ball. Lady Emily and I were going to announce our betrothal at a small family dinner, but I see we should do so now. Lady Emily has made me the happiest man in England by agreeing to be my wife."

There would be no escape for either of them. Not now.

* * *

The Shy Duchess
Harlequin® Historical #1032—March 2011

The Shy Duchess

AMANDA McCABE

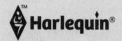

TORONTO NEW YORK LONDON
AMSTERDAM PARIS SYDNEY HAMBURG
STOCKHOLM ATHENS TOKYO MILAN MADRID
PRAGUE WARSAW BUDAPEST AUCKLAND

Recycling programs
for this product may
not exist in your area.

ISBN-13: 978-0-373-29632-3

THE SHY DUCHESS

Copyright © 2010 by Ammanda McCabe

First North American Publication 2011

Many thanks to two of my best "writing friends",
Deb Marlowe and Diane Gaston,
for creating the Fitzmanning family with me!
It's been such a wonderful, fun journey.

Chapter One

Lady Emily Carroll wished with all her might that the polished parquet floor beneath her satin slippers would open up and pull her down into the fiery pits of hell.

It would be far preferable to Lady Orman's ball.

Emily hid behind a bank of towering potted palms, the silk-papered wall at her back as she peered between the green fronds at the crowd. Lady Orman's rout was *the* invitation of the Season. Everyone who was anyone at all—and a few nobodies who managed to slip by the footmen—was gathered in the sparkling ballroom. Thousands of candles cast their light over the sheen of fine silk, the glitter of sapphires and rubies, and the snap of lace fans.

It was quite the "dreadful crush" that every London hostess longed for. The dance floor was swirling with the patterns of a country dance, while thickets of people packed around its edges to laugh and chatter and stare. Their voices blurred into a high-pitched, echoing cacophony where no words could be made out at all.

Not that it mattered, Emily thought. No one came to

such a gathering for rational conversation. They came to be seen, to have everyone know they were important enough to be invited to Lady Orman's ball. They paid a great deal of money to the modiste and the hairdresser in order to pack themselves into a ballroom like a tight row of salted fish. To have their hems trod on, their ringlets wilted in the heat, their throats made raw from shouting at one another.

And for what? For the dubious pleasure of having their names in the papers? "Mr and Mrs Whos-it were seen attending Lady Orman's ball…"

Emily sighed. There were surely many more useful, not to say more pleasant, things to do with one's time. But her parents and her brother Robert seemed to enjoy it.

She stood on tiptoe, peering through the palms to see her brother dancing with his new wife, Amy. They were laughing as they spun around, their faces alight with pleasure. Well, Amy did love society; she was good at being sociable, and that was all the better for Rob's fledgling political career. They were surely well matched, even if Amy's ancient-named family had not much money.

That was what Emily's parents, the Earl and Countess of Moreby, said anyway. Amy's family name, as old as their own, and her outgoing personality were fine assets, and a good excuse for letting Rob marry where he chose.

Besides, they would add, with sidelong glances at Emily herself, *Emily will make our fortune. She is bound to marry very well!*

Except that Emily had been a terrible disappointment to them thus far. She had not come close to marrying a title or a fortune. Or marrying anyone at all. And now the Season was almost over.

She instinctively raised her hand to nervously chew at her thumbnail, before she remembered she wore silk gloves. Her hand fell back to her side, tucked into the folds of her silver-embroidered white silk skirts. When, oh, when would that floor open up already?

The whole evening, the noise, the heat, the smell of melting candles and a hundred perfumes, bore down on her like an anvil. Soon, she would have to leave her little palmy sanctuary and join her parents. They would want to find her a partner for the next dance. That was what she did at every ball, let them match her up with rich lords—both young, spotty ones and old, portly ones— let them extol her beauty and goodness while she stood there with her cheeks on fire.

It was the least she could do, after she disappointed them so greatly last summer. They had gone to the house party at the notorious Welbourne Manor with the intention of matching up Emily with the new Duke of Manning, Nicholas.

Oh, they did not say so explicitly, of course, but it was obvious in their nervous preparations for the party. In all their words to her about how handsome Nicholas was, how great a friend his father had been to the Carrolls.

And she not only had been unable to attach the duke, she had scarcely been able to talk to him. She was always shy around men, of course, but there was something about *him* that terrified her. He was always most kind and polite, yet every time she looked into his beautiful sky-blue eyes her throat closed, and she felt that ridiculous burning blush spread over her whole body.

And then she saw his affable smile turn puzzled, and

felt him withdraw from her. That was a relief of sorts. He and his family were so very exuberant, so full of fun and frivolity, while she was so quiet and serious. They would not be a good match at all, if only her parents could see that! Such a mouse as her would never fit into such a dashing family, and it was better not to even try.

Since that house party and Rob's marriage that autumn, her parents' matchmaking efforts had taken on a desperate edge, even as paintings and ornaments began disappearing from their house.

"She is so very beautiful!" Emily overheard her mother wail one day. "Quite ten times prettier than any other young lady this Season. Why can she not bring us a single suitable offer?"

"There was Mr Browning," her father tentatively suggested.

"A *merchant*." Her mother sniffed. "With seven children."

"He is a wealthy man," her father said.

"Surely we are not in such straitened circumstances that we must bestow our daughter on a tradesman."

"Not yet," her father muttered, as Emily fled in order to not hear any more. The fact that Mr Browning was in trade did not bother her, but the seven children rather did. Plus he was twenty years older than her, and had such sweaty, grasping hands.

Unlike Nicholas, whose long, elegant fingers had clasped hers once to help her into a carriage. Yet they were both such unsuitable men for her, in their own ways. And surely her parents would not force her to marry someone she didn't care for, if they knew what had happened with Mr Lofton that time....

"I don't mean to be a disappointment," she whispered. If not for her wretched shyness, the way her mind went all blank and her throat closed up whenever she met a stranger...

"I say, the quality of the gatherings this Season have been very poor indeed," a man said, close enough to her hiding place that she could hear the actual words and not just an indistinct hum.

"I agree," his companion said in a bored drawl. "Lady Orman could once be relied upon to host only the cream of the *ton*. Now she seems to let in anyone at all."

Emily peered past the green fronds again to see Lord Barrington and Mr Fraser, two thoroughly useless dandies. She had once endured a dance with Lord Barrington, as he prattled on to her about a new way to tie a cravat or some such thing. She had no desire to listen to his gossip now, but she could see no way to slip past them. She was trapped.

"If this continues, I shall have to go see if there are more quality amusements to be had in Brighton," said Mr Fraser. "Or even abroad. Even the wine tonight is most insipid."

"I stood over there and watched the ladies pass by for an hour," Lord Barrington said, gesturing toward one of the walls with his quizzing glass. "I counted only ten that were tolerable, and only two who were truly pretty."

"Oh? Who were they, then?"

"Mrs Featherstone and Viscountess Granton," said Lord Barrington, mentioning Amy.

"True, none can match Lady Granton for beauty. She is quite the Toast. But what of her sister-in-law, Lady Emily Carroll? She is reckoned to be mightily pretty at my club."

Lord Barrington gave a contemptuous snort. "She is undoubtedly pretty, with that pale hair and white skin.

But a veritable icicle. She can't seem to bring herself to say three words to anyone, just stares at you with those cold, dismissive green eyes. At *my* club, she is called the Ice Princess, and we wager on which poor, desperate fool will marry her by the end of the Season. The winner thus far is Mr Rayburn. Undoubtedly, the marriage bed will mean the freezing off of his…"

Whatever crude word he was going to say dissolved into their snickers. Emily pressed her hands to her face, wishing more than ever that the floor would swallow her and she could vanish! She didn't feel like an "ice princess" in the least. Indeed, she felt as if her whole body was on fire with shame.

She longed to cry, to curl up and disappear, never to come to a hateful ball again.

But she was not a Carroll for nothing. Her family might not be wealthy any longer, but they certainly had a long, proud history. They had faced the Tower under Henry VIII, poverty during the Civil War, riotous parties with Charles II, and her own grandfather, a terrible gambler who had to flee to France twice to avoid creditors and angry husbands. Two giggling fops could not best her, even as she ached with embarrassment.

Emily smoothed her skirts, tucked her silvery hair back into its beaded bandeau, and stiffened her shoulders. There was nothing she could do about the hot colour in her cheeks, but she held her head high as she swept out from her hiding place and past the two men.

She might have laughed about the astonished looks on their faces, if she hadn't been so determined to get away.

Through that sheer determination, she made her way through the press of the crowd, avoiding her mother as she hurried out the double doors into the anteroom.

There were still people there, drinking the "insipid" wine, but they paid her no attention as she hurried into the corridor.

Emily drew in a shaky breath, rubbing hard at her hot cheeks. Now that it was a bit quieter, her nerves not so jangled, she knew she had to get away, even if only for a moment. She needed to be alone, to breathe some fresh air.

Not sure where exactly she was going, she dashed down the curving staircase. When they arrived at the ball, that sweep of marble and gilt was packed tightly with revellers, waiting their turn to enter the ballroom, calling out greetings to each other and loudly admiring one another's attire. Now, it was blessedly deserted; the candles sputtered low to cast dim, shifting shadows on the walls.

Gradually, the cacophony of the party faded, and Emily could hear only the whisper of her slippers on marble as she ran down the stairs. The swish of her skirt. The pounding of her heart.

So intent was she on escape that she didn't see the man at the foot of the stairs until his silhouette suddenly shifted on the white wall. Startled by the movement, Emily lost her footing on the bottom step. Her stomach lurched as her feet slid out from under her, ripping her hem and pitching her towards the cold stone floor.

She cried out, flinging her hands in front of her to catch herself. But she didn't collide with painful, unyielding stone.

She fell against a warm, well-muscled chest, arms wrapping around her to lift her up safely into the air. Shocked, Emily clung to her rescuer's shoulders, her heart racing.

"Lady Emily!" he said, his voice deep, roughly out of breath. "Are you hurt?"

She stared down at him in the fading light, the red-orange glow playing over his golden hair, the lean, elegant angles of his sharp cheekbones and knife-blade nose. His blue eyes, those eyes she remembered so well from last summer, were narrowed with concern.

Nicholas, the Duke of Manning. *Of course.* He did always seem to see her at her worst.

And being pressed so very close to him, alone in that half-light, had her far more flustered and frightened than any mean-spirited gossip. He smelled so delightful, of lemony cologne and clean starch, a faint tang of sweet smoke, as if he had sneaked away for a cigar. And how strong he was, she thought irrationally. He held her up as if she weighed no more than a snowflake—or an icicle.

Did *he* think her an icicle, too? A cold, unfeeling princess? That seemed to be the general consensus, and surely in his voluble family she would seem so even more.

That shouldn't make her feel sad, yet it did.

"I am quite unhurt," she managed to murmur. "Thanks to you, your Grace."

He smiled up at her, a bright, merry grin that reminded her of that house party. Of his laughing, teasing, romping family, and how she so wanted to be a part of all that fun. She just didn't know how, and she probably never would.

"Well, that's my duty at these routs, you know," he said. "To stand about waiting to rescue fair damsels in distress."

"You're very good at it, I'm sure," Emily said. What damsel wouldn't dream of being rescued by him? If she was a different sort of female, she surely would. He was handsome and charming and Very Ducal. And such a man would never be interested in an awkward lady like herself.

"You can put me down now, your Grace," she whispered.

Nicholas glanced down, seeming surprised to find that he still held her close to him, suspended in his arms as if he held her above the mundane, everyday world. Slowly, he lowered her to her feet, her body sliding along his. The sensation of that strange, delicious friction of silk against wool made her sway dizzily, her head spinning.

"You *are* hurt," he said, his voice concerned. "Here, sit down on this step, Lady Emily. Did you turn your ankle?"

Emily let him help her sit down on the marble she had just slipped from, smiling at him weakly. "Oh, no. It was just the heat in the ballroom...."

"Wretched, isn't it?" he said, sitting down beside her as if he had all the time in the world. "I nearly fainted myself."

She almost laughed aloud. Surely he had never fainted in his life! He glowed with robust good health and vibrant energy, as if he could conquer all the world and still have strength for a dance and to rescue a maiden or two.

"It's quite irrational how these hostesses cram so many people into their ballrooms," he said. "One can scarcely even move, let alone have a good conversation with friends."

"If you can even find your friends at all."

"Exactly so," he agreed. "At routs such as this, I'm sure I know scarcely a quarter of the guests."

"Well, I'm sure they all know *you*," Emily said.

He gave her a quizzical glance. "How on earth could they? I haven't even met half of them."

Emily laughed. Somehow, sitting beside him in the quiet and the shadows, just the two of them, she didn't feel so paralysed with shyness. Those gossiping men mattered not at all. "Everyone knows a duke. Or at least they know *of* you, and in a world where gossip races around so quickly they think it's the same thing."

Nicholas laughed, too, a surprised chuckle. "I think you are quite right, Lady Emily. People do seem far more interested in me since my father died."

From under the veil of her lashes, Emily studied the way the candlelight cast his handsome face in intriguing, shadowed angles. The hair that fell over his brow in unruly waves gleamed like an ancient gold coin. "Oh, I'm sure they were interested in you long before that," she murmured.

"I beg your pardon, Lady Emily?"

"I said—why do you attend these balls, your Grace? Surely one of the advantages of being a duke should be doing what one pleases." Unlike being an earl's daughter, who could *never* do what she pleased. Unless it was in secret.

"I'm afraid being a duke means doing a great many things one would rather not," he said, as if he read her unspoken thoughts. "There are so many expectations, obligations."

"Including dancing at crowded London balls?"

He gave a comical sigh. "Sadly, yes, Lady Emily. I fear it was one of the duties my father failed to tell me about."

It seemed to Emily the last duke had not been very *dutiful* at all, or he would not have eloped with the married Lady Linwall all those years ago! But Nicholas seemed different indeed from his father and stepmother. He wanted to do his duty the best he could—just as she did. But sometimes it was so, so hard.

Emily gave him a tentative smile. "I fear you are failing in your task then, your Grace."

"Am I indeed?"

"Yes. For you are not dancing at all, but sitting here talking to me."

"So I am," he said, laughing. "And believe me, Lady Emily, it is a far more pleasant party for it. I would much rather sit somewhere in quiet conversation than be crowded into an overheated ballroom with a lot of strangers."

"Me, too. Balls are…" *Hateful things.* "Most inconvenient."

"But a necessary evil for people such as us, you were quite right about that, Lady Emily." He rose to his feet, offering his hand to help her rise.

Emily hesitated for a moment as she studied that hand, remembering the strange, wondrous sensation of being held by him. She slowly slipped her hand into his. His fingers closed over hers, just as warm and strong as before, and she had the wild wish that they could just stand there for the rest of the night.

But they could not, of course. His touch slid away from hers. "Since I must dance, Lady Emily, would you favour me with the next set?"

"I…" Oh, how her parents would love that. Their daughter dancing with the Duke of Manning for everyone to see. But her legs still felt none too steady, and she feared that rather than inciting envy at her handsome partner and graceful movements, she would fall again and make a fool of herself.

And the last thing she wanted was for him to think her a fool. He and his family surely already thought that after last summer's party.

"I think I need to find the ladies' withdrawing room, your Grace," she said. "I seem to have torn my hem when I tripped."

He smiled at her, and bowed politely. "It is my loss, then. Perhaps we can dance at the next ball."

And perhaps cows would take wing and fly around Berkeley Square. "That would be most pleasant."

"Shall I escort you to—?"

"Oh, no," Emily said quickly. "No, I'm sure our hostess will be wondering where you are. I am quite well now, your Grace, thanks to your gallant rescue."

"I hope the rest of your evening is less perilous, Lady Emily."

Emily bobbed a hasty curtsy, and hurried away across the foyer. She knew not what direction she was going, or where. She just had to be away from him, from the way he made her head spin so confusingly, in order to think clearly again.

But she felt the warmth of his stare on the back of her neck as he watched her go.

Chapter Two

"What a charming party last night!" Emily's mother said as she buttered her breakfast toast.

"Mmm," Emily murmured. That was really all the response her mother ever required to her morning chatter. Fortunately so, for Emily didn't care for mornings—especially when she was already preoccupied with other matters.

"Lady Orman is such a fine hostess," her mother went on. "And Robert and Amy were so admired, of course. I'm sure next year they will have their own household and can give such soirées themselves. That is so essential in building a political career."

"Yes, indeed," said Emily. She was sure Rob and his wife would be most happy to get out of their parents' house, to escape. It would be wonderful beyond words to have one's own home, a place of quiet serenity and cosy little nooks for reading and thinking in peace.

Emily almost laughed aloud at her own silliness. Rob's house would never be in the least serene—he and Amy liked noise and action and parties. Emily dreamed of her own house, a place where she could order things to her own liking and be truly comfortable at last. She might as well dream of going to live on the moon. She couldn't afford even the tiniest cottage in the most obscure corner of the country, and even if she could her parents would never let her leave. Her only escape would be to marry. And that seemed distant as well.

Ever since childhood she had dreamed of a place where she could be useful, where she was needed. She dreamed of children, a home. She was still searching for that, but she was sure one day she would find it. Or at least she hoped she would. It would be the best thing for all.

Emily sipped at her tea, and remembered the terrible event that had led her to this place. She had always been shy as a child, and her mother had long urged her to open up, to make friends. Emily herself longed for friends, but knowing what to say to new people was never easy. Until she made her début in London and met a certain Mr Lofton, a handsome young man who seemed to like her very much. Too much, as it turned out. She agreed to walk with him in the garden at a ball one night, and he grabbed her and attempted to force his kiss on her.

In her revulsion, she trod hard on his foot and kicked him on the leg, making her escape as he howled with pain. "Teasing whore!" he called after her as she fled in tears. And thereafter he never talked to her again, though she never forgot the terrible smothering feeling of his kiss. If that was what came of letting her guard down, she would never do it again. She retreated into herself, and did not tell her parents or brother what had happened. She only wanted to forget it.

But sometimes, like now, the memory haunted her once again.

Her mother, who noticed none of Emily's inner turmoil, gave a deep sigh, setting the ribbons on her cap to fluttering. "But they must have a *proper* house, of course! One large enough for entertaining. One like Devonshire House or Manning House, really. If only they had someone to help them as they deserve."

Someone like the Duke of Manning, owner of that grand Manning House? Emily reached for her teacup with a sigh of her own, thinking of the look in his eyes when she refused to dance with him. So puzzled. Ladies surely seldom refused a duke, especially a young, handsome one. Yet how could she tell him of her awkwardness on the dance floor? She felt so silly when she thought of it all.

"Yes, Mama," she said.

Her mother shot her a sharp glance over the toast rack. "You did not dance last night, Emily."

Emily glimpsed the ragged edge of her thumbnail on the cup's gilded handle, and she quickly tucked in her fist to hide it. "One must be invited to dance first, Mama."

"I cannot believe you received not one single invitation! You are by far the loveliest girl this Season."

"Beauty is in the eye of the beholder, Mama."

Her mother snorted. "I may be your mother and thus biased, but I am not the only one who sees your beauty. You simply do not use it to its full advantage! If you would smile once in a while when a gentleman speaks to you, show a bit of encouragement. When I was your age I had at least ten offers, and I was not half so pretty."

"And you chose Papa?"

"He was an earl." Her voice turned wistful, as if she

was caught up in old memories. "And very handsome, too, back then. I did not know…"

Emily knew what her mother's younger self could not, that long line of feckless Carrolls who had frittered away the family fortune until there was only an old title. It merely went to show that name, title and handsome face didn't always equal a suitable match. That men could be so deceptive, just like Mr Lofton was. But her mother couldn't apply that hard-earned lesson to her own daughter now.

"I suppose there is Mr Rayburn," her mother said dourly. "He is always very attentive to you."

That was true. Mr George Rayburn *was* attentive whenever they met at parties or in the park, and he was handsome enough with his black hair and bright blue eyes, his slim figure and broad shoulders. But there was something in those fine eyes Emily did not quite trust when he looked at her, something not quite true in his smile when he kissed her hand and paid her compliments. She was probably just being foolish. All the other ladies seemed to like him very much. "I thought you did not like Mr Rayburn, Mama. He has no title."

"True enough, but he does have a fortune, or so everyone says. At this point we cannot afford to be too choosy, my dear." Her mother shook her head sadly at the prospect. "Well, there is one more grand ball left this Season, Lady Arnold's soirée. It is the last chance before everyone dashes off to the country. I insist you dance at least three times there, Emily."

"Mama!"

"Yes, at least three. And I will hear no excuses. This is our last chance, do you hear me? Our last chance."

Before Emily could answer these gloomy words, the butler mercifully arrived in the breakfast room with the morning post on his tray. Her mother seldom showed such desperation outwardly, with harsh words and eyes glittering with unshed tears. It made Emily's stomach hurt to think she had been such a disappointment, that she could not help them. She couldn't even help herself.

"There is a message for you from Miss Thornton, Lady Emily," the butler said, handing her a note on pale pink stationery.

"Oh, wonderful!" Emily cried happily. She eagerly tore open the missive as her mother separated invitations from the bills. The stack of bills was always so much higher these days.

Jane Thornton was the one good friend Emily had made in London for the Season. The youngest of three daughters of a baronet, Jane was lively and fun. She could always draw Emily out of her shell and make her laugh, both at the follies of society and at her own serious ways. Jane had been gone for a fortnight, attending on a sick aunt, and Emily had missed her. Parties were no fun at all without her company.

But now it seemed Jane had returned, and was eager to hear all about the Orman ball. What little Emily could tell her, anyway, from what she observed behind her palm tree. She definitely would not tell Jane about falling into the Duke of Manning!

"Miss Thornton wants me to go driving with her in the park this afternoon, Mama," Emily said. "May I go? I don't think we have any other engagements today."

"Yes, yes, of course," her mother said impatiently with a wave of her hand. She seemed quite distracted by her letters, which was a good thing. She usually didn't like Emily spending too much time with Jane, since the Thornton girls needed to find matches as well.

Emily took a deep breath and carefully added, "And may I go out this morning? I should visit the shops and find some new ribbon for my gown for Lady Arnold's ball."

"Certainly. Just don't pay too much for it. The cost of ribbons has become quite shocking."

"Of course not. I am always very careful about ribbon." Emily hastily finished her tea and hurried from the breakfast room before her mother could recollect some reason to keep her at home. Or worse, decide to go with her to the shops.

Emily had very important work to do that morning, and her mother could absolutely have not a hint of it.

Emily hurried down the street, dodging around the thick crowds intent on their own business, too lost in her thoughts to notice her maid Mary, who scurried to keep up, or the displays in the shop windows. The feathered and flowered hats, the bolts of rich silks and delicate muslins, held no interest for her.

She was late, and that would never do. If only Amy hadn't waylaid her as she headed to the door, intent on going over every detail of last night's ball! It was nearly impossible to get away from her sister-in-law once she settled in for a coze. And Emily could hardly tell Amy and her mother why she was in such a rush to be gone.

She turned away from the busy thoroughfare, down a quieter side street. The lane was much narrower here, the cobblestones shadowed by the close-built buildings. There were no bright shop windows, only discreet little signs by dark-painted doors announcing attorneys and employment agencies. All quite respectable, but not an area her mother would want her to frequent or even know about. To Lady Moreby, London began and ended with the fine neighborhoods of the *ton*.

With Mary close behind her, Emily turned again, to an even quieter little square. No one was around at all, except for a maidservant sweeping one stone entryway.

It was this dwelling that was Emily's destination. "Good morning, Nell," she said. "How is everyone today?"

Nell gave her a wide smile of welcome beneath her mobcap. "Good morning, Miss Carroll! All is well enough here, as always. A new girl arrived yesterday. She'll be a new pupil for you soon enough."

Emily laughed. "Excellent! I do like security for my position. I should hate to think I wasn't needed here any longer."

"Oh, that will never happen, miss! You'll always have pupils here. Everyone looks forward to Tuesdays, just to see you."

Emily couldn't help but smile as a warm, sweet feeling took hold of her and spread to her very fingertips and toes. After the tension of the ball and the cold weight of her mother's disappointment, she could feel herself finally relax. Here, she could be herself, just Miss Carroll, and be accepted for it. Needed.

"I love Tuesdays as well," she said. "Is Mrs Goddard about?"

"In the office, miss. She's expecting you."

Emily left Nell to finish her task and stepped through the doorway. It was a dwelling just like the others on the street, tall and narrow, red brick with plain windows curtained in heavy dark velvet. Next to the glossy black door, a polished brass plaque read "Mrs Goddard's School For Disadvantaged Females".

The sign did *not* say the "disadvantaged females" were former prostitutes seeking a new, respectable life within these quiet walls. Or that one of the school's teachers was Lady Emily Carroll, plain Miss Carroll, as she was known here. It would be quite ruinous if anyone ever found out her association with women of low morals.

It was her secret alone, and sometimes this work was her one truly bright, worthwhile moment all week. These women needed her—and she needed them. It was only there that she knew she was useful, where she could indulge her desire to help people.

She paused next to a looking glass in the small foyer to remove her bonnet and tidy her hair. The fine, pale strands always slipped from their pins, making her look more schoolgirl than teacher. She smoothed them back and scrubbed at a smudge on her cheek, barely noticing the curve of her dimpled chin or the wide green eyes that sometimes were the *only* things anyone noticed.

Emily paused to stare into those eyes, bright with exercise and the excitement of her Tuesdays. Her parents had always considered her—and their—best asset to be her prettiness. They had told her that since she was very young. She knew better than to put all her hopes on something so ephemeral and empty. Looks would pass soon enough, and while they were here it wasn't enough to gain her family what they wanted—a ducal son-in-law.

But what could she do except marry? How could she even begin to find out who she was, really, deep down inside? She was always lost and sad, seeking love and approval, a purpose to her life—until she was fourteen years old, and Miss Morris became her governess.

Emily had never known anyone like Miss Morris

before. The young governess was so lively, so passionate about learning, and people and the world. She'd made Emily feel passionate about them, too, had made her see the world and herself through new eyes. She was surely not just shy, mousy, pretty Lady Emily Carroll—she was herself, smart and loyal, with a great deal of love in her heart and a lot to offer.

Miss Morris took her on nature walks in the country, teaching her about the world around them, rocks, flowers, trees. In London, she took Emily on educational walks of a different sort. She took her out of Mayfair and into the poorer streets, showed her the true desperation and sadness, and taught Emily how she could use her assets to help others.

It was a great revelation, and Emily had never completely despaired of herself after that. Perhaps she did not have the lively wit society valued, the flirtatious wiles to attract men, but she did have other things to offer. And she would never settle for less than a life—and a husband—of serious purpose and calm steadiness. The Duke of Manning was surely not that.

"Emily! There you are, my dear," a voice called, pulling Emily out of her daydreams.

She turned to see Miss Morris, now Mrs Goddard, standing in the office doorway. Though the white cap on her brown curls and her grey silk dress were plain and austere, her dark eyes were bright with laughter, her lips creased in a smile.

"I'm so sorry to be late," Emily said, hurrying to kiss Mrs Goddard's pink cheek. To see her was always so wonderful, like seeing her second mother. "My sister-in-law wanted to talk, and—"

"Quite all right, my dear. I know how hard it can be to get away. Liza has got the girls started on today's lesson." Mrs Goddard led her up the stairs to the first floor, where all the classrooms lay. The women who came here seeking a new life under Mrs Goddard's charity were given lessons of all sorts, beginning with reading, writing and simple sums. They moved on to deportment, sewing, cooking, elocution, whatever might help them find a new, respectable livelihood. They also lived in the house, in rooms on the second and third floors.

When Emily first came to help her former governess last year, she taught reading and a little sewing. Now she taught some French and fine embroidery to girls more advanced in their lessons who wanted to be ladies' maids and milliners. To help them in even such small ways, to see them find a new way in the world, made her concerns about not becoming a duchess seem silly indeed! These women lived with the terror she felt when Mr Lofton tried to kiss her in the garden every day, only on a far worse scale than she could ever imagine. The women needed her help, and she was never happier than when she was here being useful.

"*Bonjour*, Mademoiselle Carroll!" her pupils called when she stepped into the classroom. A row of young ladies in fine black gowns turned to her with smiles of welcome.

Emily laughed happily. Maybe she disappointed at home, but not here. "*Bonjour, mesdemoiselles! Comment allez-vous aujourd-hui?*"

Chapter Three

"It's about time you got home. I've been waiting an age."

Nicholas had barely stepped into his library at Manning House, the afternoon post and various messages from his estate managers in hand, when he was brought up short by his brother Stephen's words. Stephen lounged in an armchair by the fire, a snifter of brandy in his hand and the newspapers open on his lap and scattered across the floor.

"I see you've had no trouble passing the time, though," Nicholas said. "I just got that case of brandy from the wine merchant."

"And excellent stuff it is, too," Stephen said with a laugh. He tossed off the last of his drink and sighed happily. "You always do have the best brandy, Nick, and the best chef, too. I had luncheon earlier, it was superb. I should visit you in town more often."

"You come often enough as it is," Nicholas said. He tried to sound grumpy about the unexpected invasion of his life and wine cellar, but in truth he was glad to see his brother. He was always glad to see any of his family. Life in town could be a lonely, dull affair, and their affectionate jokes and banter, their exuberant pranks, always kept that coldness away. With them, he did not have to think so very much. He did not have to remember. He could just be Nicholas, living in the here and now.

But they were all very busy of late. Stephen had inherited their mother's estate at Fincote Park, where she had retired in quiet sadness after their father, the duke, eloped with his lover Lady Linwall. Stephen worked hard to transform it from a place of dark memories into the finest stable and racetrack in England. Their half-brother Leo helped him in that task, travelling the Continent in search of suitable horseflesh for the stable. They sometimes heard from him, but not often.

And their half-sisters, Justine, Annalise and Charlotte, were occupied with their own growing families. They wrote often, usually to gently enquire when he, too, might enter the blessed, blissful state of wedlock as they had.

But he doubted he would ever find such great matches as theirs, love pairings all. He had tried that once, and it all ended in pain and despair. He knew his duty well enough, to provide heirs for the dukedom, and he would do it. Just not quite yet.

And since he had returned from Italy he had felt a strange distance from his family. He had lost the lightness of heart he once had with them, and he could sense their worry. He just didn't know how to reassure them—or how to find the joy in life again.

For some reason, an image of Lady Emily Carroll flashed through his mind. He remembered catching her in his arms last night as she tumbled from the stairs, the soft, warm feel of her body against his. She smelled of warm summer roses, and her bright hair brushed like silk against his cheek. She felt surprisingly sweet and alive.

In that startled moment, she had laughed and blushed, clinging to him as she found her balance. They called her the "Ice Princess", and usually he thought they must be right. She was so quiet, so watchful, her pale green eyes taking in everything around her, seeming to judge them and find them wanting.

At that house party at his family's pleasure house, Welbourne Manor, she hadn't joined in the games and laughter. She hadn't chased around the gardens or played hide-and-seek in the attic. Nicholas *did* know his duty; it had been ingrained in him since he was a child. It struck him at that party that Emily Carroll was exactly the sort of lady to fulfil that duty—pretty, well born, well mannered. A fine hostess for a ducal estate, and a fine mother for future dukes and ladies, at least as far as looks and pedigree went. Her parents had once been friends with his father, and would surely welcome the match.

But then there would be the *making* of those dukes and ladies, and Nicholas didn't relish the idea of an ice princess in his bed. He was lonely, true, yet was he *that* lonely? No, not yet.

At the ball, though, in that one moment, her quiet, pale mask slipped and he glimpsed a light deep in her eyes. Which was the real Emily Carroll?

It was maddeningly intriguing.

"You're quiet today, Nick," Stephen said, pulling Nicholas back into the present moment and away from thoughts of Emily Carroll.

"Sorry, I was just attending to some estate business

and it has me distracted," Nicholas said. He dropped the post on to his desk and sat down on its edge, crossing his arms over his chest. His valet would fuss about the crushed cravat, the wrinkled waistcoat, and cluck about how a duke should "keep up appearances".

But Nicholas feared he couldn't always be a proper duke. His father had been dead many years now, perished of a fever in Naples with his new wife Lady Linwall, and so very much had happened since then. Yet Nicholas still felt he was learning his role, still trying to fulfil all his many responsibilities.

"It was dull stuff, and I'm tired from it," he said.

"You, Nick? Tired? Never!" Stephen cried. "You're the one who could always swim across the lake and then ride five miles, all before breakfast. I would wager you were up playing cards and visiting wenches all night, and *that's* why you're tired. Here, have some brandy and it will revive you."

"I will have some brandy, before you drink it all, but I think you would be surprised at what really occupied me last night." Nicholas sat down in the chair next to Stephen's, reaching for the bottle.

"What, no gaming hells? No house of ill repute?"

"Not unless you count Lady Orman's ballroom."

"You were at a society ball?" Stephen said incredulously. "I'm all astonishment. You do need a brandy."

"Yes, I do. Our sisters are always telling me I need to do my duty and marry, so I thought Lady Orman's was a good place to start."

"They don't give a fig about your *duty*, Nick. They just have starry romance in their eyes since they married, and they want everyone to be the same. Especially us."

"Hmm." Nicholas took a deep, burning drink of his

brandy. "Is that why you're in town, then? To find a wife?"

"Good gad, no! I'm much too young to marry, though Charlotte says otherwise. I'm here to inspect a sale coming up at Tattersalls. A promising-sounding mare is in the catalogue, I hear. Though I dare say it was much the same at Lady Orman's."

Nicholas laughed, remembering the parade of giggling, white-clad débutantes and their mamas, so eager to meet an eligible young duke. And Emily Carroll, who seemed not at all interested in giggling, parading or eligible dukes.

"So it was," he said. "I'd forgotten what the London Season was really like—a giant horse sale. I've been buried in the country too long."

"You couldn't help it. Father's estates were in a bit of a mess after he died, and you had to set them right again. Not a simple task, and one I do not envy."

"Well, I wish I was still in the country now," Nicholas muttered.

"I was just there, and it's not much better than town. I stopped to see Charlotte and Drew at Derrington on my way to London."

"And how is our sister?"

"Big as a house now, and anxious for the baby to arrive. But she had plenty of energy to prate at me about the marvels of marriage and domesticity! And she had two new pugs, as well. Four is too many, I say."

"I shall be sane and avoid Derrington, then."

"That would be wise, at least for now." Stephen hesitated for a moment, then said, "Did you see no lady who caught your eye at the ball, then?"

Lady Emily's green eyes flashed through his mind again, bright and full of laughter. Not cold at all.

Nicholas shoved away the image and took another drink. "Never say you're playing matchmaker, too, Stephen."

"Of course not. I would be absolute rubbish at it. I just thought—well, it might be a good thing if you *could* find someone to help you. Someone sensible and kind. And pretty, of course."

"What lady of sense would want to put up with our family? Your pranks would drive her away in no time."

"I could control myself, and so could Charlotte and the others, if there was someone you wanted to impress. Someone you wanted to like us."

"There is no one at present. But I will keep your words in mind." And indeed he would. His sisters' concerns he was accustomed to by now, but Stephen didn't seem to notice such things. If he thought Nicholas needed "help" with his ducal work, his worries and loneliness must be showing.

That would never do at all. He never wanted to worry his family. Maybe if he did marry they would all be content for a while—until they found something else to fret about.

"We should go out tonight," Nicholas said. "Since you're in town so seldom, Stephen, you must make the most of it."

"You're not going to drag me to some stuffy ball or musicale, are you?"

"Not unless you have some terrible urge to go to Lady Arnold's ball, no. We could go to the club, maybe, play some cards. Visit Mrs Larkin's house, if you're of the inclination."

"Excellent! And I have tickets for a masked ball at Vauxhall, as well. I've heard that soprano Signora Rastrelli has a fine voice, and she'll be performing there."

"And a fine bosom, I would wager."

Stephen laughed. "That, too."

Soon after, Stephen departed for his own lodgings, since he refused to stay in Manning House, and Nicholas was left with his piles of ledgers and a brandy-induced headache. It was a good thing his brother was in town, he thought as he sat down behind the desk. Maybe what he needed was some fun, some distraction. Some drinking, a card game or two, some Italian opera singers with fine bosoms. He needed to feel like Nicholas again, and not just the duke.

But first, he did have to be that duke. He sorted through the thick stack of newly arrived invitations. The Season was winding down, yet that didn't prevent one final, frantic flurry of parties before everyone scattered their separate ways. He laid aside the few he would accept, along with bills to see to and a letter from his estate manager at Scarnlea Abbey about repairs needed. Soon enough he would be there to see to them himself.

He opened the bottom drawer of the desk to reach for more writing paper, and in the dim depths he caught a glimpse of a small gold-and-enamel case. Its deep colours, red and blue and gold, lured him to reach for it.

Usually he could ignore its call, could leave it buried in the drawer, hidden from view behind paper and boxes of sealing wax. Today, though, some deep force compelled him to take it out, to hold it in his hand.

The metal quickly warmed in his clasp, and he stared down at it for a long moment before opening it. A woman's painted pink smile greeted him, her brown eyes soft with welcome. In the miniature portrait, her dark hair fell loose over the shoulders of her red velvet gown, and she smiled eternally.

Valentina. His lost wife.

Nicholas gently stroked his thumb over the image, feeling only the roughness of the paint and no smooth, warm skin. She smiled back, always silent. In the much-too-brief time they knew each other, she was always laughing.

He put down the painting and buried his face in his hands as he remembered. He usually would not let himself think of her; it was long ago, and to remember was much too painful. But for some reason today she seemed near him.

He met Valentina Magnani on his Grand Tour, not long after his father and stepmother died and his stepbrother Brenner arrived to help them in their loss—the first time they met this son of Nicholas's stepmother's first, abandoned marriage. Nicholas was young then, barely out of university, and green as grass. Brenner thought a journey across the Continent, a time to learn more of his duties while still being largely free of them, would do him good.

And it had. At first he sorely missed his family, having never really been away from them before, but then the art and culture, the beauty of nature, enthralled him. They helped him heal from his loss, and he sent home many sculptures and paintings to adorn the ducal houses. He slowly started to find himself, who he might be apart from his family.

Then he came to Verona, Romeo and Juliet's city— and met Valentina one day at the market as she did her family's shopping. She was tall, honey-skinned, with satiny black hair and bright, dark eyes. She laughed at his clumsy attempts to speak Italian to the merchants, and helped him buy his fruit and bread. He was enchanted by her, by everything about her—her happy laughter, the glimpse of her red, ruffled petticoat at the hem of her brown skirt, the vivid, joyful life of her. She made him feel brought back to life, too.

He walked her home that day, carrying her basket for her, listening to her musical voice teach him more words of Italian, becoming more infatuated with every step. He met her mother, took tea with them. They were a respectable family of the city, her father an attorney, but they were decidedly not nobility. Not suitable duchess material.

Nicholas opened his eyes to stare blindly out at his library, the vast, dimly lit space, shadowed by soaring shelves of leather-bound books and crowded with heavy, old furniture. In the corners lurked statues from that voyage, pale marble gods and goddesses who stared back at him with their cold eyes. He had hoped to bring home more than art, more than freezing stone. He hoped to bring back life and laughter, a wife. A family.

His courtship of Valentina was quick, passionate. After all, he came from a line of people who gave all for the sake of love—his own blood ran just as hot, and he had never felt for anyone as he did for Valentina, either before or since. He craved her presence, her smile, her kiss, wanted to be with her all the time, and she felt the same for him. They went on long walks all over the city, kissing passionately in silent alleyways, in dusty museum galleries. He sat in her family's drawing room and listened to her play the harp while her siblings ran around them.

Her home reminded him of his own at Welbourne Manor, where his brothers and sisters dashed about amid the ring of laughter. They would love Valentina, he knew, even if society wasn't so accepting. They would help him make her happy even in grey, damp England, he was sure of that. So he married her in a little Verona chapel. He raised her lace veil and kissed her in the glow of stained glass, and had never been happier than in that one perfect moment.

Happiness was not to last, though. They went to a country villa for their honeymoon: long days of golden sun; warm, dusty nights of passion. Even before they returned to Verona, Valentina was pregnant. There could be no question of returning to England until she and the child could travel, so Nicholas waited to write to his family until he could announce both the marriage and the baby. Otherwise they would come rushing to him, and he wanted Valentina to himself awhile longer.

Thirteen months he was a husband, barely more than a year. One hour he was a father, to a tiny son who lived such a brief life. Then both the baby and Valentina were gone. The laughter and light were vanished as quickly as they began, and he was alone.

Well, not entirely alone. He had his family, his duty, his cursed title. After his wife and child were buried, he left Italy for home once again, his heart left behind under that cemetery cypress tree outside Verona, and he devoted himself to his family. He kept that brief marriage a secret, for he could not bear to speak of it, even to his sisters. He couldn't bear the pity he would have seen in their eyes.

Over the years, the pain faded. He learned to cherish the memory of Valentina without despairing of what might have been. Only once in a while, on days like this, did he take out her portrait and try to imagine her near him again.

It became harder all the time. She moved further into

the past. Yet a vivid fear remained, especially when he was told yet again he should do his duty, marry and produce children. How could he put another woman through the pain and fear Valentina suffered when their son was born, the agony when the baby died in her arms? How could he hurt a woman like that, watching her suffer and knowing it was his fault?

He would surely never love another as he had Valentina, but he would not marry without at least liking and respecting a lady. And he could not inflict that on someone he considered a friend.

Perhaps Stephen would marry, despite his protestations, and have children who could inherit the title. Yet that seemed unlikely. He was too busy with his racetrack scheme to consider a proper marriage.

Nicholas carefully put the portrait back into its case and hid it once more in the dark drawer. That past was gone, and he had to remember that.

But that did not mean he was quite ready to face answering all those invitations just yet. He left them on his desk and went to the window to stare down at the windswept street, at all the passers-by hurrying on their busy way. Nicholas always wondered where they were going, what purpose drove them onwards during their day.

Sometimes they stopped to peer past his wrought-iron gates, no doubt wondering the same thing about him. What did a duke do behind his grand walls? Manning House was one of the largest houses in London, a vast, impractical edifice of pale stone and copious windows his grandfather had built and which they were now stuck with for ever. It was grand and impressive, surrounded by gardens, crowned by a large ballroom and a dining room large enough for a state dinner. But it

was impossible to heat, and right now it was good only
for nieces and nephews to chase each other down the
wide corridors, once they were old enough.

It needed a mistress, a hostess to redecorate the fusty
old chambers and arrange for parties to suit its grandeur.
Yet another reason to put the past away and think of that
blasted, ever-present Duty.

Nicholas reached for the edge of the velvet drapery
to draw it across the window. Maybe if he couldn't see
outside he couldn't be distracted by what was happening on the street. As he tugged it closer, he glimpsed an
open carriage rolling slowly past on the street, carrying
two stylishly dressed ladies whispering together. One of
them turned her head slightly, and a ray of pale sunshine
caught on a blonde curl, a soft white cheek. It was Lady
Emily Carroll.

She laughed at whatever her friend was saying, her
pale cheeks flushed pink. She swept back that errant
curl with her gloved hand.

How beautiful she is, Nicholas thought with bemusement. Oh, he had always known Lady Emily was beautiful; she was famous for it, and it was easy to see in
the perfect symmetry of her heart-shaped face. He was
struck by it last summer at Welbourne, but then forgot
when she seemed not to like him.

Now, with her face alight with laughter, the sun on
her hair, he saw it all over again. What could make her
laugh like that? What could *he* possibly say to make her
smile?

It was a challenge indeed. And a Manning was never
one to back away from a challenge.

The carriage turned the corner, seeming to head
toward the park. It was nearly the fashionable hour,

when all the *ton* piled on to their horses and into their carriages and paraded past each other yet again.

Nicholas turned away from the window, and from the work that waited at his desk, and strode out of the library. All that could wait. "I need my horse saddled!" he called. "Quickly!"

Chapter Four

"Look, Emily! It's Manning House. Isn't it lovely?" Jane cried, gesturing at the vast mansion as their carriage bounced past. "Like a palace in a fairy story."

Emily laughed as she studied the gleaming windows, laid out like endless rows of diamonds in white stone expressly to show off wealth great enough to counter any window tax. She remembered a line she learned once in lessons on Tudor history—'Hardwick Hall, more glass than wall.' Somehow, it was hard to imagine the duke living there in that chilly mausoleum.

"If the fairy story is about the Snow Queen, bringing down winter from her mountain fortress," she said. "It looks mightily uncomfortable."

"But excellent for grand balls," Jane declared, her gaze still fastened on the house. "Can't you just imagine being the hostess of such a gathering? Being a *duchess*?"

"I can imagine it," Emily said, still laughing. "It sounds horrid. Everyone staring all the time, everyone pestering for invitations to those grand balls…"

"Exactly! The Duchess of Manning would utterly rule society. She could set every fashion. Wouldn't that be wonderful?" Jane sighed deeply, glancing back over her shoulder as they turned a corner and Manning House disappeared from view.

Emily's laughter faded, a sneaking suspicion setting in as she studied her friend's narrowed eyes. "Jane, have you set your cap at the Duke of Manning?"

"Oh, la, no!" Jane cried. The brief glint of calculation faded as she giggled. She straightened her feathered bonnet on her auburn curls and sat back against the carriage cushions. "I'm not such a fool as that. I'm too harum-scarum to ever be duchess material. That's *your* department, Em."

"Mine?" Emily said, shocked. "Of course not. I would make a wretched duchess."

"Nonsense. You seem born to royalty, with your looks and your quiet grace. And since there is no eligible prince at present, a duke would be the next best thing. Especially one as handsome as Manning." Jane leaned closer and whispered, "Don't his blue eyes just make you want to melt?"

Well—they did, actually. Whenever he looked at Emily she longed to sink down through the floor, robbed of any powers of speech she might once have possessed. But she would never admit that, not even to Jane. Not even to herself.

"He is quite fine-looking," she said carefully.

"Fine-looking?" Jane scoffed. "He is a veritable Greek god. My parents would be in alt if I could catch him, of course, but it would never happen. I shall have to settle for some country baronet, I suppose, like William Jameson. He seems on the verge of making an offer. What about you?"

Emily laughed. "I'm not in the least bit interested in Sir William!"

"Certainly not, who would be? That nose! But there must be someone you like?"

"No, there's no one."

"I cannot believe that."

"Believe it, my dear Jane. I have met no one this Season I could be really fond of. Perhaps I shall have to find a country squire, too. Maybe a nice curate?"

She spoke in jest, but really a curate would be just right. An earnest, sincere young man who would read to her by the fire in the evenings. Who would ask for her help with his sermons, and praise her charity work in the neighbourhood and never grab her suddenly as Mr Lofton had. It would be perfect—if he had a roguish smile like the duke…

Emily gave her head a hard shake. "That is what I need."

"A curate? Your parents would never allow it. You are the beautiful daughter of an earl!"

The shy daughter of an impoverished earl. "We'll see what happens."

The carriage turned through the gates of Hyde Park, joining the flow of vehicles and horses parading for the fashionable hour. "Don't worry, Em, the Season is not done yet. We have time to find someone better than the Sir Williams of the world," Jane said. She reached into her reticule and drew out a small square of vellum. "Maybe here?"

"What is that, Jane? Some sort of love letter?"

Jane giggled. "No, silly! Tickets to a masked ball at Vauxhall. My sister, Mrs Barnes, procured them for me, and she has agreed to chaperon us there. She's terribly easy to distract, though—she won't get in the way of our fun."

"Vauxhall?" Despite herself, Emily was terribly intrigued. She had heard of the infamous masked balls held in the pleasure gardens, of romantic assignations in dark walkways and glorious illuminations that transformed the night. She had laughed at some of the wilder tales, sure they could not be true.

But—what if they *were* true? What if she went and saw them for herself?

She glanced down at the tickets. *A concert by Signora Rastrelli*, they read in scrolling script. *Fireworks and illuminations grander than anything yet seen in London!*

Music, fireworks. It did sound wondrous. But… "Jane, I'm not sure we should."

"We'll be wearing masks! No one will even know we're there."

"My parents would never allow it."

"Then just tell them you're staying with me at my sister's house that night. Tell them—oh, I don't know! That her relation, a curate, has come to visit and has promised to read us some fine sermons."

Emily laughed, torn between her duty and the promise of a little fun. Surely an evening of music could not be harmful? She didn't plan to go off along the Dark Walk, after all.

Something deep inside of her, some tiny, terrible imp of mischief that seldom dared show itself, pushed at her. *Go on*, it whispered, soft and alluring. *Be a little daring. What harm could it do? You have been working so hard.*

But it could do a great deal of harm, she feared. Yet still the temptation was there.

"I don't know," she said. "I think—"

"Good afternoon, ladies!" someone called, interrupting her words. "Very pleasant weather we're having, are we not?"

Emily looked up to see Mr George Rayburn approaching on his horse. He had been the only suitor to really appear this Season, dancing with her at her first ball and being attentive since then. He sent flowers, fetched her lemonade at parties, things of that nature—if that could really be called a suitor. He had not made an offer, and her parents would have refused him anyway. His fortune was respectable enough, from all reports, but he had no title.

Now, though, at the end of the Season, if he were to come forward, they might be more amenable. If Emily liked him, she could probably persuade them Mr Rayburn was a reasonable match.

He drew in his horse next to their carriage and tipped his hat, smiling down at them. She *should* like him, Emily thought as she smiled back at him. He was terribly handsome, with waving, glossy dark hair and hazel eyes, a strong jaw and straight nose. He was tall and lean, athletic, much admired. He read poetry, had travelled widely, had correct opinions and impeccable manners.

And he did seem to like her. He wasn't put off by her shyness or her lack of dancing skills. Why could she not really like him? Perhaps it was that way he had of looking at her.

But maybe she was wrong. Everyone else seemed charmed by him, even Jane. Her friend held out her hand to Mr Rayburn with a happy trill of laughter.

"Mr Rayburn! We have not seen you out and about this week," Jane said.

"I fear I had to attend some business on my estate that could not wait," he answered. He seemed to speak to Jane, but his gaze lingered on Emily. "I am sure I could not have been much missed in all the flurry of the end of the Season."

"Oh, but I vow you were!" Jane said. "There were not enough gentlemen to dance with at Lady Orman's, were there, Emily?"

Emily smiled, remembering how she herself had not danced at all, no matter how many men there were. "No, I suppose there weren't. No gentlemen who were *good* dancers, anyway."

Mr Rayburn arched his brow. "You think me a good dancer, Lady Emily?"

"You managed to avoid getting your foot stomped on when we danced, Mr Rayburn, and you prevented me from tripping more than once. To me, that makes you an expert."

"I am glad I impressed you with something, Lady Emily," he answered.

Jane glanced between the two of them, her head tilted as if she puzzled something out. "Shall we all walk for a bit? I feel in need of some exercise."

Emily nodded eagerly. Perhaps if they were walking, in the midst of the crowd, she could more easily avoid Mr Rayburn's steady hazel stare. He did always seem to watch her, expect something from her when she could not fathom what it was. She only knew it made her feel fidgety, uncomfortable—and not in the same way the Duke of Manning did.

They left the carriage and set out along one of the pedestrian pathways. Emily loved coming to the park in the mornings, when the walkways were sparsely filled with nannies out with their charges and footmen

walking the employers' dogs. She loved watching the
children with their hoops and dolls, enjoying the light
and fresh air, the freedom. It made her yearn for the day
when she would have a child of her own to walk with
in the park, to love and nurture. But the park was such
a very different place late in the afternoon, when it was
taken over by stylishly dressed society figures, intent
on seeing and being seen.

A couple, laughing raucously together, brushed past,
jostling Emily. She stumbled, and Mr Rayburn caught
her arm in a hard grasp.

"Are you quite all right, Lady Emily?" he asked.

"Oh, yes, thank you," Emily said. She tried to ease
her arm away, but he held on, leading her along the
pathway to a more open spot.

"It is shockingly crowded today," Jane declared, quite
as if it wasn't exactly this crowded every day. "How
fortunate we have you to protect us, Mr Rayburn."

"And how fortunate I am to escort *two* such lovely
ladies. I'm the envy of every man here," Mr Rayburn
answered with a charming smile. "Now, Miss Thornton,
Lady Emily, perhaps you could tell me all I missed
while I was sadly away from town. Was Lady Orman's
as great a crush as everyone predicted?"

"Oh, even more so!" Jane said. "One could scarcely
even move without being trod upon."

As her friend chattered on about the ball, Emily half-
listened, her mind drifting away from the gossip, the
crowded park, even from Mr Rayburn's clasp still on
her arm. She thought of next week's planned lesson at
Mrs Goddard's, her favourite pupil Sally who showed
such promise and how well they were all progressing.
They needed more challenging material in their lessons
to keep up with them. Perhaps she could teach them a

bit of Italian? Some of them might even be able to go for governesses soon.

She was so distracted by her plans she didn't notice the tree root in her path until she tripped right over it.

"Oh!" she cried, as pain shot through her thin half-boot and up her foot. Mr Rayburn's hand tightened on her arm, holding her upright yet again. "Thank you, Mr Rayburn. You are very kind."

"It is entirely my pleasure, Lady Emily," he said hoarsely, staring into her eyes. "You do seem to need someone to look after you."

A sudden jolt of anger sizzled through her, and she finally shook her arm free of his touch. That was exactly what she did not want any longer, people always telling her where to go and what to do! "Looking after" always seemed to mean "telling what to do". She never got to do what *she* wanted, or to make up her own mind about anything.

"Thank you for your assistance, Mr Rayburn. I am very well now." Emily hurried ahead of Jane and Mr Rayburn, not knowing where she was going, only that she had to get away and shake free of that sudden, unaccountable anger. It made her feel ridiculously out of control.

She found herself near the Serpentine, its banks lined with yet more people, laughing, talking, seemingly so very pleasant and light-hearted. Underneath, though, Emily knew they were always watching, always—judging.

She walked on at a slower pace, making herself smile politely. Jane and Mr Rayburn followed her, still chattering together about that blasted ball.

In the distance, just at the edge of the clearing near the river, Emily glimpsed the Duke of Manning himself, seated on a white horse that contrasted dramatically with his well-cut dark blue coat and fine doeskin breeches. She stopped short, nearly tripping yet again as she stared in sudden dazzlement.

She just couldn't seem to help herself. It was as if all the light of the day gathered directly on him, and he was all shimmering gold.

She remembered myths of Apollo, called "Ever Bright" by the Muses, and she was sure this was what they meant. Despite the swirling crowds, he appeared to be alone in a glowing pool of serenity and light. He wore no hat, and his golden hair was windblown, falling over his brow and the collar of his fine coat. He held the reins lightly in one gloved hand, answering greetings with a faint smile on his face.

It was almost as if he was bemused to find himself in such a cacophonous scene.

"Whatever is Manning doing here?" she heard Mr Rayburn say behind her. "No one in his family ever deigns to come among the crowds here."

Emily could not blame him for that. If she was a duchess, she would never do what she didn't want to, either. But why *was* he here? She had never seen him in the park before.

"Should we say hello to him?" Jane asked. She sounded uncharacteristically indecisive. Jane always seemed to know exactly what she should do.

"And stand in line with everyone else eager to pay court? I don't think so," Mr Rayburn said dismissively. He took Jane's arm and the two of them turned away. "I thought we were going to walk. Lady Emily?"

"Yes, of course," Emily said. She started to turn away, as well, to follow them back down the path. To her astonishment, though, the duke caught sight of her and smiled.

He tugged on his horse's reins and headed straight toward her.

"My goodness! The Duke of Manning is coming *here*," Jane cried.

"So he is," Mr Rayburn muttered. Emily looked back at him just in time to catch a glimpse of a frown on his face, before it was covered in his usual sociable, practised smile. It seemed perhaps he did not much care for the Duke of Manning.

Emily wondered if he knew something the rest of society did not. Otherwise she could not account for such a reaction. What could it be?

"I think—oh, my!" Jane said. "I think he means to talk to us."

And indeed he did. He reined in his horse right next to Emily and politely nodded to her, smiling. "Good afternoon, Lady Emily. I trust you have recovered from the dreadful crush of the Orman ball?" he said. His smile widened, more of a grin really, wide and white and full of gentle, teasing humour. As if they shared some secret, as if he remembered all too well when she slipped on the stairs and fell into his arms.

A hot blush touched her cheeks, and she ducked her head to try to hide under her bonnet's straw brim. "I am quite recovered, thank you, your Grace," she said with a curtsy. "Though I am definitely enjoying the fresh air today much more!"

He laughed, and shifted easily in his saddle, as if he was born on horseback. He looked so right there, Emily thought, comfortable and elegantly powerful, while she was terrified of the huge beasts.

Horses, of course—not dukes. Though she was also

rather terrified of him, when he looked at her so intently, as if he was seeing her for the first time. It was a very different sort of terror than that she felt when Mr Lofton grabbed her in the garden, though. It was a temptation inside her own heart.

"I definitely agree with you on that, Lady Emily," he said. "A sunny day outdoors is much to be preferred."

Jane gave a delicate cough, and Emily suddenly recalled that she was not, in fact, alone at the park with the duke. "Your Grace, I believe you know my friends, Miss Thornton and Mr Rayburn?"

"Of course I do. How do you do, Miss Thornton, Mr Rayburn?" he said.

"Very well indeed, your Grace," Jane said cheerfully. "We were just going for a stroll. Perhaps you would care to join us?"

Emily shot Jane a hard glance, but Jane blithely ignored her. What if she said something foolish to him as he walked right beside her, or, heaven forbid, tripped and fell again?

"I would be happy to join you," he said. "If you are sure I would not be intruding on your confidences?"

"The path *is* rather narrow for four, your Grace," Mr Rayburn said in a hard voice.

Jane tugged sharply at his arm. "Nonsense! Every party is merrier with more, and there is plenty of room near the river. You and I shall just walk ahead, Mr Rayburn, and his Grace can walk with Lady Emily."

"Thank you for the invitation," the duke said. He dismounted and handed the reins over to his groom before offering Emily his arm. Jane had already fulfilled her promise—or threat—and led Mr Rayburn ahead. She tossed a triumphant smile back over her shoulder at Emily.

Emily had no choice. She slid her gloved fingers into the crook of his elbow and allowed him to walk beside her along the path. The other strollers watched them avidly as they went by, but she tried her hardest to ignore them. She watched the path under her feet, wary of every possible obstacle waiting to trip her.

The gossip she would just have to worry about later.

"I hope I am not interrupting important confidences between you and your friends, Lady Emily," he said quietly.

She glanced up at him, then wished she had not. His eyes really were terribly, terribly blue. "No, of course not, your Grace. Miss Thornton and I were able to confide on the way here. And Mr Rayburn is—well, he is not that sort of friend."

"Perhaps he is more of a suitor than a friend?" he said teasingly.

But Emily was not accustomed to being teased. She felt that blush flame even hotter. "I—no, of course not. I just—I… No."

"Forgive me, Lady Emily. I am so used to teasing my sisters and cousins about their admirers I sometimes forget how to behave in polite society."

His family—of course. What a prig he must think her after them. "Mr Rayburn does not *admire* me, your Grace."

"Does he not? Very foolish of him, I would say."

"I…" She hardly knew how to answer *that*. She could scarcely say she actually had no admirers to be teased about, by him or anyone! "How is your family, your Grace? I have not seen any of them since that house party at Welbourne Manor last summer."

"All disgustingly healthy, thank you. My sister Charlotte is expecting her first child very soon."

"Indeed?" Emily was astonished. She remembered Charlotte Fitzmanning, with her wild hair and untidy gowns, always with a pack of pug dogs at her heels. Emily knew she had married Andrew Bassington soon after that party, of course—and now she was to be a mother. She would have her very own family. Emily couldn't help but envy her for that.

"You must send her my best wishes, your Grace," she said. "Are you hoping for a niece or a nephew?"

"Either, as long as the child—and my sister—are healthy." He glanced towards the sun-dappled, blue-green river, where children sailed their toy boats and laughed in innocent delight. A shadow seemed to pass over his eyes, and he frowned.

"I am sure they will both be quite safe," Emily said softly. "Your sister did seem to have a most robust constitution."

That strange shadow lifted from his face, and he laughed. "That she does. I already have one niece, little Katherine, my sister Justine's child. I am sure she would like a little girl for her playmate."

"I should like to have a niece, too," she said. She gestured toward a pretty, tiny redhead toddling by the water's edge as her nurse flirted with a footman nearby. The child waved her hands and laughed in sheer pleasure. "Perhaps one like that girl?"

"A fine choice, Lady Emily." He led her again along the path, closer to the river. "I do hope *you* are quite well after the ball? That fall you took…"

A group of children ran across the path in front of them, distracting her and making her laugh. "It was nothing at all, your Grace. I fear it could have been worse, though, if you had not been there to assist me."

"That is my task at balls, to rescue fair maidens."

"You should not let that be known widely, then, or ladies would be fainting at your feet in droves in hopes of rescue."

He gave a startled laugh. "Why, Lady Emily! Was that a *joke*?"

Emily thought about it for a moment. "I think it might have been."

"A joke with an unfortunate grain of truth, I fear."

"You probably don't need to worry, your Grace. Most society ladies are not so clumsy as I am and could not fall if they tried."

"I am glad to hear it. I can't spend *all* my time saving fainting ladies. But I can't believe anyone could ever call you clumsy, Lady Emily."

"Oh, they could," she said with a sigh. "And I think—"

From the corner of her eye, Emily caught a glimpse of flashing movement, dark and strange in the bright day. She spun around, and to her horror saw a runaway curricle barrelling down the roadway—and straight toward the red-haired child. The driver, a terrified-looking young man, had lost the reins. Pedestrians dived out of its wild path, shrieking, but the little girl was terribly oblivious.

"No!" Emily screamed. She ran towards the child, but her skirt hem wrapped around her ankles and tripped her.

The duke had no such constraints. He dashed past Emily, swift on his long, powerful legs, and dived for the child as the carriage crashed ever nearer. Everyone else ran the other way, but not him. He took a diving leap for the girl and caught her up in his arms a split second before the curricle would have run over her.

His momentum carried them both over the embankment and straight into the placid waters of the river.

Terrified, Emily lifted her wretched hems and dashed towards the river, along with everyone else. The carriage had finally ground to a halt some distance away, but she didn't notice. All she could see were the waves washing over the spot where he had disappeared.

The duke leaped up, the girl held tightly against him. They were both completely soaked, but the child laughed delightedly in his arms as Nicholas sputtered for breath. A clump of weeds clung to his wet hair, now more green than gold with sludge.

To Emily, though, he did not look so very comical.

"Kitty!" a nursemaid shrieked as she ran past Emily, that flirtation with the footman forgotten. "Oh, is she hurt? Is she?"

The duke spat out a mouthful of water, wading towards shore. "I don't think so, miss," he said. "Though she is making a deuced lot of noise."

He slowly climbed up the embankment, the child clinging to his neck as she chortled with sheer joy. His fine clothes were utterly ruined, but he didn't seem to notice. He carefully handed the girl to her nurse.

"Keep a closer eye on her, yes?" he said hoarsely.

"Oh, yes, sir! Of course," the maid cried. "Thank you so much, how can I thank you? I turned my back for one moment and—"

"One moment is all it takes, I fear," he said. He sat down heavily on the grass, his head in his hands as the maid carried the child away and the crowd slowly dispersed as the drama seemed over. "One moment and they're gone."

"Oh, your Grace," Emily said. She knelt beside him, only to find she trembled violently. How close that poor child had come to disaster! If not for him, the duke... "Are you hurt at all?"

He shook his head, and he trembled, too. "Of course not, Lady Emily. I've been dunked in far worse." He slowly lowered his hands, and she saw that his face was a bit pale, but completely expressionless. He took off his boots, one after the other, and emptied out the water. He removed his coat and wrung out the sleeves.

"I did not think they would start so young," he muttered.

"Your Grace?" Emily said, bewildered. Had he hit his head on the embankment? What was he talking about?

"Seeking rescue," he said. "You did warn me."

She laughed. "Indeed. But I fear you will be the one in need of rescue if you don't get home and into some dry clothes as soon as possible."

"I am fine, Lady Emily. We should find your friends first."

Of course! She had completely forgotten about them, about everyone. Emily glanced up to find Jane hurrying towards them, her eyes bright with excitement. Mr Rayburn followed, looking considerably put out by the whole scene.

"No need, for here they are already," she said.

"Oh, your Grace! That was utterly amazing," Jane cried. "So very heroic."

"Not heroic at all, Miss Thornton," he answered as he rose to his feet and held out his hand to help Emily. "I merely acted out of instinct, as anyone would."

Yet no one else had acted at all, Emily thought. Only

him. Would she now have to revise her opinion of him as merely a pleasure-seeking, shallow duke? That would be most inconvenient.

"I heard you were at the park today, Em, when the Duke of Manning performed a most daring rescue."

Emily looked up from her book as her brother bounded into the drawing room. "So I was, Rob, along with half of London."

Her mother turned eagerly from her embroidery. "The Duke of Manning? And you were there, Emily? Why did you not say something!"

Because Emily did not know what to say. She knew her mother would become terribly excited at the knowledge she had even seen the duke today. Her mother would be sure to blow the whole incident entirely out of proportion and make it all something it was not. Emily was just too tired for all that right now, and much too confused.

And she also just wanted to keep what she had seen to herself for a while, to try to decipher what it all meant. She couldn't do that with her family chattering on about it all, as they had a tendency to do. Yet it seemed keeping quiet was no longer an option.

"Emily!" her mother said. "Did you hear me? Why did you not tell me you saw the Duke of Manning at the park? Did he speak to you?"

Emily carefully closed her book. "I suppose it all just slipped my mind."

"Slipped your mind?" her mother cried.

"You are a strange girl indeed, Sister," Rob said. He leaned over her chair to examine her book, his light brown hair flopping over his brow. He didn't look quite like an important up-and-coming politician when he did that, she thought, but like the brother of her youth. "I'm sure anyone else would definitely remember seeing the duke rescue a child from a runaway carriage. And then walking away on his arm when it was all over."

"What!" Emily's mother screamed. She tossed her sewing on to the floor. "Emily, you will tell me everything this moment."

"It did not happen quite like that," Emily protested. "And how do you know of it, Rob?"

"Amy saw Jane Thornton's sister at the milliner. But it doesn't matter how *I* know. Everyone in town knows by now. Nothing so dashing has happened at the park in ages." Rob tugged at one of her curls. "They say you wept and mopped at his sweated brow."

"He was too wet from falling in the river to sweat," Emily muttered. "And I did not weep. Though I was naturally frightened for the poor child."

"I wouldn't be too sorry for her—she's Lord and Lady Hampton's brat. It seems they're proclaiming Manning the great hero of the age."

"Already?" said Emily. "And how do you know *that*?"

"Amy saw Lady Hampton's aunt on the way home from the milliner's. Amy is amazing at discovering information," Rob said admiringly.

"You mean she is a great gossip," said Emily.

"Whatever you call it, Sister, it's immensely useful and one of the many reasons I married her. It would do you good to talk to people yourself more often."

"Enough of this arguing, you two!" their mother cried. "Emily, tell me what happened immediately."

Emily quickly related the tale of the child's rescue—a short version of it, anyway—leaving out most of her own involvement and all her emotions. Even that abbreviated account had her mother sighing.

"What a heroic tale!" she said, dabbing at her eyes with a handkerchief. "How proud our old friend, the late duke, would be. And to think you were there, Emily!"

"So was everyone else, Mama," Emily protested again.

"But no one else went to his assistance, only you, my dear. And now your name is linked with his."

"Well done, Em," Rob said.

"I did nothing at all! He scarcely even noticed me," Emily said, to no avail.

"Perhaps we should allow you to go to Vauxhall with Miss Thornton and her sister after all," her mother said. "I wasn't sure about the outing at first, but such a good deed deserves a reward. And there can be no harm if you are with respectable friends."

"Really? You are allowing me to go to Vauxhall?" Emily said, astonished. Her mother had hesitated when Emily first relayed Jane's invitation, but now she seemed quite happy to allow it.

"Of course, my dear. The duke might be there, after all. You must see what you can make of it."

Emily departed the drawing room soon after, leaving her mother and brother to their happy conversation of the doings in the park and what it might mean. They seemed to think it meant the duke had noticed Emily at last, or some such nonsense.

Once she was safe in the silence of her own chamber, she locked the door and went to stare out the window at the gathering evening. Her room looked down on their tiny back garden and the mews behind. All was quiet now, as everyone was at home preparing for their nights, their parties and dinners and theatre outings. The sky was the palest of pinks, shading slowly into grey.

What was *he* doing tonight? she wondered. Was he getting ready to go out and enjoy his hero-dom? She hoped he was staying home to rest by a warm fire, as he would surely catch a chill after his—what did he call it? His dunking?

She had a sudden vision of the duke, Nicholas, by his fire, cosy with books and supper on a tray. That was *her* favourite sort of evening. What if she was there, too? What if she could sit by him as they toasted cheese in the fire and laughed about the follies of gossip? He would reach for her hand and…

"No!" she said aloud, and laughed at her fancies. He did not seem a man to relish a quiet evening at home. Dukes were very busy and always sought after, even ones who weren't the hero of the day. His family seemed to love parties above all else, dancing and music and jokes.

And yet—yet she *had* glimpsed something different in him today, ever so briefly. She had known he was brave, of course, always riding hell for leather and racing carriages at Welbourne Manor, swimming in the lake there, climbing the hills. Dancing all night. But today's bravery was of another sort. He had put himself in danger to save a child, a person unknown to him, without an instant's hesitation while everyone else fled or froze in horror. As she had.

Only after did he seem at all shaken, as if the true danger to that little girl had only just come to him. And that girl had been most reluctant to part with her rescuer—as all ladies seemed to be with him.

Emily bit at the edge of her thumbnail as she watched the sky slide into indigo twilight. Teaching at Mrs

Goddard's meant that not only did she teach the women writing and French, they taught her things as well. They were careful never to tell lurid tales in her hearing, but she did hear some things. She heard stories of how men, especially wealthy and titled men, were not to be trusted. They used people, particularly women, for selfish ends and discarded them without a care. That was why she worked at Mrs Goddard's, to help women recover from such terrible experiences. She wanted to help however she could.

The Duke of Manning was about as wealthy and titled as a man could be, and he was the son of a famous libertine, a man who had abandoned his wife, the mother of his heir, and married his mistress as soon as that poor wife died. Yet today Emily had seen not a shred of selfishness or carelessness.

Was it only the rush of the moment that made him act thus? Perhaps tomorrow he would go back to the careless, scandalous ways of the Mannings. Or maybe—maybe that was simply how he really was, deep inside.

Emily was very confused, and she did not like that feeling at all. Maybe her mother was right, and the duke would be at Vauxhall for the masked ball. If she met him in disguise, not as Lady Emily Carroll, perhaps she could glimpse that true self, not just the face he showed society.

It seemed a harebrained scheme at best, but for now it was all she had.

Chapter Five

"You've been very quiet all day, Nick. Is something amiss?"

"What did you say, Stephen?" Nicholas said. He tore his gaze from the night-dark streets flashing past the carriage window and glanced over at his brother. Stephen was running one of his many 'lucky charms' between his fingers, back and forth, and that was seldom a good sign. But maybe Nicholas should find some kind of charm as well. It seemed he needed one.

"I said you are being strangely quiet, which is not like you. Usually no one can get you to shut up."

Nicholas threw his black satin mask at his brother's head. Stephen batted it away, laughing, but in the process dropped his charm. Nicholas scooped it up and held it to the moonlight. It was a tiny gold horseshoe, as bright as Emily Carroll's hair. "I have a great deal to think about, you know."

"Ducal things, I suppose?"

"Indeed. And if you're going to twit me about my work, I'd just like to see *you* take it on. You're the heir, anyway. You be the duke, and I'll go off and live on a sunny island somewhere, with no estates to run and no siblings to corral."

Nicholas closed his fist tightly around the charm. He was being churlish, he knew, and he was sorry for it. It wasn't Stephen's fault he was in such a strange mood. He hadn't been able to shake it away all day. He kept seeing that child, so close to danger, kept reliving it over and over in his mind.

And he kept seeing that look in Emily Carroll's green eyes as she knelt beside him, so full of horror and shock—and confusion. She had seen him at his worst, damn it all, seen him at his most vulnerable. He didn't like that, and he couldn't decipher why that would be.

Stephen sat back on his seat, his hands up in mock surrender. "Certainly not! I have not the least desire to be a duke. It's a blasted great nuisance, and apparently it makes a man surly as well. And I'm only the heir until you marry and have horrid little Mannings of your own."

Which would never happen, not after Valentina and their poor little son. Nicholas rubbed his hands hard over his face and through his hair, messing his valet's careful arrangement. "I'm sorry, Stephen. I don't know what's come over me today."

"I suppose the hero of the day is entitled to a foul mood now and then."

"I've told you before—I only did what anyone would do when a child is in danger."

"Tell that to the Hamptons. They've blanketed the whole drawing room at Manning House with bouquets in their profuse thanks. And I hear they've been proclaiming your name all over town."

"I wish they would stop, then." It seemed absurd for

Lord and Lady Hampton to thank him so ardently for saving their child, when he could do nothing to save his own. He did not feel heroic in the least.

"I wouldn't be so quick to turn modest, Nick. All the ladies will be even more in love with you than before." Stephen gave him a grin. "Maybe one in particular?"

Nicholas answered that grin with a scowl, which did not put off his brother in the least. "Who on earth do you mean?"

"I was at the club this afternoon, and heard tell that Lady Emily Carroll seemed enormously concerned for you when you took that tumble into the Serpentine. They said she cradled your head in her lap and wept."

"Oh, damn it all." Nicholas tightened his fist on the charm, the golden corners biting into his skin. That was all the blasted situation needed—rumours about him and Lady Emily. "It was not like that at all. We happened to be walking together when it happened, that is all."

"You were walking with Lady Emily Carroll?" Stephen said, sitting up straight in interest. "But she did not like you at all last summer at Welbourne! Despite all her parents' efforts at matchmaking."

"She did seem less than enthused about me," Nicholas answered. "Our family is probably not serious enough for her."

Stephen gave a snort. "Socrates would not be serious enough for her! Has she ever smiled?"

Yes, indeed she did smile—and it was like the sun came out when she did. But then it always vanished all too quickly. "I met with her at the park and did the polite thing for an acquaintance and walked with her for a time." Nicholas saw no need to mention he had actually followed her to Hyde Park, foolishly following something elusive in that smile. "I'm sorry to be the cause of any gossip about her."

"I had assumed those stories were made up out of whole cloth. I didn't realise you actually were with her at the park. Did her touch freeze when she took your arm, Nick?"

Her hand had been quite warm. Warm and delicate, trembling slightly as she took his arm. And she smelled like summer roses. "Don't be a fool, Stephen. She is not actually an ice princess, no matter what those bacon-brains at the club say."

"It seems she's called that with good reason, though. I've never seen a lady so quiet and still. They say—"

"Enough!" Nicholas shouted. "I do not want to hear any more about Lady Emily. Surely we know well enough what it's like to be the objects of idle gossip. We shouldn't subject an innocent lady to unfair slurs."

"I—yes, of course. You're very right, Nick," Stephen said, looking nonplussed and quite sorry. "I certainly don't want to be unfair to Lady Emily, especially if you like her."

"I don't *like* her. I'm just sick of the gossip. It never ends."

"And you've been working too hard, Brother. We'll have a merry time at Vauxhall tonight, it is just what you need. Some wine, some music, some pretty women— you'll be yourself again in no time. And I will help you more, I promise."

"Just make your racetrack scheme a great success. And perhaps you're right, I just need some fun," Nicholas said. But deep inside he was not so sure. His family thought a bit of fun would solve any trouble, but maybe that wasn't so true any longer. Another night out, among noise and crowds, seemed the last thing he wanted. There was never a moment to think, to understand.

Then again, maybe *thinking* was the last thing he needed.

He tossed the charm back to Stephen, who caught it neatly, and reached for his discarded mask. The bright lights of Vauxhall were drawing nearer as they crossed the bridge, the press of carriages thicker around them as everyone headed for the masquerade.

Nicholas tied the mask over his face, and drew the hood of his black cloak closer. He would drink some of Vauxhall's excellent arrack punch and find a pretty woman, as Stephen suggested. Maybe a plump, soft red-head, someone very different from a delicate, porcelain-doll blonde, and forget himself with her. It had been much too long since he did that.

And then tomorrow, he would no longer be haunted by a pair of solemn green eyes.

"Oh, Emily, isn't it terribly exciting?" Jane whispered as they stepped through the turnstile into Vauxhall, the dense line of revellers dispersing on to the walkways.

Emily twisted her head about, taking in her surroundings. It *was* exciting, strangely so. She hadn't expected very much from this outing—she had heard and read so much about the pleasure gardens she was quite sure she knew what it would be like. She'd thought it would be a mere curiosity, something to see once and be done with, since she could not get away from Jane's invitation once her mother gave her permission.

But reading and seeing were two different matters. The gardens were astonishing, like something in a dream. It was a different world from her day-to-day existence of duty and sense. Here she didn't have to be Emily. Here she could be anyone at all.

Maybe that was the real point of any masquerade. To escape for a time.

She held on to Jane's arm as they followed her sister down the entrance pathway, and tried not to stare open-mouthed like some green country girl. Off to their right was the Grand Quadrangle, their destination, and she could glimpse it through the carefully spaced trees. Thousands of glass lamps, their globes faceted to make the light sparkle, shimmered from the branches, casting an amber glow on the costumed crowds as they passed beneath them.

"It's like something from the *Arabian Nights*," Emily murmured. "It can't be quite real."

"I can't believe we're here," said Jane, tugging the folds of her Greek-goddess costume into place. "However did you persuade your parents to let you come?"

"Oh, it was not difficult." After her name was linked with the duke's in the Great Park Incident, as she had begun to think of it, they would have allowed her anything. Her mother had even given Emily one of her old gowns, an elaborate creation of green satin and ruffled gold lace Lady Moreby had worn in her own first Season, to serve as a costume. With the gown, a raven-black wig of high piled curls, and a gold silk mask, she really did feel like someone else.

Unfortunately, she had also borrowed her mother's old high-heeled shoes, and she was sure she would topple from them at any moment.

"Well, however you accomplished it, I'm very glad you did," said Jane. "We're going to have such fun tonight! Oh, look at that man over there, the one dressed as a Crusader. Who do you suppose it is? He has such deliciously broad shoulders."

Emily laughed, but in her own mind she decided the Crusader's shoulders were not nearly as attractive as the duke's. He was so very strong, the way he snatched up the child so swiftly, as if she weighed nothing at all. The way he caught her, Emily, when she fell from the stairs, and held her so easily. So close to him…

She suddenly stumbled on a loose patch of gravel, her heel sinking into the pathway. Cursing her silly, distracted state, she yanked her shoe free and hurried after Jane and her sister Mrs Barnes as they entered the Grand Quadrangle.

The Quadrangle was the centrepiece of Vauxhall. Lying in the Grove between the parallel Great Walk and South Walk, it was enclosed by four classical colonnades holding the supper boxes and surrounding yet more walkways and trees. The orchestra played in the centre, lilting dance music as the guests arrived and mingled, greeting friends, looking for new flirtations, trying to guess who was who behind the masks.

Yet more of those glittering lamps were draped in the trees and lit up the colonnades, so bright it could have been midday. Magical creatures in the garb of kings and damsels, Greek gods and goddesses, shepherds and shepherdesses, and mysterious figures in dark cloaks slid in and out of the light and shadows. Emily felt dizzy with it, as if she was caught in an ever-shifting kaleidoscope.

She stumbled again, and someone caught her arm before she could fall. Dazed, she glanced up to see it was one of those cloaked men. A black satin mask covered most of his face, giving him a slightly sinister air, like a demon dropped suddenly into the bright fairy revel.

She instinctively drew back from his touch, frightened. But then she glimpsed the eyes behind that mask. Surely only one man could have eyes of that certain shade of blue.

"Thank you, sir," she whispered. She willed him to speak. If she heard his voice, she would know for sure it was the duke. But he merely nodded and moved on, disappearing into the crowd.

"Hurry up or you'll fall behind!" Jane called.

Emily shook away the strange spell the gardens and the blue-eyed man cast on her and followed Jane into their box. It was a small space, open on one side so they could watch the concert, made even closer by the long table and close press of chairs. Mrs Barnes's friends waited for them, and to judge from the clutter of empty wine bottles on the table they had already begun the revels. They called out uproarious greetings, waving their goblets in welcome.

As Emily squeezed on to an empty seat between Jane and a lady dressed as a voluminous Queen Elizabeth, she caught a glimpse of herself in the looking glass hung on the back wall. At first she leaped up again, sure she was about to sit on some unfortunate woman, but then she laughed. It *was* her, that black-haired lady in green satin. She had forgotten she wasn't entirely herself tonight.

If that was really the Duke of Manning, surely he did not know her either. If only she could find him again, and try to find out for certain.

"Here, Emily, have some arrack punch," Jane said as she pressed a glass into Emily's hand. "Vauxhall is quite famous for it."

"As they are famous for the paucity of their refreshments?" Emily murmured as she watched the footmen in Vauxhall livery deliver their supper. Platters of tiny, bony chickens, paper-thin ham and little wedges of pale cheese.

"It's better than Almack's, I dare say," Jane said, drinking deeply of the arrack.

Emily sipped at hers—and coughed as her eyes watered. "It's—quite good."

And it certainly was, once she got past that first sharp kick. Spicy and sweet at the same time. She drank some more and nibbled at a little dry chicken as she studied the passing crowd. There were so many men in black cloaks, all of them too far away for her to see the colour of their eyes. She would never find him again! She should have followed him when she had the chance.

So distracted was she by her search that she hardly noticed when she finished her punch and her glass was refilled. She felt quite pleasantly warm and tingling, and everything seemed so very *funny*. Even the chicken was suddenly tastier.

The orchestra launched into the opening bars of an aria, and the famous Signora Rastrelli swept on to the stage amid a storm of applause. She held out her arms and curtsied deeply, a tall, bosomy woman in purple velvet and vast white plumes towering over her bright red hair.

She launched into her first song, an old lament of lost love, and everyone fell silent to listen.

"'I pass all my hours in a shady old grove, but I love not the day when I see not my love! Oh then, 'tis oh then that I think there's no Hell like loving too well…'"

Emily rested her chin in her hand, watching Signora Rastrelli in something like envy. What would it be like to look like that, sing like that? To feel things so very deeply? To have such great passion? It would surely be quite uncomfortable, but also perhaps rather marvellous.

"'Where I once had been happy and she had been kind, when I see the print left of her foot in the green, and imagine the pleasures may yet come again…'"

But I love not the day when I see not my love. Emily had never felt like that at all. She loved her family, of course, as exasperating as they could be. She wanted to please them and help them, and she knew they loved her, too, and wanted what was best for her in her life. She loved the women she taught and her work at Mrs Goddard's, it was very fulfilling. She loved trying to do the right thing, trying to do her best and help people. But she had never felt like *that*, swept away by sweet emotions so much larger and greater than herself.

And she probably never would.

Her eyes suddenly itched, her throat tightening as if she would cry. She stared down into her nearly empty glass, blinking furiously to hold those foolish tears back.

Not that anyone would notice if she did start crying. Everyone else was sobbing at the song's passion. But Emily felt like the walls of the box were closing in on her. The press and heat of the other people was too much, and she could not breathe.

"I'll be back in a moment, Jane," she whispered to her friend.

Jane glanced at her from behind her white feathered mask. "Are you all right, Emily? Your cheeks are all red. Should I come with you?"

"No, no. You're enjoying the music and I—I just have to find the necessary." Emily cringed at the indelicate excuse, but it was all she could come up with quickly. Jane nodded and went back to watching the concert.

Emily slipped out of the box and away from the crowds on the well-lit walks. The punch seemed to be working its sorcery on everyone else, too, for there were many flushed faces and loud laughs, and much leaning on each other as couples strolled past.

She still felt dizzy and silly, and on the verge of tears. She didn't know where she was going, she only knew she had to be alone for a moment.

"Why does this always happen to me at parties?" she whispered.

She saw a narrower, darker pathway through the trees ahead and stumbled towards it on her cursed heeled shoes. There were far fewer lamps here, just a sprinkling set high in the trees, and the darkness closed around her in blessed quiet. She could hear whispers and soft laughter from the shadows, but she saw no one else. A cool breeze swept along the path, rustling the leaves and branches, and she shivered in her thin satin gown.

Up ahead, she glimpsed the pale marble of a fountain, shimmering in the starlight like an oasis. Perhaps she could sit down there, get off her aching feet and breathe deeply at last. She lurched towards it, and was nearly there when her heel caught again in the gravel. This time it snapped right off, and sent her pitching head-first to the ground.

She didn't even have time to panic, let alone scream. A strong, well-muscled arm caught her around the waist and lifted her up.

Cold fear rushed through her like ice in her veins, freezing her in place. She had heard the tales—she should have known better than to wander away on to the dark walks by herself! Now something dreadful was going to happen, something even worse than what happened when she had to fight off Mr Lofton in the garden.

Emily kicked out wildly, but her feet tangled in her heavy skirts and threw her even closer to her captor. She twisted and shrieked. By sheer luck, her fist flew backwards and collided with a solid jaw.

One arm tightened around her waist while one hand clamped over her mouth. Even in her haze of fear, Emily remembered the words of Sally, her pupil at Mrs Goddard's: *You have to bite if anyone tries something with you, Miss Carroll. Bite and kick them as hard as you can. And then run.*

That had been merely a rhetorical conversation on a situation Emily was sure would never happen, but here she was. She blessed Sally's hard-won wisdom as she tried to bite down again.

But the man's hand pressed even tighter. "Be easy, minx! I mean you no harm, I promise." His voice was low and rough, his breath warm against her ear.

Emily heard Sally's warning voice in her head again. *Whatever you do, miss, don't believe their promises!*

"I merely wanted to save you from falling," he said. And this time something in that voice caught her attention and made her cease her struggling wiggles. Hoarse as it was, it sounded oddly familiar.

She inhaled, and smelled the clean, soapy, lemony scent on his skin. It was just like that faint, summery cologne she had smelled when Nicholas caught her at the ball.

Could it really be him, catching her yet again? She relaxed just a fraction, and felt the strong, lean body against her back. That panic roared back over her, but this time it burned rather than froze.

"Good," he said, a relieved tone in his voice. "If

I move my hand, will you not scream? I won't hurt you."

Emily nodded, and his muffling palm slowly slid away from her mouth. He carefully set her on her feet, his arms loosening around her waist.

Emily spun around, teetering on her broken shoe. The shadows were deep here in the trees, but a stray strand of moonlight fell across her rescuer. He wore an enveloping black cloak that gave him a rather sinister aspect, yet bright blue eyes glinted through the eyeholes of his glossy black satin mask. It *was* the duke. Nicholas. He had come to her rescue again. What must he think of her, falling all over the place every time she saw him!

Then she remembered—tonight she was not herself. She wore a raven-coloured wig and a mask, as well as her full-skirted, old-fashioned gown in a vivid colour a modern young lady would never wear. He would not even know it was her. Somehow, that thought gave her a new confidence.

"Thank you for your assistance, sir," she said, pitching her voice low and soft. "I'm sorry I bit you."

He held out his hand ruefully to display her faint bite marks on his palm. "I should not have grabbed you like that. I didn't want you to fall."

Emily nodded. She didn't know what to say next; she was utterly tongue-tied. All she could do was stare up at him in fascination. If she was not herself tonight, then neither was he. He was not the duke, he was just a man. What if they were indeed two strangers, encountering each other by chance on a pretty moonlit night? Two people with no knowledge or expectations of each other?

It was a heady, frightening thought.

"You shouldn't be alone here, miss," he said, still in the rough voice. "Unless you are meeting someone?"

Meeting someone…? *Oh!* Emily almost clapped her hand to her mouth at the sudden realisation—he could *not* know who she was, therefore he probably thought her a doxy, or at least a lady of somewhat loose principles. Being not herself was not so easy after all.

"No, not at all," she said quickly. "It was just much too warm in the supper box; I wanted some fresh air."

"Most understandable," he answered. "The crowds can be most overwhelming."

"Yes, exactly so." Emily's head was spinning, and she felt oddly fuzzy-headed and giggly. "And I was a bit giddy."

Nicholas laughed. The sound was most delightful, and made her want to laugh, too. Everything just seemed so much grander tonight, larger and brighter and louder. "Too much of the excellent arrack punch? I know the feeling well."

She remembered the two—or was it three?—large glasses she had consumed of that delicious concoction. "What's in that stuff, anyway?"

"It's quite simple, I believe, grains of Benjamin flower mixed with sweet wine and rum."

"Simple and deadly, I would say." Rum and wine? She never consumed more than a tiny bit of wine at a dinner party—no wonder she was so dizzy now.

"It *is* rather potent, especially if one is not accustomed to strong drink."

"How do you know I am not accustomed to it?" Emily said, oddly indignant.

"You don't have the look of a habitual drinker," he said. The back of his hand gently brushed over her cheek, leaving soft warmth in its wake. "Your skin is too clear, your eyes too bright." He took her wrist lightly in his hand, turning her palm up on his. "You are too slender and pale."

Emily stared down in bemusement at her hand in his, so small against his rough skin. Did he ride without his gloves, work on his estate? Singular indeed. "No, it's true. I don't generally imbibe."

"Is that how you came to stumble?" he asked, his voice full of infuriating amusement.

She snatched her hand away. "I stumbled because my heel broke. Blasted old shoe. I don't know how ladies wore such heeled contraptions all the time." She had a difficult enough time with her usual flat slippers.

"Let me see. Perhaps I can fix it," he said. Much to her shock, he knelt down before her and gazed up at her in steady expectation.

"Are you a cobbler, then?" she said tightly.

He gave her a wide grin. A tiny dimple appeared in his cheek, just below the edge of his mask. It did very strange, twisty things to her stomach. "Oh, I am a man of many talents."

"That I can believe." Emily felt that odd, bemused spell come back over her again. She didn't seem quite in control of herself, especially with her stomach fluttering so nervously like that. She slowly lifted her hem a few inches and held out her foot in the broken shoe.

Nicholas slid his hand around her ankle, his fingers strong and hot through her white-silk stocking. She shivered as his caressing touch slid over her instep. It felt as if he touched her bare skin, and it was quite shocking, quite…

Delightful.

He slid the gold brocade shoe off her foot and examined the broken heel as he still cradled her foot. She would never have thought she would enjoy someone touching her *foot*. Feet were merely utilitarian, of course, made to carry a person around. They were not especially attractive. But Nicholas touched it as if *her* foot was something beautiful and precious.

It made her feel dizzy all over again, and she reached down to balance her hands on his shoulders. The feel of those hard muscles and smooth skin sheathed in fine black wool and velvet did nothing to steady her, though. It just made her even dizzier.

"I'm afraid it is quite hopeless," he said.

"Hopeless!" she cried. Yes, it *was* hopeless, feeling this way about him. They were so entirely wrong for each other.

And yet, at this moment, she had never felt more right.

"Your shoe is broken beyond repair," he said.

Emily laughed. "Some cobbler you are, sir!"

"I said I was a man of many talents. I fear I am master of none."

"I find that hard to believe," she whispered. He was obviously a master in the art of touching a woman in a way that made her mind go all soft and misty. Every light caress he ran over her toes, the arch of her foot, sent fiery tingles up her leg that made her want to whimper.

"I beg your pardon?"

Thank goodness he had not heard her! "I said—how am I supposed to walk on a broken heel?"

"Luckily, another of my talents is ingenuity." He slid the shoe back on to her foot and gently placed it on the ground. Then he reached for her other foot, curling his fingers around her ankle. Emily let him; in that enchanted, time-out-of-time moment, she might have let him do anything.

He removed that shoe and said, "Hold on to me."

She curled her fingers tighter over his shoulders, and he let go of her foot. As she tucked it back into her skirts, he twisted hard on the intact heel of that shoe and broke it off as well.

"Voilà, madame," he said. "Slippers. Very à la mode."

Emily giggled. How very silly she felt tonight! It was really rather nice not being herself. She should do this more often. "You *are* a cobbler, sir."

"I do try my best at any task that presents itself." He reached again for her foot, but that mischievous imp that sometimes came over her took hold. Laughing, she tucked it further in the voluminous folds of her skirt, making him search through the ruffles to find it.

When he caught her by the ankle, he drew her closer to him and leaned down to kiss her instep. A great shiver rushed through her at that touch.

Shocked, she almost cried out his name before she remembered they did not know each other. Her fists curled on his shoulders as his lips slid up her ankle. It was—oh, so very delicious.

And surely not proper in the least! She shouldn't let him do that, she should—well, maybe just one more little touch. Just to see what happened.

Emily closed her eyes tightly against the sensations his touch created. His hand slid slowly, slowly from her ankle up the back of her calf. His mouth followed, open, hot through the silk. Oh, why had no one ever told her such feelings could exist! This was nothing at all like the terror Mr Lofton's kiss awakened or the slight disquiet of Mr Rayburn's touch. This was something else entirely.

He nipped lightly at the curve of her knee, and she gave a strange, strangled mewling sound. She opened her eyes and looked down to see a most startling sight. He was almost hidden by the frothing ruffles of her gown. And he was—oh, he was kissing her *knee*.

Emily's legs went weak under her, and she collapsed to the ground beside him. Her skirts dragged free of him, leaving his cloak askew. Off-balance, he fell atop her, sending them both flat on to the path with him above her.

He braced his hands to either side of her head, pushing up to stare down at her. His body blocked the moonlight, the trees, everything. He was all there was in the world, him and his wondrous eyes looking at her as if she was all he desired.

No one had ever, ever looked at her like that, as if they saw her right down to her soul. People saw her beauty, her façade; sometimes they even thought they saw who she was, and dismissed her as chilly, proper and dull.

Ironically, no one had ever looked at *her*, as he did not when she was in disguise.

Full of wonder and terrifying fear, she slowly reached up and touched his face below the edge of the mask. His skin was warm and taut as bronzed satin, roughened by whiskers along his jaw. She touched the echo of that dimple, hidden now by his sudden solemn intensity. She ran her fingertips over his lips, which parted on a gasp. They were surprisingly soft....

He lowered his head and touched those lips to hers. Emily had been kissed before, once or twice by brave suitors, and thus she thought she knew what a kiss felt like—sloppy, wet, an unpleasant intrusion.

But now she saw she had no idea whatsoever what a kiss was. *This* was a kiss.

It was slow and soft, almost gentle, as he brushed his mouth back and forth over hers, pressing little kisses to her lower lip. Those slow caresses, though, ignited something deep inside of her, some burning, frantic need. She curled her hands in the folds of his cloak and dragged him closer, her lips parting instinctively.

He groaned deep in his throat, and the kiss changed, became more frantic and needful. Shockingly, she felt his tongue trace the line of her lower lip. When she gasped, he slid inside.

It was so very intimate. She could *taste* him, wine and mint and night air, feel him as his tongue twined with hers and she tentatively responded. Her palms flattened and slid around his back. Through the layers of cloth she felt the taut shift of his muscles, the tension of his body as he held himself above her.

But she did not *want* him to be away from her! She wanted him closer. She arched up against him, holding on tightly as that kiss deepened. Through the sparkling haze that had fallen over her mind and senses, she vaguely felt his hand slide along her side to her hip. He traced its curve before curling into her upper thigh and urging her closer to him. His palm smoothed over her backside through her heavy skirts.

Emily was sure there was something—everything—she should not be doing. Her everyday, practical, shy self was screaming at her to cease at once! She should certainly not be rolling around on the ground with the Duke of Manning, kissing and letting him touch her *there*. But that scream seemed the merest of faint squeals through that fog of heady need. She wasn't Emily, not now, and he was not the duke.

His lips slid from hers, along her cheek below her mask, tracing the line of her jaw. He nipped at a spot just below her ear that was shockingly sensitive. Emily gasped at the pleasure, like a burst of ripe summer fruit, sparkling and tart on her tongue. She sought his lips with hers again, eager for another kiss.

Barely had their mouths touched when something did break through that haze—an explosion high over her head. A *real* explosion, not one in her fevered mind.

Emily's eyes flew open to see fireworks in the sky above her, red and blue and bright-white against the black night. It was as if they illuminated the truth of what she was doing.

She pushed him away. His blue eyes, lit by those incandescent fireworks, were wide with a shock that echoed her own. Their spell was broken.

"I am so very sorry…" he began brokenly.

Emily frantically shook her head. She didn't want to hear his apologies; this was all her fault. She had forgotten herself in the most appalling way. She had forgotten the lesson so hard-won with the incident of Mr Lofton.

She was never drinking again, that was for certain.

She searched for her lost shoe by the sporadic light of the fireworks. "I have to find my friends. I'm sure they will be missing me by now."

Nicholas found the shoe by the side of the path and held it out to her. She was glad he didn't try to replace it on her foot—she didn't know what she would do if he touched her again. Obviously she was a complete wanton who could not be trusted.

"Let me see you back to the colonnades," he said quietly.

"No!" Emily cried. She thrust her foot into the shoe and leaped to her feet. She swayed uneasily at the sudden movement, completely unsteady. The punch, which had made her feel so sparkly and giggly earlier, now made her feel rather sick.

He was beside her in an instant, steadying her with a gentle touch on her arm.

"I am fine, thank you," she managed to say in a semi-ordinary voice. "I can find my way back."

"I know why you would not want to be seen with me," he said. "But at least let me follow at a distance and make sure you find your friends safely."

Safely? Emily nearly laughed aloud. What more danger could she possibly find? The danger obviously lay inside of her. She was a hoyden.

The thing that truly made her sad and regretful, though, was that one moment when she imagined he really, truly saw her. He didn't even know the woman he had kissed was her, Emily. She was just a stranger to him, and tomorrow he would surely forget her and this moment in the dark woods.

But she feared she would never forget.

"Please?" he said. "You won't even know I'm there."

Emily nodded, and set off towards the colonnade. "You're going the wrong way," he called.

She spun around and headed in the opposite direction. The lights and noise grew as she came closer, the glow of the real world surrounding her again. She glanced back to see if Nicholas still followed her, but he was nowhere to be seen.

Chapter Six

He was the biggest damnable fool that ever lived.

Nicholas strode down the street. The walkway was crowded with shoppers and servants laden with packages, yet he hardly saw them or heard the greetings of his acquaintances. He wasn't there, in the fine, sunny day on Bond Street, but back in the darkness of Vauxhall, holding Emily Carroll in his arms.

Emily Carroll! Of all women, how could it come to be her? She had made it clear she disliked him, and she was not the sort of lady *he* usually liked. She was quiet, watchful, where he liked blithe gregariousness, daring and humour. Yet last night had been beyond daring—it had been sheer lunacy. How did it happen?

Nicholas rubbed his hand over his face, trying to erase the vivid memory of her mouth under his, soft, sweet, eager. The feel of her body against his touch. He knew all too well how it happened. Lady Emily was tipsy on Vauxhall's potent punch, and he was a little foxed himself. Alcohol and masks were never a wise combination. They always gave the illusion of freedom and anonymity, of lack of consequences.

Well, there was no such thing as lack of consequences. He knew that all too well. His own father had lived his life grabbing whatever he wanted, heedless of its effects on his family name or the people around him. For him, there *were* no consequences; Nicholas and his poor mother and his siblings were the ones who lived with them. When he himself married Valentina, he didn't care what happened next, he only cared about his love for her in that moment. And Valentina died because of it.

Since he lost her, he had been so careful. So determined not to be like his father. Until last night.

He had only followed Emily when he saw her stumble away from the colonnades because he was worried about her safety. He didn't want to think too closely about why he watched her all evening in the first place. Ever since they ran into each other on her arrival, he had been acutely aware of where she was, her laughter with her friends, her tears at the sad song—the glasses of punch she consumed.

He could scarcely believe it when her friends let her wander off alone, and when she went off down the dark pathway. Had she no clue of the danger that awaited a beautiful woman in such places?

Of course she did not. Most young ladies did not grow up as his sisters had, knowing the ways of the world and sophisticated about its dangers. So he had followed, to make sure she was left alone, and when he saw her fall...

He caught her. And it was as if something deep inside of him, something cold and dormant since Valentina, sprang to life. And not just the *thing* in his breeches, either.

Emily, or rather the tipsy, black-haired lady with Emily's green eyes, had put her arms around him and made him feel strong and protective and—and needed again. The power of the lust that seized him when he merely touched her foot, felt the warm, rose-scented, feminine *life* of her, shocked him. It was powerful and primitive, completely instinctive—and not something he would ever have associated with Lady Emily Carroll.

Nicholas kicked at a chink in the pavement, making passers-by veer away from him with startled glances. When he first kissed her, he hadn't been thinking at all—that burning lust completely took over, and he *had* to taste her. At first she seemed quite surprised, not sure what to do, but then—oh, hell, but then she responded to him with a gasp, reached out to him, learned the patterns of their kiss.

She learned quickly, ardently. And he forgot they were in a public garden, on the ground amid the trees. He forgot he was the Duke of Manning and she was Lady Emily Carroll, daughter of an earl who was his father's old friend. They were only a man and woman who wanted each other, needed each other.

He had, blast it all, touched her backside. And a lovely, shapely backside it was. If the fireworks hadn't gone off, who knew what would have happened. Lady Emily fled and rightfully so, though he watched to make sure she rejoined her friends and seemed unharmed, though shaken.

He had first followed to make sure no one attacked her on the dark walks, and it turned out he was the attacker. He was just like his father after all. No, he was worse. His father's *amours*, culminating in his elopement with Lady Linwall, had all been worldly women at his own level.

He himself seemed to lust for young, innocent ladies tipsy on arrack punch, who did not even know who he really was. He was a fool and a cad.

He paused before a jeweller's window display to compose himself. People were beginning to look at him like he was a wild animal as he strode past them muttering to himself. After the gossip over his "heroics" in the park, he did not need any more attention at all.

But there in that window, nestled on a cushion of white satin, was a square-cut emerald pendant surrounded by diamonds. The stone was the exact colour of Lady Emily's eyes, brilliant, summery grass-green. If she was any other woman he was trying to apologise to, he would buy that and send it to her with a poetic letter. Probably one written by someone else, since he had no poetry in him at all, but the sentiments would be heartfelt.

Lady Emily, though, was definitely not just any woman. She didn't even know it was him last night, and was probably ill with mortification today. The last thing she needed was an emerald the size of an egg landing on her doorstep.

No. If he did not want to be like his father, there was only one thing to do. Go to Lady Emily, confess his identity and propose to her. Her parents would surely be ecstatic.

But Emily would not be. She did not like him, and if she found out it was him at Vauxhall she would like him even less. Yet she would feel obliged to marry him—and they would end up as mismatched and unhappy as his own parents had been.

He thought of his mother, alone and miserable at

Fincote Park. He would never wish that on Emily, would never want that bright flame he glimpsed so brightly last night to go out.

What was the right thing to do? He was damned if he knew, and the pounding headache from all that punch now throbbing behind his eyes was not helping him at all. There was only one thing he could do at the moment. Go in the shop and buy that pendant. Just in case.

By the time he emerged after purchasing the emerald, as well as gifts for his sisters and his little niece, Katherine, the crowds had grown thinner. It was late in the day, nearly time for Society to converge on Hyde Park again.

Would Emily be there? he wondered. And would she be with George Rayburn? He remembered when he first encountered her at the park, before the runaway carriage. She had been walking with Rayburn, and the man had a damnably lustful, possessive glint in his eyes when he looked at her. He hadn't seemed at all happy when Emily walked away with him, Nicholas, though Emily herself had given no indication of how she felt towards Rayburn, or indeed towards anything at all. Was the man a serious suitor?

How would she have reacted if it was *Rayburn* at Vauxhall last night? That thought sent an unexpected, blinding jolt of raw jealousy through him.

"Why, your Grace! What a pleasant surprise to see you here this afternoon," a woman called from behind him.

Nicholas spun around to see Emily's mother, Lady Moreby, along with her pretty but gossipy daughter-in-law, Viscountess Granton. *Blast it all*—it seemed he had no luck the last few days.

The ladies fluttered towards him, all ruffled parasols, feathered bonnets and excited smiles. He would have to make polite conversation with them, all the while knowing what he had done at Vauxhall.

The emerald seemed to burn right through his coat.

"Lady Moreby, Lady Granton," he said with a bow. "How very nice to see you again."

"And you," said Lady Moreby. "Doing a bit of shopping, your Grace?"

She glanced up at the jeweller's sign, then she and her daughter-in-law exchanged one of those speaking, cryptic glances. He was almost certain he did not want to know what it meant.

"I will be seeing my sisters soon, and wanted to bring them a gift from town," he said.

"Ah, yes, your dear family!" cried Lady Moreby. "I so enjoyed seeing them again last summer, and was very sorry not to encounter them this Season."

"I fear family matters have kept them in the country," Nicholas said.

"Of course. And the Season is almost over, and we shall be going to the country ourselves soon." She exchanged another look with Lady Granton. "We will miss everyone so very much that we are giving a little farewell dinner party next week, a few days after Lady Arnold's ball. Just to say goodbye."

"It will be a very intimate affair, your Grace," Lady Granton added. "Only the closest of friends and family. It is shockingly last minute, I know, but perhaps you could attend? We should enjoy it so very much— especially my sister-in-law, I think."

Nicholas was certain Lady Emily would *not* enjoy it very much—especially once she learned the truth about Vauxhall. But he could hardly refuse, not with the two ladies looking at him so expectantly, and not with the old friendship between his father and the Carrolls. Perhaps it would be a chance to make some amends to Emily, as well.

"I should like that very much, Lady Moreby," he said. "Thank you for including me."

Lady Moreby laughed, her heart-shaped face glowing. For an instant, he glimpsed Emily in her. She must have looked just like her daughter in her youth, and even now had that classical, fair prettiness. Perhaps that was what Emily would look like in comfortable middle age, with her family around her.

"I will send a card round to Manning House, your Grace," she said, and the glimpse of a future Emily vanished. "How fortuitous to encounter you here today!"

"And we are so happy to see you have recovered, your Grace," added Lady Granton.

Recovered? For an instant, he feared she knew about last night. "I beg your pardon, Lady Granton?"

"From the incident at Hyde Park, of course. Your heroic rescue of that poor child. And my sister-in-law there to witness it all! I am sure I would have fainted quite away if I was there," said Lady Granton. "We are all so full of admiration, your Grace."

"Anyone would have done the same, Lady Granton," he said yet again.

"Well, you must tell us all about it at our dinner," said Lady Moreby. 'We shall just let you finish your shopping now, your Grace. I am sure you must be terribly busy."

They all made their farewells, and Nicholas started to walk away. But a breeze caught Lady Granton's whisper as she leaned towards her mother-in-law under their parasols.

"Was he buying a ring there, do you think, Mama?" she said.

Lady Moreby glanced back at him, her pretty, rosy-round face suddenly tense. "Oh, my dear Amy. We can only hope."

A ring. Nicholas hurried on, pulling his hat low over his brow. Blast it, he should have got one of those as well. Who knew if he might need one?

Chapter Seven

"Je suis, il est, elle est, nous sommes, vous êtes. Oh! Is that quite right, Miss Carroll? I'm just not sure."

Emily pulled herself back to the present moment, listening to her pupil Sally recite her French verbs in the school room at Mrs Goddard's, only to find she was biting her thumbnail again and heard scarcely two words out of ten. She still seemed to be back on the dark pathway at Vauxhall.

She quickly curled her thumb into her fist and gave Sally a reassuring smile. "Yes, that is exactly right. You've made amazing progress, Sally."

But Sally wasn't fooled. She peered closely at Emily with those brown eyes so much older and harder than her twenty years. When she first came to Mrs Goddard's, her hair was tinted a bright red-orange and her accent was harsh and thick. Now, with the curls back to a light brown and her voice carefully modulated to a soft pitch, clad in plain, pale muslin gowns, she seemed much like any respectable young lady. She worked tremendously hard to better herself, had a kind way with the younger girls, and was Emily's best and brightest student.

But still Emily often had the sense that Sally knew so much more than she herself ever would.

"You aren't ill today, are you, Miss Carroll?"

"No, no. A bit tired, that is all."

"And no wonder, miss! I'm sure there are parties every night," Sally said with a laugh. "Dancing and card playing and such."

"I wish there were not," Emily muttered. "They are quite dull."

"Dull, miss? Surely not." Sally twirled her pencil thoughtfully between her fingers. "Aren't those toff parties meant to help you find a suitor?"

Emily had to laugh, too. "So my mother says. Yet I have not found them especially helpful."

"Miss Carroll! Surely you have a suitor. Lots of them, I would wager, with your looks. Why, if you were at my old place at Mother Logan's you would have made a fortune!" Sally suddenly clapped her hand over her mouth, her cheeks turning pink. Emily would have thought Sally could never blush. "Oh, I never meant to say that! Forgive me, miss."

Emily laughed harder. "Nothing to forgive, Sally. I just fear a 'toff' ballroom requires more than a pretty face. A dowry and some conversation help, too."

"Well, isn't there at least someone you might like? Just a little bit?"

Emily studied Sally's face for a moment, those knowing eyes. She did so long to confide in someone about the duke, to ask advice from a woman who might be able to help. She could not ask her mother or Amy, of course. Nor could she ask Jane. Much as she liked her friend, Jane was a bit prone to over-excitement when it came to romantic affairs, and she was something of a gossip. Besides which, she probably did not know much more than Emily herself.

But Sally would know. And she would never tell.

"May I ask you something in confidence, Sally?" Emily whispered.

"Of course, Miss Carroll." Sally leaned closer, her own voice soft. "I'll help you in any way I can. It's the least I can do after all you've done for me."

"I am not entirely ignorant, you understand. I read and I hear things. I've even been kissed, a few times anyway. But..."

Emily feared Sally must be laughing at her, her own experience was so much greater than anything Emily would ever possess. But Sally merely gazed back at her solemnly. "Yes, miss?"

"Does it mean something when a man kisses a woman's—foot?" Emily whispered. "I have never heard of such a thing before. Is it an—odd thing to do?" It had certainly felt most odd, and wonderfully pleasant, when Nicholas kissed her foot and caressed her ankle. She hadn't been able to stop thinking about it.

Sally's eyes widened. "Did a man do that to you, miss? At a *ball*?"

"No, not exactly." Emily took a deep breath and told her the whole story. Well, not the *whole* story, of course—she did not tell her Nicholas's identity or quite how much punch she had drunk. But it was all enough that by the end Emily's cheeks were very hot indeed.

"Cor!" Sally breathed, her fine new accent lost. "You mean he did all that not knowing who you were?"

Emily nodded miserably.

"But he didn't—finish?" Sally said. "He didn't force you into anything?"

"No! He stopped the instant I told him to, and made sure I returned to my friends. He thought I didn't see him watching me go, but I did."

"Amazing. I never met a man who could do that." Sally's gaze sharpened again. "You wouldn't want to tell me who he is, would you, Miss Carroll? I know a lot about more men of the *ton* than you would think."

"I really should not." Though Emily was horribly tempted to know what rumours there might be about the duke that she would not know, rumours among the darker denizens of London. But what if there was something there, something really dreadful? Did she truly want to know?

"Well, he sounds like a real gentleman to me, miss," said Sally. "Unique, I would even say. You shouldn't let him go."

How could she let something go when it was not hers? When it was not meant to be hers at all?

Emily left Mrs Goddard's even more confused than when she arrived, if such a thing was possible. She made her way back to the more respectable part of town with Mary trailing behind her, hardly seeing where she was going.

Until a fine carriage rolled to a stop beside her, an open barouche painted in glossy black with a gold-and-green crest on the door. The coachman drew in the matched black horses, and a man leaned out to sweep off his hat to her. The sunlight caught on his bright hair, and she saw to her shock it was the Duke of Manning himself, conjured up by her daydreams.

"Good day, Lady Emily," he said. "Out for a bit of shopping?"

"Er…yes, your Grace," she answered, then realised

neither she nor Mary carried any packages. "Though I did not find what I was looking for, I fear. We were just on our way home."

"Is that so? Then may I offer you a ride back to your house? It seems quite a long walk from here," he said.

A ride in his carriage? Sitting close together? Emily was not at all sure that was a good idea. It was obvious from Vauxhall that sometimes she had trouble controlling her hidden wanton tendencies. Not that she would jump on him in an open carriage for everyone to see, but…

Well, one just never knew what might happen. The more time he spent with her the more likely he was to discover she was the woman in the black wig. And she would never want him to know that. She was determined to keep her secret, and how could she do that if she was always with him?

She glanced back down the street, but there was no help forthcoming there. And Mary looked at her pleadingly, as if she longed to cease walking.

Emily sighed. There was simply no escape. She would just have to be as careful and circumspect as possible. The ride would not last for ever.

"Thank you, your Grace," she said. "That is very kind of you."

Nicholas immediately swung open the carriage door and leaped down, not even waiting for a footman, and held out his hand to help her up, his hand strong on hers. Mary was ensconced next to the driver on the box as Emily settled herself carefully on the velvet cushions. It was a remarkably fine vehicle, much lovelier and more comfortable than her parents' ancient, lumbering berlin. As they moved smoothly down the street there were no bumps or jolts at all, and as she ran her gloved fingertips over the plush upholstery, she could almost see why her family wanted her to marry a duke. He probably had dozens of vehicles like this one.

Not that fine carriages were any excuse for something as serious as marriage. Emily peeked at Nicholas from beneath the brim of her bonnet to find him watching her closely, his eyes an even brighter blue in the daylight. A handsome face was no excuse, either, even though his was so extraordinarily handsome.

And he kissed so very, very well.

Emily curled her fists hard against that fine velvet, trying to think sensibly again. "It is very kind of you, your Grace," she said carefully.

"I was going in that direction, Lady Emily, and it would have been very rude to let a lady walk such a distance," he said. Strangely, he sounded equally careful. "It was the least I could do after the great kindness your mother showed me today."

Alarm bells rang in Emily's mind. The duke had met with her mother? "Kindness?"

"Yes. She invited me to your dinner party."

"Dinner party?" Emily said dumbly, feeling rather like Jane's mother's trained parrot. They were having a party? Had she simply been too distracted to notice any preparations or invitations going out? Or was this some new scheme of her family's?

Nicholas frowned. "You are not aware of the event, Lady Emily?"

Emily curled her hands even tighter to resist the urge to bite her thumbnail—or tear her hair out. If this was some sort of scheme, he could never find out! "Oh, my mother and my sister-in-law are in charge of our family's social engagements. They seldom require my assistance, which is good since I am so forgetful. Of course you are more than welcome at our dinner party, your Grace. But surely you are very busy. I hope you would feel no obligation to accept if you have a previous engagement."

"Not at all. I am very happy to accept. A small dinner with friends will be most welcome after so many large balls."

And so many amorous encounters at Vauxhall? To cover her blush, Emily turned to look out at the passing street. That was almost worse, though, as everyone they passed stopped in their tracks to watch the carriage with the ducal crest go by. They would all see it was Lady Emily Carroll riding with the Duke of Manning, which would give her mother even more fuel for her matchmaking fire.

"Are you sorry the Season will end soon, your Grace?" she said. "No more parties or gatherings."

"I'm looking forward to going to the country. There's much work to be done at my estate. And if I do find a sudden craving for town, I can always return. There always seems to be a few interesting people around, no matter what time of year."

"That is true. And if *you* were here, there would suddenly be many more."

Nicholas laughed. "All the more reason to stay in the country, I think. Do *you* prefer town, Lady Emily?"

"Not at all. I like the quiet of the country, being able to walk and read and do whatever I like." Though she feared this particular country sojourn at Moreby Park would be longer than most, after her parents' disappointment over her failed Season. She might not be able to leave again.

And this might be one of the last times she saw the

duke, too. The cold wave of disappointment at that thought was most disconcerting.

"You're able to walk there without bossy dukes insisting on driving you home?" he said with a teasing smile.

Emily had to smile, too. She never could be solemn around him for very long. It simply felt too good when she was with him. "It is a very different, and much more pleasant, thing to walk in the country."

"So it is."

"And will your family join you at your estate?"

"Not this year. My sister Charlotte and her husband are at his estate at Derrington, waiting for their baby to arrive, and my other sisters are travelling with their husbands. My brother Lord Stephen will be returning to his own estate soon. It will be terribly quiet for me, I fear."

Emily could hardly imagine him without his noisy, energetic family. They seemed such a part of him—and yet another reason a match between him and her would be a bad idea.

The carriage drew to a smooth halt at the doorstep of her home. She thought she glimpsed her mother's face at one of the upstairs windows, but then there was only a swaying curtain.

Nicholas stepped down and held out his hand to help her alight. She stared at it for a second, unsure if she should take it. She had proved over and over she was not in her right mind when he touched her.

A bitter little smile touched the corner of his mouth. "It won't turn into a snake and bite you, Lady Emily, I promise."

Feeling even more foolish, she took his hand and let him lead her to the pavement. Even through their gloves she could feel the hard strength, the heat of his touch, and she remembered what his bare hand felt like on her skin.

He held on to her for a moment after she stepped to the pavement. "You see," he whispered in her ear. "Quite safe."

That she did not agree with at all. She swallowed hard past the sudden dry lump in her throat. "Thank you for the ride in your carriage, your Grace," she said quickly, before she lost her breath. "I look forward to seeing you at our—our dinner party." Whenever that impromptu event might be.

"I look forward to it as well."

She peered up at him, trying to detect any signs of sarcasm that might be lurking there. Any hint that he might know it was she at Vauxhall and was merely toying with her. He smiled back at her, all smooth politeness—just as he always was with her.

She knew she should feel quite reassured, safe with her guilty secret, but she did not. She only felt more nervous, more uncertain, than she ever had before. That little, nagging hint of disquiet simply would not leave her alone.

The front door swung open, and for a second Emily feared it was her mother, coming to urge the duke to stay for tea. But it was the butler, with no trace of any of her pesky relatives lurking behind him. They were there somewhere, though, watching. She just knew it.

"Thank you again, your Grace," she said quickly. "Good day."

"Good day, Lady Emily," he answered. He looked as if he would say something more, but Emily hurried up the steps and into the doubtful safety of the house. Only once the door was shut behind her and she heard the carriage rolling away did she relax, slumping against the nearest pier table.

"I should be happy," she whispered. She had discovered her own strength—she *could* be around him without leaping on him in lust, or bursting into flames from blushing. She could keep secrets when she had to. It had all gone rather well, considering, and now she had her first meeting with the duke after their little encounter out of the way.

Why, then, did she feel like such a wretched ninny?

"Emily, dearest, there you are!" her mother sang out. Emily glanced up to find her hurrying down the stairs, all wreathed in smiles and fluttering cap ribbons. "I see I don't have to ask if you had a good outing."

Emily turned away from her mother to the looking glass hung over the table. Avoiding her own eyes, she untied her bonnet and stripped off her gloves. The thin kid still seemed to smell like him. "It was quite all right, I suppose, though I found nothing at the shops."

"But you did not have to walk home, you sly girl," her mother said, just a hair short of crowing. "I never thought I would see my daughter arrive home in a *ducal* carriage! I do hope Lady Verney across the street saw. She has been so boastful of her daughter's betrothal to a mere viscount."

"Mama, it was a ride that lasted all of ten minutes, in an open carriage covered with servants, including Mary," Emily said. "Not a betrothal or an affair of any kind." She spun around and hurried into the drawing room, where the maids were laying out the tea things by the fire.

Her mother followed at her heels. "Well, it is a very good sign. You should have invited him in for refreshments. Your papa is in his library, as usual, but I am sure he would have enjoyed saying hello to the duke."

"I would have thought a dinner party would be quite enough for him," Emily said, plumping down in her chair. "Mama, why did you not tell me we are having a dinner?"

Her mother sat down across from her, still with that maddening expression of satisfaction on her face, even as she tried to hide it by fussing with the teapot. "It was rather last minute, my dear. An impromptu way to say goodbye to our friends before we are buried in the country."

"Impromptu when you met the duke and waylaid him outside the shops?"

"Not at all! Really, Emily, you are becoming quite cynical and suspicious. It is not becoming; it will cause wrinkles." She reached into her sewing box and drew out a sheaf of papers. "Amy and I have been working on the menu. Do you think the duke likes lamb with mint and rosemary sauce? He did seem to enjoy something similar at Welbourne Manor last summer, but I am not sure it is quite the thing now. And we will have to bring in desserts from Gunter's, of course. Cook is all very well with plain dishes, but not with the puddings. I'm not certain what to do about flowers. Pink roses? You do look lovely with pink, Emily, but lilies are fashionable."

Emily sighed and poured herself a very strong cup of tea. She certainly needed every fortification she could find, as there was no stopping her mother now. Not when she started to speak about lilies. She smiled and listened to her mother's plans, knowing that her family needed her help.

Chapter Eight

There was no doubt about it. Lady Arnold's ball was *the* event of the Season.

Traditionally the final grand event before society fled London and the gathering heat of summer for country estates and the pleasures of Continental travel, everyone always went for one last chance to wear their fine clothes before they were out of fashion and hear the latest *on dit* before it became old news. Lady Arnold had one of the largest ballrooms in London, after Manning House, and she always filled it with the best orchestra, the most flowers and the finest guest list. Anyone who had the merest pretence of being anyone at all was there.

Even Emily, though she could find no potted palm to hide behind at all. It seemed palms were now *passé*. Lady Arnold instead decorated with loops of ivy intertwined with white roses and white-and-gold ribbons, draped in lacy patterns around the room. Very pretty, but useless for hiding places.

Emily sat on one of the small white brocade chairs lined up along the walls, among the chaperons and wallflowers. Perhaps, she thought, her white muslin gown would help her blend into the upholstery.

That, however, did not seem to be the case. Very few people spoke to her, especially since Jane and Amy were dancing, Mr Rayburn had not yet arrived, her father and brother were off in the card room and her mother had flitted off somewhere with her friends, but many stared and whispered. It appeared the tale of her carriage ride with the duke had spread, and along with the Park incident it all made for delicious gossip. She should have known, of course, that this would happen.

The duke would not care. He and his family had been causing far worse scandals for decades. Emily, though, was achingly uncomfortable.

She shifted on her chair, opening and closing her lace fan. She tried to watch the dancers, the swirling kaleidoscope of their bright gowns and brilliant jewels, tried to distract herself and think of other things. She glanced surreptitiously at the ornate clock against the far wall, and saw she had actually been there less than an hour. And her mother and Amy would never want to leave until one or two at the earliest.

Emily snapped open her fan again and wafted it vigorously in front of her face. Why had she not brought a book with her? She needed to get on with her lesson plans for Mrs Goddard's, there was not much time left before she departed London and they would have to do without her for a few months.

The dance ended, and Amy's partner left her at the empty seat next to Emily's. "Lud, what a great crush it is tonight! I can scarcely breathe," Amy cried. "My slippers will be in shreds by the end of the evening."

"Where is Rob? Does he not care to dance tonight?" Emily said.

Amy snapped open her own fan. "You know how he is at these affairs, always off talking about politics somewhere, never any fun. I think he is in the card room with your father. Besides, it is not the thing for husbands to dance with their wives, at least not more than once."

Emily plied her fan harder as more people strolled past them, still staring. Amy took her hand to hold her still.

"Emily, darling, you will quite disarrange your hair, after I took such trouble with it," Amy said. Indeed she had spent an hour before they left the house pushing Mary out of the way and fussing with curls and ribbons herself, saying Emily should try to be more fashionable. She straightened the pink rosebuds and loops of pearls caught in Emily's fine, blonde hair.

"It hardly matters, Amy. The one you hope to impress with my fashionableness is not even here."

Amy scowled, not even bothering to deny it. "Where could he be? Everyone comes to Lady Arnold's ball. It is vital to one's social life."

"Perhaps it is not so vital for a duke?"

"Of course it is! Why, is that not Wellington himself over there? That is why the Duke of Manning needs a duchess to help him organise his engagements properly."

"And you think I would be the one to do that? I have no idea how one even goes about being a duchess."

Amy tsked as she gave Emily's hair one last tweak. "Of course you do. You give yourself far too little credit, Sister. You are an earl's daughter, and very pretty, if rather quiet. You know how to run a fine household and move about in society, even if thus far you have chosen not to. Anything you do not know already would be easy enough to learn."

"Is there a 'how to be a duchess' book on the shelves at Hatchards, perchance?"

Amy laughed. "If there was, I would have read it long ago! But really, Em, this is a fine chance for you and for all of us. Rob would be such a good influence in politics, if he had a proper patron to help him, and your parents deserve a comfortable retirement. You should have your own house, before it is too late." And before she was Amy and Rob's responsibility and burden, though she did not say that aloud. Emily knew very well it was true, all of it.

"Em, I do think you should—" Amy began, only to be fortuitously interrupted.

"Good evening, ladies," a deep, masculine voice said smoothly. "May I say how very charming you both look tonight? Quite the loveliest in the ballroom."

Emily turned away from Amy to find Mr Rayburn standing before her. She hadn't seen him since that dramatic day in Hyde Park, though he had sent flowers. She had supposed the gossip about the duke and herself had put him off, yet here he was, bowing and smiling at her most charmingly, as if nothing had ever interrupted his sporadic courtship.

How much easier life would be if she could like Mr Rayburn in that way, Emily thought sadly. If he made her pulse race and her cheeks grow hot as the duke did. But life was not often easy. And there was something about him that made her feel so unsure.

Amy frowned at the interruption, but quickly covered it in a polite smile. "Mr Rayburn! We have not seen you in a few days."

"I was sadly called away from town for a short time,

Lady Granton, but I did have to return in time for Lady Arnold's ball. It is my last chance this Season to beg for a dance with Lady Emily, if she would so favour me." He never took his gaze from Emily's face, which was rather disconcerting. Could he read her thoughts there?

"That is very kind of you, Mr Rayburn," Emily said. "But I don't mean to dance this evening."

"Emily, I am sure the exercise would do you good," said Amy. "And Mr Rayburn is right, this is the last ball of the Season…"

"His Grace, the Duke of Manning," Lady Arnold's butler suddenly announced. The ballroom doors opened, and the duke appeared at last. He wore a simple, perfectly cut evening coat of deep blue velvet that nearly matched his eyes and a gold-shot ivory waistcoat that sparkled in the candlelight. All the light in the room seemed to gather directly on him, leaving all else in shadow.

His gaze slid over the company—and landed right on Emily. She was so startled she had no time to look away or even disguise what she was feeling. That sudden excitement at seeing him, the fear, the giddiness—surely it was all written right there on her face.

Then Lady Arnold hurried over to him and he was surrounded by the crowd. Emily's fist tightened on her fan.

"Perhaps you are wise not to dance after all, Emily," Amy said quickly. "I seem to have torn my hem in that last quadrille. Will you come with me to the ladies' withdrawing room and help me mend it? If you will excuse us, Mr Rayburn."

His face darkened, and Emily noticed his gloved hand flex. But he merely bowed and said, "Of course. Perhaps we can take a turn about the room later, Lady Emily."

Emily hastily nodded as Amy took her arm and hustled her away. Her sister-in-law dragged her through the heavy press of the crowd, frantically looking side to side as she no doubt searched for the duke.

"Amy!" Emily whispered. "That was terribly rude to Mr Rayburn."

"Oh, pooh," Amy whispered back. "Mr Rayburn has no title and not enough fortune. It was one thing when he was your only suitor, but now…"

Emily glanced back over her shoulder to see Mr Rayburn still watching them, nearly obscured by the throng. Jane stood with him now, saying something into his ear.

"Ah, your Grace!" Amy cried. Emily whipped her head back around to find they were right in front of Nicholas. Lady Arnold watched them with a smirk, but Emily hardly even noticed. She could only see him.

Amy tugged sharply at her hand, pulling them both into low curtsies.

"Lady Granton, Lady Emily," he said. "How very good to see you again."

After a few more pleasantries about the weather and the size of the party, Lady Arnold was distracted by more new arrivals and Amy, just as Emily feared, seized her chance.

"Your Grace, Emily was just saying the ballroom is so crowded she feels rather faint," Amy said, all sweet concern. "We were on our way to seek some fresh air, but sadly I must now repair my torn hem."

Emily tried to free her hand, to protest, but Amy just tightened her grip.

"If Lady Emily feels faint, I would be happy to escort her on to the terrace for a moment," Nicholas said. "I am not especially fond of such crowds myself."

"Your Grace, there is no need…" Emily began. Her words were cut off by another of Amy's pinches. She was frightfully strong for such a small lady.

"So kind of you, your Grace!" Amy said happily. "I will rejoin you both momentarily."

She danced away, and Nicholas held out his arm to Emily, watching her expectantly. Emily glanced around, but there was no escape. Everyone around them seemed to be watching to see what she would do, and there was no place to run. There never was.

She took his arm and let him escort her to the half-open doors to the terrace. She was quite sure he must feel trapped by her family's machinations; she knew that feeling all too well herself. Yet he gave no sign of resentment, no indication he wanted to leave her in the nearest corner at the first opportunity. He held on to her arm and talked of light, polite matters, not even minding her minimal, murmured responses.

Maybe dukes were taught to be excessively polite, even ones from notoriously wild families. Or maybe they just developed finer acting skills than most people, all the better to manage all the demands placed on them. If only there really *was* a guidebook to such things, as she had wished for! Then she wouldn't feel so lost and confused around him.

Then again, it was not the *duke* who confused her. It was Nicholas himself. She glanced at him sideways, secretly. He seemed so careless, so easily, socially polite, yet she was so sure there was something else underneath that ducal surface. She had seen it too briefly at Vaux-hall, a raw, passionate loneliness that touched something she hid down deep in herself.

Every once in a while, when he thought no one

watched, it flashed in his eyes. But only for an instant, then he concealed it again.

They slipped through the doors on to the terrace. It was a space that only Lady Arnold's house possessed in London, a wide, enclosed walkway with tall windows opening on to the garden. They could be closed against the chill even as they let in the moonlight, or they could be open to the night breezes as they were now.

It seemed all the potted palms had been moved out here as well, for they lined the walls and made intimate little pathways. Chairs and tables were hidden in leafy nooks, perfect for quiet conversations. The noise dropped suddenly in that space; the roar of the crowded ballroom muted to soft murmurs and laughter. Couples strolled past slowly, pale flashes between the dark green palms.

"I've thought of building something like this at Manning House," Nicholas said.

"It is certainly lovely," Emily answered. "Are you planning to entertain more at Manning House?"

He laughed wryly. "I suppose it's my duty to, or so everybody keeps telling me."

"Hmm," Emily said thoughtfully. *Duty*—that is what everything always seemed to come to. They could pretend to be free, to choose, but duty always caught them in the end. "Duty is quite important, though I suppose giving a party once in a while would not be a very onerous one."

Not like marrying someone you didn't want because your family demanded it. Not like having to keep teaching work secret because it was not *proper*.

"And that old behemoth of a house seems good for nothing else," he said. "My family hates to visit it, and who can blame them? It's huge and draughty."

"They won't visit you at Manning House?" Emily asked in surprise. The Mannings and Fitzmannings didn't seem to care where they were, as long as they could pile in on each other. "That is not very kind of them."

"Not at all, Lady Emily. I would much prefer to visit them in *their* houses, which are much cosier and happier. But I do think a party might lure even them to Manning House."

They stopped at the far end of the terrace where two corner windows met, sheltered by a thick bank of palms. It was very quiet there, no voices except the whistle of the wind past the glass. She could almost imagine they were alone there, just the two of them as they had been at Vauxhall. It was disconcerting, making her quite nervous—yet also strangely comforting. In the midst of the vast crowd she felt so terribly lonely. Here, with just him, she did not feel alone at all.

She peered out into the night, at the swaying shadows the trees made against the star-lit sky. "This would be a fine space for a Venetian breakfast on a sunny day. Or maybe a little dance party, where everyone could see the moon as they ate their dinner." She could see it in her mind, her own party planned her own way. Her own home, where she could run things. Surely she would be good at it!

"It would also be a perfect place for me to set up my new telescope," he said.

"Telescopes? You mean those tube things scientists use to study the sky?" Emily was intrigued. She had read of such things and how they worked, and had wondered what it would be like to see the night sky closer, really study it and know what it was.

"You know of them?"

"Oh, yes, I have read of such things. They sound marvellous. But I did not know that anyone at all could possess one. They sound quite—rare." And expensive.

"I ordered mine specially made in Italy. My—well, some friends there told me of a glassmaker who can grind lenses to exact specifications. It is nothing as large as something the Herschels would have possessed, but it gives me an excellent view of the stars. I even glimpsed a comet once, streaking across the sky—" He broke off with a rueful laugh. "Forgive me, Lady Emily, for boring you. My newest enthusiasm has me carried away, I fear."

"I am not bored." And indeed she was not. She was fascinated by this deeper glimpse of him. "You actually saw a comet?"

"Right over there." He pointed past her shoulder, out the window to a cluster of bright stars in the east. "I wasn't sure what it was at first. But when I studied it through the telescope—oh, Lady Emily, I wish you could have seen it. It was the most glorious thing."

"I can imagine it must have been." Emily stared up into the sky, leaning her cheek just a tiny bit against his sleeve. She couldn't help herself. "Do you ever wonder what it would be like to drift away up there into the stars? To escape this place and just—*be*?"

She had never said such a thing to anyone before, never hinted of any such fanciful yearnings. She didn't know what made her say it now, but Nicholas didn't make fun of her. He just nodded.

"Of course I do," he answered. "Doesn't everyone think of things like escape once in a while? Wonder what it would be like to find a different world?"

"Not everyone," Emily said, thinking of her own family. They didn't imagine being anyone but who they were, which was why they fought so hard to hold on to their place in society. And that gave her a cold reminder of the way Amy had practically pushed her on to Nicholas.

She turned to face him, putting her back to that fanciful night sky. "You don't have to stay here with me, your Grace. I know you have many important people you must speak to."

He gave her a crooked grin, and that ridiculously alluring dimple flashed in his cheek. Just as it had at Vauxhall, below the edge of his mask—right before he kissed her foot.

Suddenly weak, Emily leaned back against the window. The glass was cool through her thin muslin gown.

"People more important than Lady Emily Carroll?" he said.

"Oh, please, your Grace, don't tease me!" she burst out. "I know my sister-in-law practically forced you to come out here with me. My family can be so—overwhelming. But I don't want you to feel obligated…"

"Lady Emily." He caught her hand in his, and she was so surprised the words strangled in her throat. "Do I look as if I am easily—overwhelmed? That I can be forced to do something I don't wish to?"

"I…" She thought of that steel behind his easy affability, so seldom glimpsed—and all the more formidable for it. "No, I suppose not."

"Then is it so unbelievable that I would rather be here watching the stars with you than chattering like an inane fool in a crowded ballroom?"

"Yes," she blurted.

He laughed, and raised her hand to his lips for a quick kiss. His mouth was warm and surprisingly soft through her silk glove, reminding her all too acutely of how it felt, and tasted, against hers.

"How little you know me, then, Lady Emily."

"I don't know you at all, your Grace. Which is surely for the best, for both of us."

His brow lowered in a frown. "What do you mean?"

"I mean…" Emily closed her eyes tightly. That confusion she felt whenever he was near came over her yet again, just when she most needed to be clear-headed. "Oh, your Grace! Nicholas. It was me, and I am so sorry."

"It was you?" he said. He sounded as confused as she felt. "What do you mean? What was you?"

She opened her eyes and forced herself to look him in the face. He was gilded by the moonlight, his face and hair all molten gold like an ancient statue of some pagan god. She could bear it no longer. She had always been a terrible secret-keeper, except when it came to her teaching, and somehow keeping secrets from him was harder than anything. He was *not* like Mr Lofton, she reminded herself, or like Mr Rayburn. He deserved the truth from her.

"It was me at Vauxhall," she whispered. "In the broken shoe. I didn't mean anything by it, I promise, your Grace. I'm not sure what came over me, I just…"

Much to her shock, he laughed. *Laughed!* He kissed her hand again. "Shh, Lady Emily. Enough."

She snatched her hand away. "Why are you laughing? I am completely serious!"

"I am not laughing at you. You just look so very— earnest, my lady. When I am the one who should confess and apologise."

"You should…?"

"Yes. You see," he said, ducking his head with a slightly sheepish expression incongruous for a duke. "You see, I discovered it was you before you confessed, and I must apologise to *you*."

He knew? All along? And he had just let her stammer guiltily, let her feel terrible for days? "You knew it was me?" she cried, completely forgetting they were in a public place.

Emily suddenly felt angry. Anger was unladylike and, worse, unproductive. It did nothing with her family, and it never improved anything. Only work did that. But now she felt—yes, she felt *angry*! She pounded her fists against his chest. It hurt her hands, but he was so surprised she was actually able to drive him back a step before he steadied himself.

"Emily!" he said roughly. "Calm yourself. I never meant—"

"You never meant *what*? Never meant anything by kissing me, by letting me feel guilty about keeping it secret from you?" She hit him again and then again. "You were probably laughing at me! You and all your family."

"Emily, be fair," he said. He sounded angry now, too. *Good*—she didn't want to be alone in this tantrum. His calmness only made her feel worse. "I have told no one, and will tell no one."

"You tell your family everything, I know that." She hit him yet again, that fury spiralling out of all reasonableness. It was as if every wrong, every hurt she had pressed down had broken free and was rising up now to choke her.

"Emily, please!" He grabbed her hands as she raised them to hit him yet again. Emily jerked away, but he held fast and pulled her close against his chest. He wrapped his arms tightly around her, as if to subdue her with his strength and heat.

"Please, calm down," he said tightly, his lips pressed to the top of her head. "I swear, I never meant to hurt you. That would be the last thing I would ever want, to hurt someone again."

Emily buried her face in his shoulder, trying to hold back her sobs. Her anger was ebbing away, as fast as it had come upon her, yet she still shook with it.

She had been vulnerable to him, not once, but twice now, and she did not like the feeling. It wasn't safe.

But she couldn't seem to move away from him. He seemed an anchor in the shaking storm of emotions. She curled her fingers into the front of his fine waistcoat and held on.

He held on to her, too, his arms tight around her. Was he afraid she would hit him again, start behaving like a shrieking fishwife once more?

"Did I hurt you?" she whispered. "I've never hit anyone before in my life."

He laughed hoarsely, his breath stirring the curls at her temple. "I've endured worse. I have very lively brothers, remember?" He was silent for a moment before he went on, "I would not tell them about Vauxhall, I promise. Nor anyone else."

"I would not want you to feel obligated in any way, just because I had too much punch and acted like a fool."

"Lady Emily, I do not feel *obligated*. But I must say—"

Emily leaned back in his arms and uncurled her hand from his waistcoat to reach up and press her finger to his lips.

"I don't want to talk about this any longer," she said. "It is over and past."

"No, I must—"

She didn't know what else to do, so she went up on tiptoe and kissed him. It was soft and tentative, a way to make him be quiet. But the taste of him, the way his mouth felt on hers—it sent her back to the Vauxhall woods and she fell down and down into that blurry abyss of need.

His hands closed over her shoulders, as if to push her away. Then he groaned, a wild sound deep in his throat, and his arms came around her again and dragged her against his body.

His mouth hardened on hers, his tongue tracing the curve of her lips before plunging inside to taste her deeply. The fire of her anger turned to desire, and she wanted more of his kiss. More of *him*.

He pressed her back against the window, his open mouth sliding from hers to trace her jaw, her arched neck. He lightly nipped at that sensitive little spot just below her ear and then licked it when she moaned.

How did he *do* this to her? She was never herself when she was with him! She wasn't even sure she liked it—it was too wild, too uncontrollable—but she couldn't seem to stop it.

She twined her fingers in his hair and dragged him up to her lips again. He went most obligingly, eagerly, kissing her with a heated artlessness and need that ignited her own.

She pressed herself even closer to him, wanting to be ever nearer and nearer. Wanting she knew not what. But her sudden movement sent him off balance, and he stumbled backward into the bank of potted palms.

Emily landed hard atop him, and the impact, along

with the crash of plants to the floor, shocked her awake.
It was like a cold rain suddenly falling over her head.

"Your Grace?" someone said in a hushed, shocked
voice.

Emily, still lying prone on Nicholas's chest, peered
up through the loosened skein of her hair. At least ten
people stared back, including Nicholas's brother Lord
Stephen, Jane and Mr Rayburn, and their hostess. Lady
Arnold covered her open mouth with a trembling hand,
looking as if she was about to faint at this terrible dis-
ruption to her elegant ball.

This was a nightmare. It simply had to be. It couldn't
be real, couldn't be happening to *her*. Not to the Ice
Princess, the most proper lady in all London.

She closed her eyes, tugged her rumpled sleeve back
up on to her shoulder, and prayed for deliverance from
the bad dream.

But when she opened her eyes it was all still there.
She was trapped, frozen.

Nicholas lifted her off him and rose to his feet in one
smooth movement. He held on to her hand and kept her
firmly by his side.

"Lady Arnold," he said. He sounded only the merest
bit unsteady. "I am sorry to disrupt your ball. Lady
Emily and I were going to announce our betrothal at
a small family dinner, but I see we should do so now.
Lady Emily has made me the happiest man in England
by agreeing to be my wife."

"Oh!" Lady Arnold exhaled. Her dismay vanished
in an instant, replaced by utter delight. Her ball's fame
would be assured by such a momentous announcement.
"Oh, Lady Emily. Your Grace. Let me be the first to
wish you happy."

Emily suddenly found herself clasped in Jane's arms

as her friend rushed forwards to kiss her cheek. "Emily! Why did you not tell me? Oh, my darling friend! When is the wedding to be? Shall I be your bridesmaid?"

Over Jane's shoulder, Emily saw Nicholas swept into the jubilant crowd, which had suddenly swelled in numbers. His brother clasped his hand. Lord Stephen smiled, but Emily saw the strained look on his face as he whispered in Nicholas's ear.

Mr Rayburn, her erstwhile suitor, stood off to one side, not even trying to smile. His face was dark with anger.

And, curse it all, her mother and brother appeared in the terrace doorway, looking absolutely, disgustingly jubilant.

Emily did not know how *she* felt at all. One instant, she was kissing Nicholas, all thought flown away, and now she was engaged to him. Engaged. To the Duke of Manning.

"Now, your Grace, you must dance with your fian-cée," Lady Arnold cried. "I absolutely insist."

And now she had to dance, too? Emily's legs were so weak she was sure she couldn't take a step let alone dance. "No," she whispered.

Nicholas took her hand again, holding her close as if he sensed her stunned state. The look in his own eyes was also quite disbelieving. There would be no escape among the stars for either of them, not now.

"I think my bride is a bit tired from all the excitement this evening," he said. "Perhaps a glass of water and a place to sit down is more in order."

He smiled at her, and she forced herself to smile back. Yes—no escape indeed.

Chapter Nine

Nicholas lunged forwards with his sword, driving his opponent back in a furious volley of attacks and blows. The clash of steel rang loud in the humid air, echoing and reverberating like thunder. Sweat dripped down his brow and into his eyes, hot and stinging. His linen shirt clung to his back. Yet still he fought on.

It was as if a demon rode him onwards, driving him with an angry frustration that would not be defeated. His opponent could only raise his own blade in an attempt at defence, trying to hold his ground.

Nicholas swung his arm in a wide arc, knocking the other man's blade out of his way as easily as if it was made of paper. He bashed against it for good measure, relishing the loud clang, the reverberation of impact up his arm, before pressing the tip of his sword to his opponent's throat.

The other man dropped his blade to the floor and threw his arms wide. "A hit, your Grace! Very well done indeed."

Nicholas fell back a step. He wiped at his damp brow

with the back of his arm, sucking in a deep breath as he tried to push away the remnants of that blood-lust. It still pounded in his veins, a loud rush in his ears.

"Thank you, Mr Watson," he said. "The exercise was just what I needed today."

"Your form was a bit off, if I may say so, your Grace," Mr Watson said, stripping off his heavy leather gloves. Watson was the fencing master at Gerard's Saloon for Gentlemen, and had been tutoring Nicholas in the art of swordsmanship for many months.

The Saloon was a great retreat from his ducal duties and the demands of society. It was a place where Nicholas could box or fence, could feel the raw physical life in his muscles and forget everything else. The rest of the world could be left at the doorstep.

Usually. Today, the world insisted on following him inside and riding on his shoulder as he fought. He was betrothed. To Lady Emily Carroll.

Every time he swung the sword he remembered that fact. He saw her pale, stricken face in his mind, felt her cold hand in his as she stood beside him and faced all those deluded well-wishers at the ball. She had said scarcely anything for the rest of the ghastly evening, and she never looked him in the eye.

Was that only last night? It felt like a century ago. That ball, so full of happy smiles and congratulations from everyone but the prospective bride, seemed to last a decade in itself.

He and Emily would not have chosen each other in a perfect world. *She* would certainly never have chosen him, as her frozen, statue-like demeanor last night showed all too clearly. And he, despite the strange way he seemed drawn to her despite his better judgement and prudence, would never have married at all. The title of

Duchess of Manning seemed cursed after the fates of his mother and stepmother.

This was not a promising start to their match. If there was any way to honorably cry off he would certainly do it. But there was not, and he was not his father. He would do the honorable thing, whether he—or Emily—liked it or not.

Even if it killed him.

He stood up straight, balancing the hilt of the sword on his palm. "Shall we go another round, Mr Watson?"

Watson laughed. "I fear not, your Grace. You have quite exhausted me today, and I would recommend you not exhaust yourself. I understand you have a wedding to plan."

"How do you know that?" Nicholas said. He cursed soundly at the speed gossip spread, even to the Saloon. There was no escaping it anywhere.

"I think everyone knows, your Grace. They do say the lady is enormously beautiful."

"Yes." Nicholas thought of Emily's pale, heart-shaped face, her bright green eyes, her slender figure. So beautiful, and so fragile. "She is."

"May I offer my congratulations, your Grace? Everyone here at the Saloon wishes you great happiness."

Great happiness? Nicholas almost laughed aloud. They all might as well wish he could go to the moon. Married happiness in his family, it seemed, had already been taken up by his sisters.

"Thank you, Mr Watson," he said.

"Nick!" Stephen called.

Nicholas glanced over to see his brother at the edge of the room, just beyond the other practising fencers.

He tossed his blade to Watson and hurried over to Stephen.

"You were fierce out there today," Stephen said. "I thought you were going to skewer poor Watson. Angry about something, perhaps?"

"Never mind about me," Nicholas said impatiently. "Did you get it?"

"Yes, and in record time, too. Being a duke, or bearing a duke's letter, certainly has its advantages." Stephen reached inside his coat and drew out a folded and sealed document.

A special licence. Now he and Emily could be married wherever and whenever they chose. And if word of their betrothal had spread even to the Saloon and its environs, the wedding would have to be soon.

"I fetched this as well, as you asked," Stephen said. He held out a small jewellery box. "I'm not sure it's a very good idea to use it, though. Seems very bad luck indeed."

Nicholas opened the box and stared down at the ring it held, a twist of gold studded with small diamonds like raindrops on a branch. His mother's ring. It had been his grandmother's before that, and his great-grandmother's, Manning brides for generations.

It had seemed a fine gesture of continuity, but now that he saw it he was sure Stephen's superstitions were quite right for once. He could only picture it on his mother's finger. She had worn it long after her marriage disintegrated, a symbol of a spectacularly failed match.

He didn't want to see it on Emily's hand. They had enough against them already with the cursed title of Duchess.

He snapped the box shut. "You're right, Stephen. A new ring would suit her better. Maybe an emerald."

"You know, Nick," Stephen said slowly, as if he was reluctant to say it but felt he should, "you do not have to do this."

"Of course I have to. You were there, you saw what happened. I will not be another in the long line of Manning cads."

"You are not like that!" Stephen protested. "But remember how it was with our parents, how unhappy they were. And how that unhappiness infected their children, too."

Children. Nicholas shook his head hard, trying to dislodge the sudden, hideous image of Emily white and still, a dead infant in her arms. *No.* That would not happen again. He would not hurt another woman like that again, he would find a way to stop it.

"It won't be that way for Lady Emily and me," he said. "We can live contentedly together after a time, I'm sure. Besides, I'm the duke. You and our sisters have been telling me I need to marry, to find a duchess. Why not her? She is quite suitable."

"Suitable!" Stephen burst out. "Nick, she is pretty, of course, and of good family. But she is so—so cold. How can you find contentment with someone they call the Ice Princess?"

Nicholas laughed. Emily was certainly not cold. Sometimes she burned like the hottest summer day, until she remembered herself and drew away again. "Things are not always as they appear, Brother. I *will* marry Lady Emily, because I must, and I will find a way to make the best of it for us both. You and the others have to welcome her into our family."

Stephen scowled, but at last he nodded. "I will do my

best, for you. And Justine always cares for everyone. I'm not sure about Annalise or Charlotte, though."

Nicholas's youngest sisters did have minds, and iron wills, of their own. But they always did what was best for the family in the end. "Once they come to know Emily, all will be well."

"I hope you are right," Stephen said doubtfully.

"Of course I am. Dukes are always right," Nicholas said with confidence. Inside, though, he was simply not so sure. Emily was a strange lady, impossible to read or decipher. One minute he was sure he understood her at last, and then she went and did something utterly unpredictable.

"Let's go," he said. "It seems I must shop for a new ring."

"I think you should go home and bathe first, Nick," Stephen said. "You smell like a dockside tavern after all the sweat you've shed today."

Ah, yes—*that* was what families were really for. Keeping things honest in a painfully polite world.

"Fine," he said. "Home first, then the shops. Then I must call on my bride."

They soon left the Saloon, Nicholas moderately tidied up, and set off for Manning House. The carriage had been left at home that day, so they were on foot. After the fifth person stopped them to wish him happy, though, he thought better of that decision.

"Shall we hire a hackney, Stephen?" he asked. Then his gaze was caught by a figure moving purposefully down the street, dodging around the other pedestrians as if she did not see them at all. But the light glowed on the golden curls peeking from beneath the plain straw bonnet.

It was Emily striding along so quickly, as if she was on some urgent errand. She was simply and soberly dressed in a dark blue pelisse, as she had been when he gave her a ride home in his carriage, no fine gowns or jewels or feathers to call attention to herself. Her maid scurried behind her, and Emily didn't look in the shop windows or at anything at all. She just looked ahead.

Where could she be going?

"Nick, are we going to find a hackney or not?" Stephen said.

Nicholas held his hand up for silence. Something in him urged him to follow her now. "Come with me, Stephen," he said, and took off after her.

He pulled his hat low over his brow and drew the collar of his coat high, hoping for a modicum of disguise. He stayed close enough to see where she was headed, but far enough behind that he could blend into the crowd. She never glanced back, though, and didn't seem to sense he was there.

She left the most fashionable shopping area and moved into a quieter neighbourhood of narrower streets. Nicholas kept up with her until she turned down a walkway between two tall brick buildings. Her move was unexpected, and he had to rush to catch up to her.

By the time he slid around the corner, she was nowhere to be seen. She wasn't in the small square at the end of the alleyway, either. There was just a maidservant sweeping the front steps of one of the quiet establishments. It was as if Emily had just vanished.

But why had she even come to this part of the city, practically alone? What was she playing at?

Nicholas remembered the black-haired woman at Vauxhall, the girl in white at the Arnold ball. And now the purpose-driven lady who disappeared on some mysterious errand. It appeared his new fiancée was a woman of many parts—and even some secrets.

"Well," said Stephen, as he skidded to a halt next to Nicholas, "I don't know what your bride is about, but this is the first time I have ever seen her do anything in the least bit Manning-like. Do you suppose she is up to some mischief?"

"That, Brother," Nicholas muttered, "is just what I would like to know." Yet it seemed he would not find out today, unless he wanted to go door to door and seek her out. That would never do; he didn't want to scare her off. Not yet.

"Come along," he said, turning away. "Let's visit the jeweller. It seems I need to buy a ring today."

Chapter Ten

"Emily, there you are! Where were you for so long? We have a great deal to do today," Emily's mother called through the drawing room door before Emily even had a chance to take off her bonnet.

Emily peeked in to find not only her mother and Amy, but three other people. They appeared to be merchants, with open cases and unfurled bolts of silks and laces. The wedding madness had already begun.

She sighed, and gave her hat and gloves to the butler. She fussed with her hair for a time as an excuse to keep from going to her mother just yet and drowning in those fabrics.

Ever since the ball last night—had it really only been last night?—she had moved about in a deep state of numbness. It didn't feel real, the fact that she and Nicholas were to marry.

She wasn't sure how she got through the rest of the ball at all. She vaguely recalled Amy snatching her away to the ladies' withdrawing room to tidy her hair and dress, and then people pressing in on all sides to offer good wishes and glasses of celebratory wine. Her parents' smiling faces, Nicholas's hand on her arm holding her steady—it was all a fizzy blur.

She had no memory of coming home, only her family's happy chatter in the carriage. The chatter continued at breakfast, until she knew she *had* to escape, and ran away to Mrs Goddard's. No one there knew yet about her engagement, so she didn't have to smile and seem happy. But she couldn't stay at Mrs Goddard's for ever.

"Emily!" her mother called again. "Whatever are you doing out there?"

"You must choose the fabric for your gown," Amy added. "These silks are all quite delicious."

At least someone took pleasure in the events, Emily thought. She was quite sure Nicholas did not, despite his great gallantry last night. He had done her such an enormous kindness. How could she repay him by shackling him to a wife he did not love, who he could not be content with?

And yet how could she not? They were both trapped.

"Here I am," she said, hurrying into the drawing room. "It looks like you two have been busy today."

"Somebody had to be, once the bride herself disappeared," said Amy. One of the merchants unfurled a bolt of yellow muslin for her inspection.

"I had some errands," Emily said. "Has the duke called?"

"No, but he sent a message," said her mother, comparing two shades of blue feathers. "He will call on your father this afternoon, but he will take the liberty of procuring a special licence as soon as may be."

"So you can marry before the end of the Season!" Amy cried. "Isn't that delightful?"

"Delightful," Emily whispered.

"The duke has offered Manning House for the wedding, which would be grand," said her mother, with a touch of regret. "But it is not at all the thing to have the ceremony at the bridegroom's home. We must have it here, even if there is much less space."

"That will make the guest list smaller, which is surely very desirable," said Amy. "More exclusive."

"And not so much food for the wedding breakfast," said her mother. "Now, Emily, which do you like for your gown? The pink or the blue? Or maybe this lovely sea-green? You do look nice in green."

Emily had barely begun to examine all the many fabrics and trims when the butler announced another caller.

"Mr George Rayburn to see Lady Emily, my lady," he announced, holding out the card on his silver tray.

"What, now?" her mother cried, frowning fiercely. "We are much too occupied at present for callers."

Emily lowered the pair of slippers Amy was showing her to her lap, her stomach twisting. Mr Rayburn had looked so shocked and angry when she glimpsed him at the ball. She would not have expected that; she had never given him encouragement or at least she did not think she had. But perhaps he had expected something from her anyway?

Whatever the case might be, she didn't want to hurt anyone. Yet it seemed she caused harm every time she turned around, to Mr Rayburn, to herself—and to the duke.

"It is quite all right," she said. "I will speak to Mr Rayburn."

George Rayburn came into the room and bowed to her mother and Amy, commenting politely on the wares spread before them, as correct and charming as ever. But his smile definitely looked strained.

Emily knew how he felt. She felt stretched and strained herself, so brittle she feared she might snap. She led him to a quiet corner near the windows, away from her family's avid ears. She stared down at the street below, at the passers-by so blithely going about their business in the pretty sunlit day.

"Have you come to offer your good wishes, too, Mr Rayburn?" she said. "That is very kind of you."

"I can do that if it's what you want, Lady Emily," he said. "But is it, really?"

There was a tone to his voice Emily had never heard before, intense and dark-edged. Surprised, she spun around to stare at him.

He leaned closer, so close she could feel the heat of his body. He seemed to press her in against him even as he did not really touch her. It filled her with a primitive urge to run.

She braced her hands on the window sill behind her, feeling faint. Her mother was nearby, she told herself; she was not alone, not really in danger. Yet she couldn't shake that feeling away.

"I'm not sure what you mean," she said.

"I mean—do you really want to marry him? Or is it something they are forcing you into?"

"You really should not speak to me like this, Mr Rayburn. It is not proper."

"I am through being proper!" he said, and leaned even closer, pressing her against the window. "You did not look happy last night when your betrothal was announced."

Emily struggled to maintain her dignity. If she was to be a duchess, as it seemed she must, she would have to learn to be perfectly dignified even under duress. She might as well start now.

"I was merely surprised by the manner of the announcement," she said.

"So you want to marry him?" His voice softened. "Lady Emily. I have long intended to offer for you myself. My admiration for you is so great I hardly know how to express it. I could not say anything until now, because of—certain matters, but now I see I must. You cannot marry him."

"Mr Rayburn, please!" Emily said desperately. "Please, do not say any more, I beg you. I have said I will marry the duke, and I can't go back on my word."

Not now, anyway. Any vague hope she had of wriggling out of this ridiculous engagement was gone when she saw the overly bright light in Mr Rayburn's eyes as she stared at her now. No man had ever looked at her like that, with raw possession, and it was frightening. Not exciting-frightening, as when Nicholas looked at her, but just…

Just plain frightening, as when Mr Lofton had grabbed her in that dark garden so long ago. For an instant, sheer fury flashed across his face, twisting its handsome lines into something unrecognisable. He grabbed her hand hard and pulled her towards him.

"Mr Rayburn…" she squeaked, her throat closing.

"I know you have seen my regard for you—what woman could *not* see it, even one who pretends to innocence as you do?" he said in a low, harsh voice. "You seemed to return it. Were you just playing with me, using me to hook a bigger fish?"

Emily had no idea what he was talking about. She looked frantically across the room to where her mother prattled with the merchants. Amy caught her eye, half-rising from her chair.

The butler suddenly opened the door again and announced, "His Grace the Duke of Manning, my lady."

As Nicholas stepped into the room, Mr Rayburn's hand suddenly tightened on Emily's, a punishing grip she could not escape. He raised it to his lips and whispered, "This is not over—my lady."

Under cover of her skirts, Emily kicked him on the shin and drove him back away from her. She hurried as far from him as she could, her cheeks hot. She had the great urge to scrub the hand he kissed on her skirt.

"Oh, your Grace!" her mother cried. "We have been expecting you. Would you care for some tea?"

Nicholas's solemn, dark blue gaze swept over Emily and her blush, and the clutter of wedding fabrics, and Emily had the sinking sense he was thinking she had been in a lover-like embrace in the shadows even as she shopped for the nuptials. He did not smile as he bowed over her hand.

"Thank you, Lady Moreby, but I fear I am interrupting your day," he said. "Please do not go to any trouble. I see you already have a caller."

Amy shot a hard look at Mr Rayburn, who still lurked by the window. Emily could feel him watching her. "Mr Rayburn merely stopped by to give his good wishes. He was just leaving," Amy said.

"Indeed I was," Mr Rayburn said. His tone held none of the fierceness of just a moment ago—it was all smooth politeness again. "I did merely come to give Lady Emily my very best wishes, and you as well, your Grace. You deserve each other, I am sure."

With that, he at last took his leave, and Emily fancied

the room filled up with fresh air again. She could finally breathe.

But Nicholas still watched her closely, unsmiling.

"There, now, we have plenty of space again," her mother said. "My husband is waiting for you in the library, your Grace. Perhaps after you speak with him you will take tea? We would so like to hear your opinion of our preparations."

"Of course, Lady Moreby," Nicholas said. "I am happy to help in any way I can, though I fear I am completely useless when it comes to ribbons and feathers. Perhaps Lady Emily would show me the way to the library?"

"She would be happy to," her mother said with a delighted smile.

"It's this way, if you'll follow me, your Grace." Emily spun around and hurried out of the drawing room. Her hands still trembled, so she tucked them into the folds of her skirt as she led him up the stairs. "It's in a rather odd place, so far from the drawing room. Papa does need his quiet."

She heard the fall of his booted footsteps on the stairs behind her, the soft sound of his breath. What he must think of her, seeing Mr Rayburn holding her hand like that! She felt she should say something, explain, but what could she possibly say? She did not understand it herself. She had no words.

And theirs was not a *real* engagement, anyway. Not a meeting of two minds and hearts, united in one purpose in life. It was a mere mistake. Surely he did not even care if she held hands with another man! Surely he did, and would do, far more than that with other women. She knew all too well from her work at Mrs Goddard's and from her own experience that that was the way of men.

Her stomach suddenly hurt at the thought of Nicholas with some other woman, someone like Sally or like the red-haired Lady Anders-Holt. There had been rumours of something between her and Nicholas last year, though Emily had seen nothing of it.

To cover her confusion, and what felt so oddly like anger, she said quickly, "The library is just up there, your Grace, the door at the end of the corridor. You may have to knock quite loudly, my father is rather hard of hearing. Or perhaps he just pretends to be, so he doesn't have to talk so often to my mother.…"

"Emily." Nicholas suddenly reached for her hand and turned her to face him. His touch was cool and gentle, not like Mr Rayburn's, but it made her flinch with surprise. He immediately drew away. "Emily, do you think we could forgo the 'your Grace'? I think we are definitely past that now."

"Of course, if you like," she said. "What should I call you?"

"Nicholas, I suppose. Or Nick, as my family sometimes does."

"Nicholas," she said slowly, testing the sound in her voice. She had thought of him as that, sometimes in unguarded moments, but still it felt strange to say it aloud. "Nicholas."

At last a tiny smile touched the corner of his lips. "That was not so difficult, was it?"

She smiled, too. "Not terribly, I suppose."

"I brought something for you." He reached inside his coat and brought out two small velvet jewel cases. "I should wait until after I speak to your father, I suppose, but now seems as good a time as any."

Emily took them carefully, as if they could bite her. "For me?"

"For you—if you wish to accept them."

She opened them and peeked inside, and gasped in surprise. They were both emeralds, large and square-cut, surrounded by ice-like diamonds, one in a pendant and one in a ring. They were brilliant as summer leaves, flawless and glittering.

"I have never seen anything like them, your— Nicholas," she whispered. "They are wondrous."

"Do you like them? The jeweller said pearls were more the thing these days, but somehow these seemed better. They're the colour of your eyes."

Her eyes? He had noticed her eyes were green? How very unusual. "I think they are too grand for me."

"Too grand for a duchess? Nonsense. They say my grandmother wore ruby tiaras to breakfast. Of course, they also say she was half-mad."

Emily bit her lip to keep from laughing. Sometimes she thought *he* was half-mad, too. She closed the boxes. "About this duchess business…"

"What of it? I promise you don't have to follow Grandmama's example. You can wear whatever you like to breakfast."

Emily shook her head. When he teased her like that, she quite forgot the serious things she had to say. "It was most honourable of you to say we were betrothed at the ball. I would have been quite ruined otherwise."

Nicholas frowned. "Considering I was the one doing the ruining, it was the least I could do. Did you think I was the sort who would abandon a lady in such a situation?"

"I— No, of course not. That is, well, I don't know you very well, do I? Nor do you know me. It seems terribly harsh that you should be tied to me for your whole life because of a moment of forgetfulness."

"Two moments, if I am not mistaken." He reached for her hand again, the one free of the jewel cases, and this time she let him hold her. The gold signet ring he wore was cold on her skin, but his hand was warm. "Is there perchance someone else you care for, Emily?"

He meant Mr Rayburn, of course. "No! No, not at all."

"Then there is no reason why we shouldn't rub along well enough," he said. "My sisters tell me I should marry, and our families have known each other for a long time. You know all our Manning quirks and foibles. And I will try to make you happy."

Rubbing along well enough—yes, that was what marriage really meant, didn't it? Family business, compromises, things of that sort. *She* had been taught that all her life. Why should she feel disappointed now?

And yet she did, most unaccountably.

She heard a burst of laughter from downstairs, her mother and Amy enjoying themselves as they chose wedding clothes. Her family was so happy. She had made them happy at last. She couldn't ruin that now.

"Then, if you are sure, I will marry you," she said.

"Very sensible," he said with a grin. He took the emerald ring from the box and slid it on to her finger. It just fit, the stone heavy on her hand. Then he fastened the pendant around her neck, its green fire flashing. "I was right. They *are* the colour of your eyes."

Emily was so moved he had noticed the colour of her eyes, and had even matched her betrothal jewels to them. The necklace lay on her skin, warm and special, the most wonderful gift she had ever been given. He raised her hand to his lips and pressed a lingering kiss to her fingers. Then he turned it on his palm and kissed her wrist, the pulse that pounded there just under her skin.

The bargain was well and truly struck. There was no escaping now.

She was lying.

Nicholas watched Emily as she made her way back down the stairs, until she turned at the landing and was out of his sight. She glanced back once before she went, and gave him a tentative smile.

Their betrothal was settled now, for better or worse, and their fate was sealed. She seemed resolved to make the best of it, as he was. There was no choice, not now.

Yet he had seen how close she stood to George Rayburn in the drawing room, how they looked at each other so intently as they held hands. And she had slipped away along the streets earlier—to meet with him? Was she in love with Rayburn? Had she wanted to marry him, before she was swept away by Nicholas's actions?

He had seen with his own parents what happened when two people followed their family's dictates in marriage rather than their own hearts. Scandal and sorrow were the results. He didn't want that for himself, or for Emily, either. She deserved better than a husband who had lost all his joy and lightness in life.

But if she would not confide in him and tell him the truth, he had to do the honourable thing and marry her. And hope one day they could be honest with each other.

Nicholas faced the library door with heavy resolve. Perhaps it was best Emily had not told him the truth after all, for then he would have to tell her about Valentina.

And he had promised himself never to mention his wife again. She was gone, and he would never repeat his mistake. The terrible mistake of loving someone so much their loss destroyed the whole world—and of hurting them.

He would try to be friends with Emily and do his best by her. That was his resolution now.

He knocked on the door, loudly so Lord Moreby could hear. "Come in!" the man bellowed. "It's you, is it, Manning? I've been expecting you."

"I imagine you have, Lord Moreby," Nicholas almost shouted. He shut the door against any hidden ears that might be listening. If this place was anything like Manning House, he knew there would always be listeners ready to pass on what they heard.

"I have, yes," said Lord Moreby. He pushed aside tottering piles of books and papers on his cluttered desk. "But there is no need to shout, your Grace. I can hear you very well."

"Indeed, Lord Moreby? I was told you might be somewhat…"

"Deaf? Not at all. Just something I put about so I don't always have to listen to Lady Moreby. That might be something for you to remember in married life."

Nicholas laughed, and sat down in one of the worn-out armchairs across from the desk. "I thank you for the advice. I think I need as much counsel as I can find for the married state."

"I don't think you need fear with my Emily. The girl is not a chatterer, she never was. In fact, I seldom know what she's thinking at all. Rather disconcerting, that. But she is a good girl, and smart. She'll run your houses and raise your children with no trouble at all." He suddenly pinned Nicholas with his surprisingly bright green gaze, so much like Emily's. "You *have* come to ask for her hand, I take it?"

Nicholas took a deep breath. "I have, Lord Moreby. I will be most honoured and happy if Lady Emily would be my wife, and, er, run my houses and raise my children." Not that there would be any children, not after Valentina. But no one had to know that.

"Excellent. I consent, of course. You seem patient enough, and honourable. You should make her a good husband." He scowled at Nicholas across the desk. "I must warn you, though. I am fond of my Emily. She is my only daughter, and I won't have you treat her as your father did your mother. He was my friend, God rest his soul, but I did not care for that."

Nicholas remembered his mother, weeping in her darkened room at Fincote Park. "No, Lord Moreby. I promise you I will never do that to Lady Emily. She will always be honoured and respected as the Duchess of Manning."

"Then we will have no quarrel, your Grace! Welcome to the family, may God help you." Lord Moreby pushed back from the desk, his warning obviously delivered and his business done. "Now, let's have some brandy before we go downstairs into all that wedding fol-de-rol. I have a very fine bottle I've been saving for just such an occasion."

Chapter Eleven

"Oh, Emily, my dear! I cannot believe tomorrow is your wedding day," Emily's mother said with a sigh as she ran the silver-backed brush through Emily's hair. She had dismissed Mary for the evening, saying she would help her daughter herself.

Emily laughed. She pressed her hand over her dressing gown, where the precious emerald pendant lay against her skin. "I can't believe it myself, Mama. The days have gone so quickly." *Too* quickly, passing in a blur of lace and flowers and visitors. She had seldom seen Nicholas in all the confusion, and had never been alone with him at all. Even last night, at the impromptu dinner party that had become a betrothal celebration, they had only had one stolen moment together where he kissed her cheek and asked her once more if she was quite sure.

She was not sure, of course, not in the least. But this wedding juggernaut was utterly impossible to stop. Her fate was decided and she had to make the best of it now.

In the dressing-table mirror she glimpsed her pale blue silk and white lace wedding gown, hung on the back of the wardrobe door. It fluttered a bit, as if to entice or mock her.

"You have been working so hard on all the preparations, Mama. You must be very tired."

"I am not tired in the least! In fact, I am more energised than I have been in years. My little girl is to be married, and to a duke. I knew when you were born, and I held you in my arms and saw how beautiful you are, that you were meant for great things. And I was right."

Great things? Emily doubted that. She had to learn how to be a good duchess, but she was a hard worker and she was quite sure she could do it.

Her mother tied off her braid and kissed her cheek. "Come sit by me for a moment, Emily dearest. I want to speak to you about something very important."

Emily's stomach clenched. Whenever her mother had *that* tone in her voice, Emily knew she wouldn't like what she heard. "Oh, Mama, I am very tired, and tomorrow is such a busy day. Can it not wait?"

"No, it cannot," her mother said sternly. "This is very important. Now, come sit by me on the bed and listen to me carefully."

Emily went with her in silence, letting her mother hold on to her hand. Her fingers were very tight, pressing the emerald ring into Emily's skin.

"Now, my dear, a wife has many duties, especially a wife who is a duchess," her mother said. "I have taught you to run a house properly, to dress fashionably and to remember to be charitable and kind. But there is one last, most important duty I must tell you about, as my mother did for me the night before my wedding."

Emily very much feared she knew what was coming now. "Oh, no, Mama."

"Yes." Her mother's lips pressed together grimly. "You will have your duty in the bedchamber. Now, Emily, I warn you it will not be pleasant. It will hurt, and be rather messy. You must lie back and do as your husband tells you, and it will soon be over."

"Mama!" Emily groaned. "I don't really need to know—"

"No, Emily, let me finish. There are ways to make it easier. I used to close my eyes and plan a party."

Emily stared at her mother numbly. "A party?"

"Yes. I would choose the china and the silver, and design flower arrangements and guest lists. Then I would devise a menu, and decide on my gown. By the time I knew what to serve for dessert, it was all over and I scarcely felt a thing! As a duchess, you could plan very elaborate parties indeed. Balls, even. Manning House has a lovely ballroom."

Emily closed her eyes, trying not to shudder. She knew the rudiments of anatomy, of course; she often visited museums and galleries full of classical nude statues. And she knew the basics of the marriage act, what went where and so forth.

But... "Mama, what exactly happens that I must fear?"

"Oh, my dear, you needn't fear! It is our natural duty, and we must bear it. The duke will show you what to do, and I am sure he will not demand anything—extra of you."

"Extra?" Emily choked out.

"Yes. You must not—touch things, or move about too much. That just makes it last longer. You are his *wife*, not a hired mistress. All will be well, Emily dearest, and in the end you will have beautiful babies, as I did. That will make everything worthwhile."

Emily was utterly stunned. "Is that all, Mama?" It was surely quite enough.

"Yes. Just remember—party planning. That is the key. Now, get into bed. Tomorrow is a very great day and you will need your rest! It would never do to have red eyes and a blotchy complexion for your wedding."

Emily slid under the sheets, letting her mother tuck the bedclothes around her and kiss her cheek. She blew out all the candles as she went, leaving Emily alone in the dark shadows. Her blue gown shimmered like a ghost.

She clutched at her pillow, trying to drive her mother's words out of her mind. Pain, and—and *mess*? It sounded appalling. She could hardly reconcile it to the pleasurable sensations she felt when Nicholas kissed her or the delight she felt when she saw a baby and imagined it as her own. How could they possibly all be part of the same process?

But maybe the kissing was meant to lull an unsuspecting woman into complacency, so she would not run away screaming from what happened next? She certainly didn't enjoy party planning enough to thoroughly distract herself.

She pulled the blankets over her head, completely frightened.

She had to escape.

Emily hurried along the street as quickly as she could without running like a hoyden. Her parents' house was filled with the bustle and noise of wedding preparations, servants rushing about to hang garlands of flowers and greenery along the banisters and over the doors and fireplaces. The heady scents of roasted meats and sugary cakes wafted up from the kitchens, and with the sweet smells of roses and lilies it made Emily lightheaded.

Her mother and Amy rushing about, giving and countermanding orders and fussing about with her hair didn't help.

So she pleaded an "urgent errand" and left to visit Sally at Mrs Goddard's for an hour. She was on her way there now, and even the relative quiet of the streets after the chaos of the house made her feel steadier. It was too early in the day for many people to be out, and the air felt cool on her face.

She had almost convinced herself that all would be well in the end, that she and Nicholas would find a way to rub along together. That this wedding could be a beginning, and not a disastrous end. Then her mother's voice would echo in her mind again. "It will not be pleasant. It will hurt and be rather messy."

And all her optimism turned grey. She did want to be a good wife and do her duty, but—messy? And *hurt*? She couldn't quite reconcile that horridness to the delicious way she felt when Nicholas kissed her at Vauxhall.

She certainly didn't enjoy planning a party enough to help her get through anything unpleasant.

"Surely Mama must be wrong," she whispered to herself. She would ask Sally, who surely had more experience of such things and could be more helpful. But first she had to find the courage to say the words aloud.

She stopped to study a shop-window display of fabrics and feathers. One of the bolts was a rich swath of gold-shot green silk, bright and bold. It made her think of the beautiful emerald pendant Nicholas gave her. It was certainly the most exquisite thing anyone had ever given her, and not just for its value. It was as if he found a jewel to match *her* and her secret desires to be confident and sparkling. A duchess to reckon with.

The pendant gave her a hope that she really could be that duchess, that Nicholas believed in her and they could come to truly know each other.

But that would never happen if she couldn't even get through the wedding night.

Emily studied the green silk again. It was too bright for a young miss, but surely it would be just the thing for the Duchess of Manning. She weighed her reticule in her hand, and felt the weight of the precious coins her father had given her as she left the house. Perhaps it was enough to buy at least a small amount of the silk. It could be a sort of talisman for the future.

Or maybe imagining dressmaking, rather than party planning, would get her through The Act.

A half-hour later she stepped from the shop with a package of the silk tucked carefully under her arm—and found herself face to face with Nicholas himself. He seemed to have come from the building across the street, Gerard's Saloon for Gentlemen, where Emily had heard men of the *ton* engaged in the wild behaviour of swordplay and fisticuffs. Nicholas's golden hair was damp and brushed back from his face, revealing the sharp, elegant angles of his aristocratic looks. His blue eyes were narrowed, his lips turned down at the corners in a slight frown, as if he was preoccupied with his own thoughts.

Did he, too, struggle with doubts today? Somehow that thought made her feel more hopeful rather than less. Perhaps they could learn to conquer those doubts together. *If* she could learn to trust him, trust her own feelings—and show him he could trust her.

He looked up and saw her standing there across the street. That frown transformed into a bright smile and he waved at her.

Emily waved back, torn between wanting to see him so much and wanting to run away from that first delicate touch of tenderness in her heart. She couldn't leave, though, as he hurried towards her, dodging carriages and horses until he stood by her side.

"Lady Emily," he said, bowing over her hand. "Such a nice surprise to see you here this morning. I thought there were a thousand things to do to prepare for a wedding, or so my sisters always said."

"Oh, yes, so there are, your Grace," Emily answered. "But my mother and sister-in-law have all that well in hand. I just seemed to be in the way, so I decided to do a little shopping."

"Well, I am glad to see you, though I fear my brother would say it's ill luck to meet with the bride before the ceremony."

Emily laughed, remembering Lord Stephen's predilection for superstitions. "Do you believe that?"

"I'm not so sure. I suppose we'll find out soon enough. If the wedding meal is burned or the vicar trips and falls at the altar, we'll know it's all the fault of our meeting. In the meantime, shall I see you home? My carriage is waiting just over there. Perhaps we could take a very long detour through the park on the way, and thus you would miss most of the preparations."

Emily glanced uncertainly down the street, which grew more crowded now. She remembered her plan to visit Sally and ask for her advice on the wedding night. But as Nicholas smiled at her, she began to hope it might not be so bad after all.

She had to learn to trust him, or their future could

never be bright. And she had to learn to trust in herself.

"Thank you, your Grace," she said, accepting his offered arm. "A drive through the park sounds most pleasant."

Chapter Twelve

"Will you take Nicholas to be your husband? Will you love him, comfort him, honour and protect him, and forsaking all others, be faithful to him as long as you both shall live?"

Emily held Nicholas's hand in hers, the vicar's voice sounding far away in her ears. She felt as if she floated underwater, as if everything came to her all muffled and distant. His clasp on her, so steady and warm, was all that held her tethered to the earth. All that was real.

Behind them sat her parents, her mother softly sniffling into her handkerchief, Rob and Amy, Jane and her parents, and Emily's deaf old Aunt Lydia.

Over Nicholas's shoulder she saw his brother, Lord Stephen, trying not to look doubtful, and his half-sister Justine and her husband Brenner, Lord Linwall. They were Nicholas's only family there, and for that she was grateful. She probably would not have been able to speak at all if they were all there, watching her, thinking her not right for their beloved brother. At least Justine had a gentle, easy air about her, a kind smile as she embraced

Emily when they met. Lord Linwall seemed stern and quiet, but when he looked at his wife there was a soft, joyful light in his eyes.

Surely no one would look at *her* like that now. She was binding her life to the man who stood beside her, so stalwart and serious.

A sudden tense hush over the drawing room reminded her that she had not answered.

"I will," she whispered, and listened numbly as Nicholas repeated the same words, vowing to take her as his wife.

"In the presence of God and before this congregation Emily and Nicholas have given their consent and made their marriage vows to each other. They have declared their marriage by the joining of hands and by the giving and receiving of rings. I therefore proclaim that they are husband and wife. Those whom God has joined together let no one put asunder. Amen. Your Grace, you may kiss your bride."

Nicholas's hand tightened on hers and he bent his head toward her. His lips touched hers, dry and surprisingly soft. It was a kiss nothing like the heated, insane embraces they were swept into at Vauxhall and the Arnold ball. This was a gentle salute, a sealing of an official contract. A lifelong contract.

He drew away, giving her an odd little half-smile, and she was engulfed in her mother's tearful embrace.

"Oh, my dearest girl!" she said. "Such a lovely bride. Who would ever have thought I would call my own daughter her Grace the Duchess of Manning?"

Emily laughed. Had that not been what her mother had been hoping and working towards for months? "You have made a perfect wedding for me, Mama."

"I'm just sorry more of our friends could not see it,"

her mother said with a regretful sigh. "St George's would have been grand."

"Oh, Mama, only social-climbing mushrooms have large affairs at St George's," Rob said, kissing Emily's cheek. "Better to have a private ceremony."

Amy also kissed her, and fussed a bit with the wreath of white rosebuds in Emily's hair. Then she found herself embraced by Justine.

"Lady Emily, welcome to the family," she said, her soft voice ever so lightly touched with a French accent. "We shall try very hard to make you happy with us."

"We're a strange lot, but not so bad once you get to know us," said her husband. Emily remembered it had been his mother who eloped with Nicholas's father so long ago, causing such great scandal and shattering two families. Yet he seemed such a part of the family now, despite all those old wounds. How had he done that?

Maybe she could learn from him. Perhaps she could never really be one of them, fit in with them and their fun-loving ways. But she *could* be an exemplary duchess and set a good example. Show them how hard she was willing to work to be perfect for their family name.

"Oh, I just realised!" Justine said. "We cannot call you Lady Emily now. You are the Duchess."

"No, just Emily, please," Emily begged. "I think it will be a long while before I accustom myself to 'Duchess'."

"You are quite monopolising my wife, Jussy," Nicholas interrupted, taking Emily's hand in his again.

"You will have her to yourself long enough at Welbourne," Justine said with a laugh. "I must get to know her now. Annalise and Charlotte will want a full report when I write to them. They are so desolate to miss the wedding. We thought we would never live to see this day!"

Emily had been relieved his whole family could not come on such short notice, but now she almost wished they had. They would keep Nicholas from leaving too soon for their planned honeymoon at Welbourne—and what came next. Terror and duty, according to her mother.

She noticed Lord Stephen standing by the fireplace, and she excused herself to go to him. She wasn't entirely sure why; he didn't seem to like her very much, and she was usually paralysed with shyness around such a jokester. But right now he seemed oddly wistful.

"What a lovely, quiet spot you've found, Lord Stephen," she said. "Isn't it strange how even small weddings feel like such a crush?"

He smiled at her, putting her a bit more at ease. He was not so fearsome when he smiled. "It's the weight of family expectations, Duchess. The whole rest of our lives pressing in on us."

Duchess—she was already fed up with the sound of that word, and it had only been her title for less than an hour. "Do you think you might call me Emily?" she asked.

"Of course. You are my sister now, and you must call me just Stephen." He reached into his coat and took out a tiny box. "A small wedding gift for you—Sister."

"Oh, no! Your family has given me too much already." The wonderful emerald pendant from Nicholas that she wore, pearl earrings from Justine, a painting from Annalise and the ducal ruby tiara, which Nicholas said his grandmother had once worn to breakfast. It had been brought to the house under guard, and her mother wanted her to wear it for the wedding. Emily insisted on the flowers.

"It is only a small token," he said, holding out the box to her. "I'm sure you will like it more than what Charlotte is planning to send."

Emily studied him warily, remembering Charlotte running around Welbourne with her hair flying and her snorting pug dogs at her heels. "What would that be?"

"A puppy," Stephen whispered. "One of her blasted pugs is to have a litter any day now, just like Charlotte herself. But don't tell Nicholas, it's meant to be a surprise."

"Indeed it will be." Emily took the box and shook it lightly. "No snorting or barking. You're right, I do like it better."

Stephen laughed. "Open it, then."

It was a tiny gold horseshoe, set with an emerald chip, hung on a thin gold chain. "How very pretty!"

"It's for good luck. You should wear it all the time. Everyone needs a good-luck charm, especially when they embark on something as perilous as a marriage."

"Will you help me put it on?" she said.

"Certainly." As he fastened the little clasp and the horseshoe fell beside the emerald pendant, he said, "Our family has not always had the best of luck at marriage. But I hope you know, Emily, that my brother has a good heart. He cares about us, and I think he works very hard to take care of us all. He never thinks of himself."

Emily pressed her palm over the horseshoe, and remembered that terrible day at the park: Nicholas rescuing the child, diving in front of a carriage to snatch her to safety. Nicholas saving *her* at the ball, saving her reputation at the expense of his own freedom.

"Yes, I know," she whispered. He was a good

man—and now he was trapped with her, a woman he did not love, who did not know how to be a good wife to him.

"He needs someone to look after him, to be kind to him," Stephen said.

Emily stared up at him, at his handsome, earnest face that looked so much like his brother's, and she remembered her promise to herself. She would learn to be a perfect duchess. Even if his family could never like her, they would respect and accept her.

"I will try my hardest to be a good wife and duchess," she said. "I will never hurt your brother, or make him ashamed of his wife."

"Thank you, Emily." He kissed her hand. "That is all we can ask."

"Are you monopolising my bride, Stephen?" she heard Nicholas say.

Emily turned and smiled at him. He smiled, too, but the look in his eyes reflected her own feelings of the day—relief, fear, a brittle, tense expectation. The wedding was over, the dice were cast—what would come next?

"Your brother gave me a gift," she said, showing him the charm. "Isn't it pretty?"

"Ah, Stephen, you and your amulets," Nicholas said, laughing.

"I fear that she will need all the luck she can find, married to you," Stephen retorted. "I should have given her a dozen."

Emily took Nicholas's hand and held it very tightly. She feared not even a dozen horseshoes, ringed around with spells, could protect her heart now.

Chapter Thirteen

Nicholas paced the floor of his bedchamber at Manning House, the hem of his black-brocade dressing gown sweeping in a wide arc every time he spun around and stalked back the other way. He felt a bit like the brooding villain of one of the romantic novels his sisters loved, lurking and scheming outside the heroine's chamber.

From behind the door that connected his room to the duchess's next door, he could hear soft feminine voices and laughter. Emily's maid was helping her change from her wedding gown, and there were mysterious rustles, gasps and laughter, and bursts of some fresh, rosy fragrance under the door.

He had only been married a few hours, and already his house—and his life—were being transformed.

Nicholas strode to the window and stared out into the night, the darkness that spread out over the garden and on to Green Park beyond. It was cloudy tonight, threatening rain, and there were no guiding stars to be seen even with his telescope. He was on his own, with his new bride.

A burst of wind swept past the window, rattling the old glass and making the draughty chamber even danker. Manning House certainly needed to be transformed by a mistress's guiding hand, refurbished and made into some sort of home. But maybe he was wrong to bring Emily here for the wedding night. He didn't want to frighten her away before they even began.

He thought of her as she had looked during the ceremony, her face pale as milk, her hand cold in his. It seemed she was already frightened even then, and would bolt at any moment.

But then it looked as if she resolved on something in her own mind. Her shoulders stiffened, her back straightened and her jaw was set in a determined line. She looked like a soldier in her fluffy silk-and-lace gown and white rosebuds.

"I will," she had whispered, and they were bound together.

Nicholas drew the old, dreary, brown-velvet curtains across the window. If she was resolved, then he would be, too. He had not been a good husband the first time; there had to be a way he could atone for that by making Emily happy, and by keeping her safe from the curse of being Duchess of Manning.

But how was he to make her happy? Titles and jewels didn't seem to excite her. Manning House was unlikely to entice her, with its dark gloominess and chilly hallways. But tomorrow they would travel to Welbourne Manor. Welbourne was small and pretty, filled with good memories. They would be relatively alone there, and he could start to get to know Emily. To try to decipher what would make her happy.

In the meantime, he had a task to perform. Nicholas

tightened the sash of his robe, feeling a bit like a soldier armouring for battle, and went to the connecting door.

All was silent now on the other side. He knocked, and heard her call softly, "Come in."

He slowly turned the handle and pushed it open. Aside from the last few days, when he had inspected the room for cleaning and the installation of new curtains and hangings, he hadn't been in the duchess's chamber since he was a child. Then it had belonged to his mother, and no one had used it since. Not until tonight.

Like the duke's chamber, it was a vast, high-ceilinged, echoing space, barely warmed by the marble fireplace. He had tried to make it less gloomy than his own room, which had not been changed since his father last used it in the unhappy final days of his first marriage. There were new yellow-taffeta curtains at the windows and draped from the old carved oak bed. The triple-mirrored dressing table was hung with green satin tied with yellow bows, and a yellow-velvet counterpane with green satin bolsters and cushions was spread over the bed. Emily's trunks and bandboxes were stacked by the silk-papered wall, ready to go to Welbourne.

The counterpane and the new, lace-trimmed linen sheets were turned back invitingly. But Emily didn't rest under them. She sat perched on the edge of the high bed, her feet in their kid bedroom slippers resting on the steps. Her hands were folded on her lap, her fine, pale hair brushed over her shoulders.

Nicholas stared at her in startled fascination. How very beautiful she was. He had always known that, of course, but now, in her pale-green dressing gown trimmed with waterfalls of white lace, she looked like an ethereal fairy princess.

A pale, delicate fairy princess. Valentina had been

tall and robust, yet even she had not been able to survive childbirth. How could a dainty fairy?

Her lower lip trembled, and she quickly bit down on it. Her hands tightened in her lap, the knuckles white. Nicholas remembered his resolve to make her not regret their ill-begun union. He wasn't making a very good start to that resolution, staring at her like a callow schoolboy.

He smiled at her in what he hoped was a reassuring manner, and slowly went to sit beside her on the bed. She did not move away, but he could feel the stiff wariness of her body.

"I'm sorry we had to come here to Manning House tonight," he said. "There was no time to see about much refurbishment, and I fear it's not very comfortable. When we return to London you must make any changes you like."

"I'm not sure I would know where to begin," she said softly. "This room is very pretty."

"New fabrics were brought in, but there was no time to replace the furniture."

"I like it. And I do hope the wedding was to your taste, and that of your family. My mother would have preferred something more elaborate, but like the furniture there was no time."

"Would *you* have preferred a bigger wedding?"

Emily shook her head. "Not at all. Everyone is talking about it quite enough as it is. But I would not want your family to think it was not done properly."

Nicholas laughed. How adorably earnest she looked, his serious new duchess! "My family has never given a moment's care to what is proper. They're just happy I am married at last. They will love you."

"Will they?" she said doubtfully. "Your brother said

Charlotte is going to send us a puppy. Is that love? Or some sort of warning?"

He laughed even harder. "One never really knows with Charlotte. I can tell her not to send it. Her dogs do shed a copious amount."

"No, don't do that! I don't want to offend her when she is being kind." Emily glanced around the dark room, the crackling fire doing its gallant, futile best to warm the space. "Besides, a dog might liven up the place a bit."

"Emily." Nicholas gently took her hand in his. It was still cold. Her emerald ring and a thin, new, bright gold band sparkled on her finger. Stephen's good-luck gold horseshoe flashed amid the lace ruffles at her neck. "I know we have not started well, but I want you to know I will do my best to make sure you are content. Whatever you want, you must only tell me and it will be yours. I don't want you to regret this bargain we have made."

Emily stared at him with her wide, solemn green eyes, her fingers curled around his. "You mean, if I want a carriage or a diamond necklace?"

"I suppose so, yes. Whatever might make you happy."

Her hand tightened. "I don't want those things, though I will admit that when you gave me a ride in your carriage I thought it was very fine indeed! All I want is to do my best as your duchess, to never make you ashamed."

He gently brushed his fingertips over her soft, white cheek. He watched in fascination as a pink, warm blush followed his touch. "How could I ever be ashamed of you? Look at you—there could be no more perfect duchess. I would just think you would be ashamed of *us*, as harum-scarum as we are."

Emily shook her head, her hair rippling down her back. "I will work very hard at this, Nicholas, you'll see. I am ready to do my duty."

She slowly laid back on the bed and untied the ribbons of her dressing gown. The green silk drifted away to reveal a thin, low-cut, white-muslin chemise that clung to her slender body. It was a body as lovely as the rest of her, tiny-waisted and long-legged, with high, white breasts that pressed against the lace neckline. He could see the berry-pink shadow of her nipples through the fabric, and he remembered how it felt to kiss her at Vauxhall. The heady heat of it, the sweet taste of her.

His own body responded, immediately hardening. He wrapped the folds of his robe closer over that rebellious erection. "Emily…"

"I am ready to do my duty," she said. "In all things."

She laid her arms along her sides, palms flat to the sheets, and closed her eyes. Somehow Nicholas was reminded of Ophelia, pale and perfect, sinking below the waves amid her floating flowers.

He smiled, but quickly suppressed it. He didn't want to make her indignant with his amusement again.

She seemed to sense it anyway. She opened her eyes and frowned up at him. "I know what I have to do as a wife. My mother and—and a friend told me all about it. I'm quite ready."

He shuddered to think what her mother and this "friend" had said to her. It made his resolution to not hurt or frighten her even harder.

He leaned down and gently, softly kissed her lips. Her body was stiff under his, and he was sure he knew now what her mother had advised her—to lie back and think of England. But that was not the way he wanted his marriage to be. Despite his vow to never hurt Emily as he had Valentina, to never force his fairy princess to bear his child, he wanted them to be friends. To form some sort of partnership so they could be content together.

And, blast it all, he had not been with a woman in much too long! Emily was so beautiful, and she smelled so sweet. His body ached to have her, to feel her heat closing around him and lose himself in the pleasure.

Slowly, he told himself sternly. *Carefully*. She was Emily, his wife, not one of the girls at Mrs Larkin's or an opera dancer he could make his mistress, who understood everything and was sophisticated in the ways of the world.

He kissed her again, a little deeper, and laid his palms lightly on her shoulders. She trembled under his touch, but he felt her lips part a bit, felt her begin to relax. He slowly slid his caress down her arms, smoothing away her dressing gown.

The chemise was sleeveless, and her bare skin under his touch was soft and cool. He kissed the corner of her mouth, the curve of her jaw. He lightly touched that soft spot just below her ear with the tip of his tongue. She had seemed to like that before, and he knew she still did when she sighed. A shivering ripple went through her body, and he nipped at that spot before sliding his open mouth along her throat. She tasted of roses and sugar, of sweet femininity.

In the hollow at its base, her pulse beat frantically just beneath her skin. He swirled his tongue there, tasting the hot life of her. That scent of roses grew stronger, headier around him, intoxicating, and his own desire rose up inside him like an irresistible tide.

Her arms wound around his shoulders, holding him against her. But he could not have left even if he wanted to. His desire for her had been growing and growing ever since Vauxhall. He had fought to suppress it, but now it would not be denied.

He kissed the swell of her breast above that lace, tasted the hollow between them. There was a tiny freckle hidden there, pale amber on her white skin, and he licked at it.

"Nicholas," she gasped. Her hands curled tight on his shoulders, and her neck arched against the pillows.

He touched that spot he had just kissed, caressing, testing the weight of her breast on his palm. She was so very soft, so warm—perfect. With one fingertip he traced the edge of her pink aureole. Her nipple puckered tight and hard against the thin muslin. He closed his mouth around it, tasting her deeply at last, rolling her taut nipple over his tongue.

She moaned. Her hands fell away from his shoulders and twisted in the sheets, her head tossing on the pillow. He doubted she was thinking of England now, and that gave him a deep, primitive feeling of satisfaction. His plan to make her happy seemed to be going rather well.

And he felt quite happy himself. His body was hard as iron with need for her. He eased the straps of her chemise down, baring her body to his avid gaze. She was not so very pale now. Her skin was flushed a delicate pale pink everywhere, over her full, high breasts, her flat belly.

She suddenly grabbed his hand before he could draw the fabric over the dark triangle between her thighs. "Y-you're not supposed to remove my clothes, I think."

"Emily, my dear," he whispered against her breast. "I wish you would *not* think. Not just at this moment. But you do have a point."

"I do?"

"Yes. It is unfair for me to be clothed while you are not."

Emily stared at him as he rose up on his knees beside her and reached for the sash of his robe. She squeezed her eyes shut as the velvet loops pulled free.

Nicholas laughed, and shrugged out of the heavy garment. He tossed it to the floor. "It's quite all right. I'm not that frightening, I promise."

She peeked warily. Then she closed her eyes again. "Not frightening according to whom, exactly?"

He took her hand and pressed it flat against his chest, right where she could feel the pounding of his heart, the rise of his breath. It was hard to breathe easily with her touch on his bare skin, with her so near him. Curse it all, but he did want her, more than he had ever thought possible. More than he had ever wanted any woman.

More than he ever *wanted* to want her.

"I'm just a man, a human being," he said. "And I want to make you happy, Emily. I want to give you pleasure, if I can."

Her eyes opened, and she stared up at him in raw astonishment. "You want to give *me* pleasure? But my mother and Sally said—"

Nicholas swooped down and covered her mouth with his, kissing her with all the passion of his pent-up hunger until she moaned. "Emily," he muttered, "I want you to forget what your mother and this Sally person told you. Trust me now. Please."

Slowly, she nodded, and he kissed her again. He slid his tongue over hers, tasting her deeply. When he felt her body relax beneath his again, he gently slid down her chemise the rest of the way and cast it to the floor with his robe. He caressed her shoulders, her waist, the soft flare of her hips.

He lowered himself between her thighs, nudging them apart, and softly touched her very core.

She gasped and tried to pull away, but he refused to stop kissing her, to let her go so easily. He combed his fingertips through the damp curls before easing inside. She was soft, wet—and very tight.

She made a strange mewing sound deep in her throat as he touched her, as he tried to find that one perfect, sensitive spot. When she cried out against his mouth, her hips arching, he knew he had found it. She felt like hot satin against his skin, and he could smell the delicious musk of her desire. The desire that rose up to meet his.

"I'm sorry, Emily," he whispered. "I can't wait any longer."

She nodded. "It's all right, Nicholas. I'm ready."

He reached between their bodies and guided himself carefully into her. It took every ounce of his strength to move slowly, to be careful, to not drive himself forwards and find his pleasure in her body. She was very tight, her virginal body pressed around him, and the heat of her made him groan.

Beneath him, she squeezed her eyes shut again and clutched at the twisted sheets. She made no noise.

Nicholas braced his arms to either side of her, holding his weight away from her. Beads of sweat trickled down his bare back as his desire screamed at him to move, to take her!

Her lips parted, and he barely heard her whispered words over the blood pounding in his ears. "Soon be over," she said, just as he drove through the thin barrier of her maidenhead. He slid deep inside of her, a hot pleasure greater than any he had ever known washing over him.

And Emily screamed. She grabbed at his shoulders, her nails digging into his skin.

"Oh, sweet God, Emily! I am sorry," he shouted. He tried to pull away from her, but her nails still held him fast, and her knees were clamped to either side of his hips.

He had *known* he had to be careful with her, that she was a delicate lady. He had told himself to go slowly, to not frighten her. And then he forgot all that the minute he touched her, and jumped on her like a barbarian.

"Emily, you have to let go of me so I can move away," he said tightly, through his own cloud of pain. She had a surprisingly strong grip for someone so small. And there was his own, overwhelming sexual need, which would not be pushed away so easily. Not when it was so close to glorious fulfillment.

She turned her head to one side, and to his horror he saw a tear trickle from the corner of her eye. It glistened there, a tiny diamond on her pale cheek. She bit her lip.

"Emily, please," he said, as gently as he could. "You have to let go of me."

At first he thought she couldn't do it. Her fingers dug into his shoulders as if he was all she had to cling to now in the world.

And he felt the same. As he stared down at her pale face, she was all he could see. She was all he knew.

Finally, she nodded and her hands slid away to rest at her sides. She seemed to be holding her breath, and she made him think of a delicate bird, wary and poised for flight. Her eyes closed tightly.

Feeling like a brute, Nicholas eased himself off her

and sat on the edge of the bed, his fists braced on his knees as he struggled to calm his raging desire.

"Oh, Em, I am sorry," he said. He reached for his robe and pulled it back over his naked body. "I'll leave you now so you can rest. It's been a very long day." And it looked to be a very long night, one he would spend alone with his unfulfilled need for her—and his guilt.

To his shock, she said, "Nicholas, wait." He heard her sit up against the pillows, the rustle of the sheets as she drew them around her. "Must you go?"

She sounded so forlorn he knew he couldn't leave her. He scooped up her chemise and handed it to her. Only once he heard her draw it over her head and lay still again did he turn to look at her. Her hair was tousled over her shoulders and the blankets she had drawn close gave her the look of a wild, rebellious fairy. She stared down at her lap.

"I would think you would want me to go as quickly as possible," he said. "That you wouldn't want to see me right now."

"I suppose it is not the thing for husbands and wives to stay together all night," she said. "But, well, this room *is* very large, and—and I just don't want to be alone in it. Could you stay with me until I fall asleep?"

Stay with her? That was all he wanted. As he looked at her now, so beautiful and vulnerable, so alone in a situation not of her own making, it was all he wanted. To hold her and comfort her, to keep her safe.

Only it seemed he was no good at that at all.

"I'll stay with you," he said, "if that's what you want."

She nodded, and slid over to make room for him on the vast bed. He climbed beneath the sheets with her, and carefully put his arm around her shoulders. Much to his surprise, she snuggled close to him and rested her head on his shoulder.

"Everything is so very strange tonight," she murmured sleepily. "But things will look better tomorrow, yes? And every day I will find my way clearer."

"I think we both will," he said. He slid his arm around her and held her against him. She was so soft and warm in his embrace, so wonderfully alive. "I seem to have much to learn about being a husband."

Emily laughed softly. "And I know nothing about being a wife. Maybe we can learn together, though. Maybe we can be partners of a sort? Learn to trust each other?"

Nicholas wasn't sure she *could* trust him, not if he jumped on her in lust every time he saw her. Something inside him just couldn't seem to help it, a physical, beastly side that wanted her so fiercely.

And he remembered her furtive behaviour the day he followed her through the streets to that mysterious house. Would she ever trust him enough to tell him what that was? Could he trust *her*?

"That is not an easy task, learning to trust," he said.

"No, it certainly isn't easy." Emily propped her chin on his shoulder to gaze at him steadily. Her green eyes were so clear and bright, just like those faraway stars. "But it seems we're stuck with each other now."

Nicholas wrapped one of her long golden curls around his finger. The fine, spun-sugar hair clung to him. "How would you suggest we begin this task of trusting?"

A tiny frown drew a crease between her eyes. "Well— perhaps you could tell me a secret."

He laughed in surprise.

"Yes," she insisted. "Something no one else knows.

Then you will see that I will tell no one. That your confidences are safe with me."

"I don't have a secret."

"Not even one?"

Of course he did have one. A big one. Valentina and his marriage to her. But that was so very large, and buried so deep. Nicholas wasn't sure he could even say the words aloud after so long keeping them silent.

Yet Emily watched him steadily, hopefully. *She* was his wife now, and their future had to be built together.

Nicholas pushed the pillows behind his back and sat up against them, gathering all his inner strength. Emily slowly sat beside him, her eyes wide and solemn.

"I do have a secret," he said, "one I have told no one, not even my siblings. But you are right. We must be partners now, and you should know."

Emily nodded. "I am listening, Nicholas."

He took a deep breath and plunged ahead. "I fear you are not my first wife."

"Not…" Her face turned even whiter, but Nicholas saw that she, too, had hidden wells of strength. She did not move away or raise her voice. She curled her hands tightly on the sheet and said, "Are you saying you are already married? That you have a wife hidden away somewhere?"

"No! I am not the villain of a horrid novel, Emily. My wife died, many years ago."

"Oh, I see." That frown between her eyes deepened as she struggled to decipher his words. "But if you were married to this lady…"

"Valentina. That was her name."

"Valentina—how did your family not know about it? If you loved her enough to marry her…"

"I did love her, very much. But no one knows about

her, not even Stephen. No one, until you." He took her hand, gently urging her to sit closer to him. He could tell the story better when she was not watching him quite so sadly.

"Why did you tell no one about her?" she said.

"It happened when I was in Italy, on my Grand Tour, not long after my father died. Brenner thought I should go then, that the travel and education would be good for me after such a loss, before taking on my full responsibilities," he answered. "It was so quick. I had never met anyone like Valentina, so very alive and bright and honest! I fell for her, just like that, with one dance, one laugh. She was the daughter of a respectable attorney of the city, and at first they weren't sure about me and my intentions, a wild young Englishman who seemed crazy to them. But I persuaded her to marry me, to return to England with me as my wife. I thought we could tell my family then, when we arrived home. It didn't seem the sort of thing to put in a letter, and I knew if they met her they would accept her right away."

"I see. And then what happened?"

Nicholas rubbed his hand over his face, as if he could erase the old memories. They were still there, and yet they seemed faded and distant. It was as if the mere saying of the words, the sharing the memories to the light of day, made them grow further and further away.

But he was suddenly weary, and couldn't go on with the rest of the sad tale. Not yet.

"She died," he said. "Before we had been married a year. And I returned home to my family. They seemed to realize something had happened while I was gone, but for once they didn't press me about it. It was too hard for me to speak of her, and as time went on I did

not even know how to begin. It seemed easier to keep
her hidden in my heart, my own secret. Now I suppose
she is yours, too."

Emily was silent for a long moment. She stared down
at their joined hands as if she was stunned by his tale.
He wondered if he had made a mistake, if she would
run from him.

But she gently kissed his cheek and he saw the sheen
of tears in her eyes. Everyone who called her icy was so
wrong, he thought. So very wrong.

"Your secret is safe with me, Nicholas," she said
simply. "And I thank you for telling me."

Nicholas nodded. He had no more words now, no
more emotions. Only a deep, weary peace. "Shall I leave
you now? You need to get some sleep."

Emily shook her head. "You need rest, too. Stay with
me." She slid down among the rumpled bedclothes,
drawing him with her.

He wrapped his arms around her, holding her close.
He gently kissed her forehead, and she smiled as she
held on to him, already drifting into sleep.

"Goodnight, wife," he whispered.

"Goodnight—husband," she whispered back. And
that word sounded sweeter than he'd ever thought it
would again.

Chapter Fourteen

The dawn light crept from the window, a thin, pale pink line between the heavy curtains that flowed over Nicholas's sleeping face. Emily leaned her elbow on the pillow, gazing down at him.

He looked younger in his sleep, more peaceful, as if the burden of his position was eased when he lost himself in dreams. His bright hair was tousled over his brow, his arm stretched out as he sprawled across the mattress. She lay very still, trying hard not to disturb him in his rest.

How silly she had been last night! She had known what to expect, thanks to her mother and Sally, and first it wasn't at all what they said. It was quite—pleasant when he touched her and looked at her naked body with such raw hunger. It made her feel really beautiful for the first time, made her feel full of light and pleasure. Maybe marriage would not be so difficult, after all!

He had shared his deepest secret with her. Surely that meant something very great. He told her about his first wife, his Italian Valentina, something he had shared with no one else. It was a very sad tale, and she was certain she could not compare with a lost love of that sort. But maybe they were learning to trust now. If only she could tell him *her* secrets, too....

Emily heard Nicholas stir beside her, felt his lean, hard body stretch and shift next to hers. He gently kissed her brow, and without opening her eyes she reached out to touch his face. His skin was warm, roughened by a morning growth of beard. Somehow touching him that way, waking up next to each other like this, felt more intimate than anything. Something very profound had changed last night, emotionally.

"Have you been awake long?" he murmured.

"Just for a little while."

"It's still early. You should try to rest a while longer, before we journey to Welbourne."

"I'm not sure I can sleep in such a grand room," she said. "It doesn't feel like my own. I would probably get lost if I tried to even cross to the window."

Nicholas caught her hand in his and kissed it, his lips soft and lingering over her knuckles. "I want you to do whatever you like to make the room feel like your own," he said, holding her hand against his cheek. "Make this whole cursed house your own! And Scarnlea Abbey, too. They *are* yours now, you are the duchess."

Emily opened her eyes to find him watching her closely, his eyes very blue and very serious, in the ripening morning light. "What if you don't like the changes I make?"

A tiny smile quirked at the corner of his lips. "I can't imagine not liking anything you did. But even so, you must do whatever you want. Whatever will make you happy."

She hardly knew what to say. No one had ever trusted

her taste or judgement before, or given her free rein to do anything at all. But she was sure she could make Manning House worthy of the title.

Nicholas watched her now with an open, serious confidence, as if he believed she could do that, too. Even after everything—the hasty wedding, the disastrous wedding night. The tale of his secret marriage.

"Thank you," she whispered, and kissed his cheek. Those whiskers tickled at her lips and made her giggle. He reached up and brushed a stray curl back from her cheek, a gentle touch that still made her shiver.

How could the slightest, gentlest touch from his hand do that? It made her want more, made her greedy to be closer and ever closer to him.

And he seemed to feel the same. His gaze sharpened, and his fingertips trailed over the curve of her cheek, along her throat to her shoulder, bound by the thin strap of her chemise. His stare followed his touch, hungry.

Emily was hungry, too. Filled with a terrible, aching longing for *him*.

"Emily, I'm sorry for my behaviour last night," he said. "You must have thought me a brute. And then when you listened to my confidences, let me unburden myself—I felt so much more free than I have in a long time."

She laid her fingers against his lips, stopping his words. She wanted no words today to shatter her fragile fantasy, her silly dream that this was some kind of real marriage. That illusion would vanish soon enough when they left this room.

"We spend half our lives apologising to each other," she said. "Please, Nicholas, not today. I'm glad I could listen to you. Your secrets are always safe with me."

He grinned, and she felt the soft movement of his lips under her touch. "No apologies, then."

Overcome with emotion, with painful longing, Emily leaned closer and kissed him. She threw her caution to the wind and put all that longing and all those foolish dreams into that kiss, and he responded. He took her tightly in his arms, pulling her close to his hard body until there was no longer anything between them. Nothing holding them apart. Maybe she *could* banish the memory of his first wife, at least for a time.

The tip of his tongue lightly traced the curve of her lips, sliding inside to taste and tease. Tentatively, she used her own tongue, making him groan, which in turn made her feel even bolder. She caressed his bare shoulders with her palms and trailed her touch lower, over his chest. His skin was hot, like smooth satin over hard steel, roughened by a light sprinkling of pale gold hair. She felt the powerful beat of his heart under her touch, the strong, vibrant life of him.

She traced the edge of his flat, puckered nipple with the side of her nail, and it tightened under her touch. Nicholas groaned against her mouth, and pulled her closer until she lay right on top of him. Their kiss turned harder, more frantic, deeper. A hot, humid, desperate need swept over Emily, and all her senses were filled only with him. The way he tasted, smelled, the way his body felt against hers. *Nicholas*—her husband.

He caught her by the waist and rolled her beneath him, their legs and arms entangled. His kiss slid from her lips along her throat as she arched her head back in surrender. She felt the heat of his tongue over the curve of her shoulder, the sudden chill of the air on her skin as he drew her bodice lower.

His mouth soon chased away any hint of cold. He

kissed the soft swell of her breast, making her gasp at the fireworks-sparkling sensation of it. She combed her fingers through his hair, holding him to her.

Nicholas captured her aching nipple deep in his mouth, rolling it over his tongue, biting at it lightly. Emily could hardly breathe, she was seized with the terrible pleasure of it all. She arched herself against his body, her legs falling apart instinctively to cradle him.

Through her bright haze, she felt him reach down to catch the hem of her chemise, pulling it up over her legs, her hips, baring her to his gaze, his touch. He caressed the soft underside of her knee, the curve of her thigh as she pressed it against his hip. His fingertips lightly skimmed her backside, touching her fleeting, teasingly, *there*.

"Oh," she moaned at the jolt of lightning sensation. It was like nothing she had ever felt before. "Again, please."

He laughed and touched her again, a little deeper, a little harder. It was—wondrous.

She traced the groove of his spine, feeling the damp, fevered heat of his skin, the shift of his body. She swept her exploring caress over his own backside, and the hard muscles tightened under her touch. She felt the velvety length of his rigid manhood against her inner thigh, and rather than make her afraid it delighted her. He *did* still want her.

"Please, Nicholas," she whispered. "Now, please."

He drew back from her a bit, his bright blue gaze wary as he stared down at her. "After last night? Emily, you'll be sore."

"That doesn't matter. I just—I just want this. I want it to be better for you this time."

He gave a humourless laugh. "Oh, believe me, Em. Last night was fine for *me*. But for you…"

"Then show me now. Show me how it can be," she whispered. "Please."

"Oh, God help me," he groaned. He slid her chemise over her head and tossed it to the floor before kissing her again. There was no careful art to this kiss at all, only sheer, raw need. They fell back on to the bed, wrapped around each other.

He nudged her legs wider and slowly eased himself into her. There was some pain, a stretching sensation, but no shocking tearing feeling. Emily knew what to expect now, and she arched her hips to draw him even deeper.

He braced his arms to the bed, and held himself very still for a long moment as she became accustomed to that sensation of fullness. And any trace of pain flowed away, leaving only him and her, together. Slowly, he eased back and rocked forwards again, and then again.

With each movement he was a little deeper, a little faster, until she learned his rhythm, they learned each other. That delicious, tingling pleasure spread through her whole body, to the very tips of her fingers and toes, and she sobbed with the joy of it.

She closed her eyes and tightened her legs around his hips as he plunged into her, faster and faster. "Nicholas!" she cried out. "I don't—I can't…"

"Just let it happen, Em. Let it—free!"

And she did. She let go of all her control, all her inhibitions, and let it all burst free in a fiery white explosion of pleasure.

"Emily!" he cried. His body tensed above hers, taut as a drawn bowstring. He suddenly pulled out of her and groaned deeply. "Emily."

Then he fell to the bed beside her, their limbs still entwined. She felt the heat of his breath on her shoulder, as ragged as her own. His arm slid around her waist, holding her close, and she slowly reached out to touch his hair, to twine her fingers in the damp, silken strands.

She felt weaker and more tired than she ever had in her life, and yet she also felt—lighter. Freer. As if she could run and dance and shout! As if she could do anything at all.

His breath slowed as he slid into sleep, and Emily bent her head to kiss his brow. His arm tightened.

She wished she could find words to thank him, to tell him what a great gift he had given her! But there were no words. They were all jumbled about in her tired mind.

"Mama was so very wrong," she whispered. And she curled up against him as she tumbled down into a dark, peaceful sleep.

Chapter Fifteen

Emily leaned her elbow on her travelling case as she peered out of the carriage, trying not to press her nose to the window glass like a silly, eager girl. She had been to Welbourne Manor before, of course, but never as a real part of it. It made her feel so very excited to be almost there now. She was a duchess now; she had to be dignified.

Not that she had been terribly dignified that morning, in her bedchamber. She peeked at Nicholas from under the hood of her cloak, trying not to blush as she remembered the things they did together in that ridiculously vast bed. The way she clutched at him and cried out. And now that hours had passed, now that they were on their way to Welbourne, truly husband and wife, she did not know what to say to him. She only knew she couldn't mention his secret again. That was in the past now; she wanted to build a future.

So she resorted to the weather. "Such a fine day we're having," she said. "I was afraid it would rain."

Nicholas laughed. "It never rains at Welbourne. Especially when a honeymoon is planned there."

"Have there been many honeymoons at the estate?"

"My sisters, I suppose. They were all married there."

Emily watched as the carriage turned in through the gilded gates of Welbourne, wide open in welcome, and rolled down a wide gravelled lane lined with shady trees. Beyond she glimpsed rolling green fields dotted with a few fluffy, picturesque sheep. In the distance was a small lake and a shimmering summerhouse, all custom-made for fun and pleasure and frivolity.

"Would you have liked to be married here, too?" she asked. "In a place that belongs to you?"

Nicholas reached over to take her gloved hand, bringing her gaze to his. He gave her a smile. "I thought our wedding was just right, don't you? No crowds to stare at us."

Emily had to laugh at that. She *was* glad for a small wedding—she would surely have tripped and fallen in front of a crowd. "Yes, I did like that."

"And Welbourne is not mine. It belongs to my whole family." He gestured out the window, and Emily saw that the house itself had come into view. A shimmering white Palladian villa rising like a wedding cake above bright flower beds, soaring exterior staircases and a profusion of sparkling windows. It looked like an illusion, a dreamhouse.

"Now it's yours, too," he said.

Emily watched, entranced, as the house drew closer. No, it could never be hers; she could never really belong there, not as Nicholas and his siblings did. But she was touched that he *wanted* her to belong there, that she was not being shut out immediately. She was touched that he trusted her.

The carriage drew to a halt at the foot of the marble steps, and footmen in blue livery immediately dashed over to open the door and lower the steps. Nicholas stepped down first and helped Emily to alight, holding on to her arm as they went into the house.

The entire staff waited in the soaring, light-filled foyer, which was bedecked with flowers and greenery. Footmen and chambermaids, the chef and kitchen girls, even the scullery maids in clean mob caps and aprons were arrayed to greet them.

The butler, clad in his black coat, gave them a low bow. Emily remembered him from the house party, a quiet, efficient presence who seemed to know every inch of the estate. "Your Grace, may we offer our congratulations on your nuptials? Welcome to Welbourne Manor, Duchess. The staff is entirely at your disposal, and we hope you will be very happy here."

"Thank you, Gelray," said Nicholas. "I would imagine you all never thought this day would come, eh?"

Gelray stiffened indignantly. "Certainly not, your Grace. We would not presume." An older lady in grey silk stepped forward to curtsy. "Duchess, this is Mrs Courtney, the new housekeeper here at Welbourne."

"I will give you a tour of the house as soon as you are rested from your journey, your Grace," Mrs Courtney said. "You must let me know if there are any changes you wish to see made."

Emily remembered her wish for a guidebook to being the perfect duchess. She certainly wished she had one now. "Thank you, Mrs Courtney. I am sure everything is perfect just as it is."

The housekeeper's lips pursed, as if that was not quite the right answer. Maybe she wanted a bossy, demanding duchess? "Let me introduce the rest of the staff, your Grace."

Emily was quickly introduced to Signor Napoli, the famous chef she remembered from her last visit as being quite temperamental. Today he was all smiles, promising to make her his *divino* trout à l'orange for dinner. She also met a vast array of people, whose names and faces blurred together in one vast whirl. Emily could hardly believe it. Welbourne was a small pleasure villa; what could the staff possibly be like at the grand ducal estate, Scarnlea Abbey, and at Manning House?

"Your lady's maid is waiting for you in your chamber, your Grace, if you would like me to show you there now?" Mrs Courtney said, as the staff rushed off to their duties, now properly introduced.

Emily glanced at Nicholas, who nodded. "I will see you later at tea, Emily."

She hurried up the winding stairs behind Mrs Courtney, her head pounding. It was a relief to find the long, shady corridors silent and dim, lit only by chalky rays of sunlight from the high windows. Last time she was here, the halls and chambers rang with loud laughter and running footsteps as people played raucous games of hide-and-seek and blindman's buff. Now it felt like she was all alone there.

"It has been quite a while since the carpets were changed, your Grace," Mrs Courtney said with a sniff. "And the curtains are becoming a bit faded."

Emily studied the limp draperies and pale carpets, the outdated furniture. "I see what you mean, Mrs Courtney. Perhaps new ones can be ordered soon, if His Grace's sisters agree."

"But you are the duchess now," said Mr Courtney. "It's a very good thing for Welbourne to have a proper mistress at last. Ah, here is your chamber. I hope it will be quite satisfactory."

Mary already waited for her there, along with Emily's trunks and boxes holding her new trousseau. It was a pretty chamber, all pink and white, filled with yet more flowers. Over the white marble fireplace hung a painting by Annalise, a view of Welbourne in the rich glow of an autumn day. The dressing table was draped with pink-and-white tulle, her brushes and pin boxes already on its glass surface.

"Very nice, thank you, Mrs Courtney," Emily said. At least the housekeeper did not suggest changes in here! Emily liked it just as it was.

"I will send up tea and refreshments, your Grace. You need only ring the bell if you require anything else at all."

Emily sighed as the woman shut the door softly behind her. "It's terribly grand here, isn't it, my lady?" said Mary, voicing Emily's own hidden thoughts. "I mean— your Grace. It didn't seem that way last summer."

"No, it didn't." Emily took off her cloak and gloves and dropped them on to a little marble table next to a pair of cavorting china shepherdesses. Welbourne had seemed chaotic and shabby and fun last summer. Even her parents' country house, the seat of the Earls of Moreby for centuries, did not seem so grand now. "I guess we'll just have to be what this house needs, according to Mrs Courtney."

Mary gave her a doubtful glance as she shook out the cloak. "And what is that, your Grace?"

"A proper mistress. Whatever that means."

"...and this is the small sitting room. Miss Justine— Lady Linwall now—often uses this room when she visits Welbourne," Mrs Courtney said. She opened the last door along the long upstairs corridor, letting Emily peek inside.

Her head was spinning with all the rooms she had seen on this whirlwind tour before dinner, all the large, airy chambers just made for parties and dancing. The house seemed too silent with only Nicholas and herself in residence, as if it waited breathlessly for the influx of laughing, merry guests. She was sure she could never be that "proper mistress" for such a place!

But this room felt different. It was just as bright as the rest of the house, but smaller, cosier. A chamber for quiet conversations, for reading or sewing, or just thinking.

Yellow brocade chairs clustered around the carved white-wood fireplace, while a small piano sat by the windows and a delicate gilt desk waited for a lady to sit there and plan the household menus or write letters. Yellow-and-white curtains were looped back, letting in the waning daylight outside.

Emily's gaze was caught by two portraits hanging over the mantel, and she went to examine them closer. Both the women wore the same silver satin-and-lace gown, and Emily recognised one as Charlotte Fitzmanning, with her heavy dark hair and watchful brown eyes. The other was a beautiful blonde lady, a lace fan in her graceful hand and a teasing smile on her lips.

"That is Miss Charlotte—Lady Andrew Bassington now," said Mrs Courtney. "And her mother, the late duchess. Miss Charlotte wore the same wedding gown last year."

"It's very beautiful," Emily murmured. She studied the duchess's painted eyes, so full of life and happiness. She was a lovely lady; it was no wonder she had turned this whole family upside-down as she had. Her presence still seemed to hover over the house, like the memory of an exotic perfume.

Emily almost laughed at herself. She might have this lady's title now, but she would never take her place. Not until she stood up for herself and made changes to suit herself. There had to be a new way of being Duchess of Manning. She had already made a beginning there.

"If you would like to use this room, your Grace, I can have it dusted and aired," the housekeeper said.

Emily gave the last duchess one more long look. Could she use this room, with those laughing eyes watching? Perhaps it would be a good thing, and remind her that she was part of this family now, too, for better or worse.

"Yes, thank you, Mrs Courtney," Emily said. "I would like that very much. I will have some new furniture ordered from London, too, so we can do some updating."

"Very good, your Grace. Shall I take you to the dining room now?"

Nicholas waited for her there, standing at the head of the table as the servants carried in platters of Signor Napoli's richly sauced creations. Emily laughed to see the shining, polished expanse of the table, vast enough for a great banquet and set with the finest of china and crystal, with heavy, gleaming silver and a vast bouquet of spring flowers. A half-dozen candelabra cast a golden candle-glow over the palatial scene.

And her own place, at the foot of the table, seemed miles away from Nicholas.

"Are we expecting company?" she said, watching as more footmen arrived with yet more food, more wine. "A battalion, perhaps? Or the king?"

Nicholas laughed ruefully. "I told them we didn't want anything grand. But Signor Napoli was eager for the new *duchessina* to sample his creations."

"I look forward to it. The food was splendid at your party last summer." Emily took her seat, and as she suspected she could barely glimpse her husband. "I think the company might be even better now, though, if I could only see to be sure."

"Oh, this is ridiculous!" Nicholas leaped up from his chair and strode along the length of the table to take her hand. "We are on our honeymoon, we should at least be able to talk to each other at dinner."

Emily giggled and let him lead her to a chair to the right of his. The servants scrambled about in confusion to move her place setting.

"That is much better, don't you agree?" said Nicholas.

"Much better indeed. I don't feel quite so alone as I did way down there."

One of the footmen poured out goblets of rich red wine, and Nicholas raised his to her in a toast. "Here is to honeymoons, and our first night at Welbourne."

"To Welbourne." And honeymoons, even when they did not feel quite real.

"And how do you like the house, now that you have seen it all?"

"It's quite lovely, of course." Emily took a sip of the wine, which was sweet and rich, unlike the vinegary stuff her parents served. She was hoping it would make her feel bolder, more—wife-like. "But then I always thought that."

"You must make any changes you like, order new furniture, carpets, whatever."

"Oh, no, I could not do that here! This is your family's home. But I did tell Mrs Courtney I would use the small sitting room, if your sister would not mind."

"Emily." Nicholas reached over and covered her hand with his. "How many times must I tell you? No one will mind whatever you do. This is *your* house now, as is Manning House and Scarnlea Abbey. You are the duchess now."

"Yes. I keep forgetting, I fear. I don't feel at all duchess-ish yet," she said.

"I think it might take a lifetime to feel like that. I don't feel like a duke in the least."

Emily laughed, feeling happy to see he trusted her with decorating at least, and took a small bite of Signor Napoli's delicious trout. That was a definite perk of being duchess. "But what are your own plans while we are here, Nicholas?"

As they talked of calling on neighbours, of fishing in the lake and perhaps going on a picnic the next day, Emily slowly relaxed. The light talk, the wine, the candlelight—it all worked its spell on her until that strain of worrying about the right thing to do, which she seemed to live with every minute since she had met Nicholas, drained away. She was not a new duchess, in a new home, she was just Emily. And he was just Nicholas.

But the wine also worked to make her very sleepy after the long day.

By the time the raspberry cream pudding was served, she was yawning secretly behind her hand.

Not secretly enough, though. "Would you like to retire, Emily?" Nicholas asked, draining his own glass of wine. "We can play cards after dinner tomorrow."

Emily smiled at him drowsily. "Yes, I think I could

not keep my eyes open tonight, it has been such a long day. And I am entirely full, thanks to Signor Napoli's excellent fare. We should make him come back to London with us."

"I doubt he would do that. He declares London to be a vile cesspit where no one appreciates the art of his cooking."

"That can't be true anywhere." Emily hesitated as she pushed back her chair to leave the room. "Perhaps I will see you later, Nicholas?"

He looked surprised, but not entirely unhappy. "Certainly, if you like. Goodnight, Emily."

"Goodnight."

Later, after Mary had helped her change into her nightdress and brush out her hair, Emily lay under the bedclothes and listened for Nicholas to come upstairs, for any sound from the chamber next door. She remembered what had happened in their bedroom in London, the unexpected delight of it all, and it made her smile into her pillow.

Surely he would come to her soon, and it would happen again. Then she could see if that was only some kind of oddity, or if by some miracle lovemaking was always like that.

And if only she was not so tired…

Emily's chamber was silent as Nicholas eased the door open and peered inside. The candles had sputtered low, casting flickering shadows on the walls that spread down over the bed.

She lay there in the middle of the high feather mattress, the curtains tied back and the bedclothes drawn around her. Her golden hair lay in shimmering waves over her shoulders and the lace-trimmed gown she wore, and a little smile was on her lips, as if her dreams were sweet ones.

Nicholas sat down on the edge of the bed, careful not to wake her. She had looked so tired at dinner, even as she laughed with him, and he didn't want to interrupt her dreams, even though his body ached with desire for her.

He tightened the belt of his robe, drawing it closer over his erection. "There will be time for that tomorrow," he whispered. Tomorrow, and for a long time to come. He wouldn't make the mistakes with Emily he made with Valentina. He wasn't a foolish, callow youth now, even if it felt like it with his lust raging inside him as he stared down at her beautiful face, the swell of her breasts under the gown.

Their marriage had not begun well, and it was still on unsteady ground. Maybe it would never be the love match he had had with Valentina, that his siblings had with their spouses. Maybe he had made a mistake in marrying her. But at least there was one area in which they were compatible, and it was a start.

He gently kissed her brow, smiling as she murmured in her sleep and burrowed deeper under the blankets. "Sleep well in your new home, Emily," he muttered. He tucked the bedclothes closer around her and silently left the room.

But that unruly desire wouldn't abate so easily, no matter how fiercely he wrestled it down. He feared she was making him feel again, for the first time in a very long while.

Chapter Sixteen

"Hold it at a slight angle, like this." Nicholas's arms came around her, his hands lightly adjusting hers on the wooden curve of the bow she held. Though his touch was soft, strictly practical, Emily could feel it all the way to the very core of her. Whenever he touched her now, she felt so shy and yet so bold at the same time, even if it was just the brush of his hand as he passed her the marmalade at breakfast that morning or helped her try to launch an arrow straight now.

It made her feel terrified—and hopeful. Their marriage seemed to have begun rather well, all things considered. Surely it could go on like this? Maybe even grow better and better?

But she had found that whenever she allowed herself to hope something might change in her life, she was left disappointed. She couldn't bear it if that happened now, with something as important as her marriage.

And she couldn't help but remember waking up alone in her new bed this morning.

She forced away the cold memory of that confusing

moment, the instant where she drifted between dreams and waking and couldn't remember where she was, and focused on the cool, sleek bow in her hand. When Nicholas had offered to teach her some archery this morning, she was quite sure it would not end well. The welter of scattered arrows on the grass, far short of the target, proved her fears right. Yet she wanted to spend this time with Nicholas, show him how hard she was willing to work.

If only the feel of his soft breath on the back of her neck would cease distracting her!

"You're tensing your fingers again," he said gently. "Just relax, like so. Grip the bowstring lightly, about here." He slid her fingers into place, covering them with his own. "Draw back in one smooth, slow movement and—release."

Emily pulled back on the string as far as she could, trying to keep her focus on the target, and let go. The arrow flew straighter than the others, its green-feathered end iridescent in the sunlight, and landed in the target. Still far from the red centre, of course, but definitely in the target and not on the ground.

"I did it!" Emily cried. She dropped the bow to the grass and clapped her hands in joy. "Look, Nicholas, it's in the target!"

"So you did," he said, an unmistakable note of pride in his voice. "And on your very first try."

"It was my eighth try. But it's lovely of you to ignore that." Without thinking, she spun around and threw her arms around his neck. She kissed his cheek over and over, making him laugh. Every moment with him made her feel more confident, more sure of herself and what she could do as a duchess. "Next time I will hit the bull's-eye itself. And maybe you could teach me to row on the lake, too?"

"One thing at a time," he said. "Maybe some tea now?"

Emily glanced over his shoulder to see some of the servants setting up gleaming silver trays on the shady terrace. They were absolutely polite and professional, but she saw two of the maids smile at their employers' antics.

Emily quickly stepped back from him and smoothed the skirt of her new yellow-muslin gown. "A little refreshment does sound welcome."

She scooped up the bow from the grass and took Nicholas's offered arm as he led her to the waiting terrace. Cushioned chairs were set up companionably around the damask-draped table, laid out with tiered trays of sandwiches and cakes, along with a delicate Italian porcelain teapot and cups and a crystal pitcher of lemonade. The servants at Welbourne were obviously very thorough.

"Do they always have so much food for two people?" Emily said with a laugh. "Last night could have been a banquet for Henry VIII."

"I don't think Signor Napoli and his staff are quite used to only serving two. Usually when anyone is in residence at Welbourne there's a vast crowd to follow, sometimes at a moment's notice. I suppose they wanted to be prepared."

"It must seem terribly quiet to them now, and to you." Emily poured out the dark, steaming India tea, adding lemon to his as she remembered he liked. "Perhaps you would rather have a party come to join us?"

"And ruin the rare luxury of quiet? Not at all. Unless you are feeling lonely."

Emily took a long sip of her tea. "I am almost never lonely," she said, not quite truthfully. She was often lonely, but that merely seemed the way of things.

She stared out over the rolling lawns of Welbourne, all fresh green and glistening under the sun. They sloped all the way down to the lake, with its tree-lined shore, docks and the little white summer house. Swans glided placidly on those waters, while sheep grazed on the fields nearby.

She hadn't noticed all that perfect loveliness last summer, it had been so crowded with people. Now she saw its true beauty.

"I see why you like it here so much," she said. "I've never seen such a peaceful, pretty place. I'm surprised you and your family aren't here all the time."

"We would be if we could. It's our favourite place—the only place where we can really be ourselves."

"I haven't noticed any of you behaving with particular inhibition anywhere else," she said teasingly.

Nicholas laughed. "No, we don't often curb our emotions. But here no one judges us for them, or talks about our parents behind our backs. Here we can pursue our own passions without hindrance. Not that I have any creativity myself."

"Nor do I. I cannot even embroider or net a bag like my sister-in-law Amy. But you are very good at archery. That surely takes a great measure of creative visualisation."

He leaned back in his chair, watching her curiously. "How so?"

"You must picture the arrow flying straight on its course and landing in the target. Something I have yet to master."

"It's my sister Charlotte who is the true archer. That's

her bow you are using. Our father had it made especially for her."

"Oh." Emily glanced down at the bow, only just noticing the small C.F. burned into the wood and gilded. "I hope she will not mind that I borrowed it."

"Not at all. She'd be glad to share our father's gift." Nicholas took another drink of his tea, staring thoughtfully over the lawn. "My father didn't have much time to spend with us, he was always so busy with his duties and later with…"

With his mistress? "Personal duties?"

Nicholas smiled ruefully. "Something like that. But the time he did have for us we loved so much. My father was a man of such boundless energy and enthusiasm, so much younger than his years. He always entered into our games with gusto, teaching us archery and riding, how to swim. Every day felt like a holiday when he was with us."

"And your mother? Did she play games with you, too?"

Nicholas shook his head, a frown flickering over his face. "My mother was always of a rather melancholy disposition. She tired easily, and the sunlight pained her head. But when my brother Stephen and I were young she would often read to us and tell us tales."

"What sort of tales?" Emily asked.

"Oh, mythology mostly. She did love old stories of knights and their damsels fair, beset by dragons and evil magicians, contending against spells and fighting great battles. I think that may be where my brother gets some of his more interesting notions."

Emily rubbed her little gold horseshoe pendant between her fingers. "What happened to her—later?"

"After my father met Lady Linwall, you mean? She

was very unhappy. Her whole life had been her position as the Duchess of Manning, her whole reason for being to uphold the family's position and reputation. My father's other mistresses were nothing, opera dancers and milliners, liaisons that were quick and discreet and did nothing to hurt the façade of the family. But Katherine—Lady Linwall…"

Emily swallowed hard, her throat tight. "He loved her."

"Yes, in an overwhelming way no one could ever have predicted, least of all my father. She was so vivid, so full of life and laughter, and she loved him just as much. They were like a force of nature, a blizzard or an earthquake, that could not be denied. My mother retreated to her own estate at Fincote Park, which Stephen now owns, and never went into society again. The shame made her too ill."

Emily stared out over the gardens again, those verdant lawns and bright waters that sparkled so brilliantly. But there seemed to be a faint grey cloud passing over it all. There seemed to be a hard lesson for her in that sad tale—duty and hard work were not always enough.

She looked over at Nicholas, who also stared off at the lake with a shadowed look in his eyes. A bar of light fell over his golden hair, turning it to molten sunshine, and he rubbed a hand over his jaw. How would it feel if she lost him? Lost him to some glittering, glamorous lady who was all she could not be? Someone like his lost Valentina?

Which was ridiculous, of course. He was not hers to lose. Still, the imagining was painful.

"What of your own parents?" he asked suddenly, sitting back in his chair.

"My parents?"

"What were they like when you were young? I have talked quite enough about myself today; now it's your turn."

Emily had to laugh. "My parents are not quite as interesting as yours. My mother likes to go out in society and to talk a great deal. My father likes to be quiet and read. He is usually in his library and she's in the drawing room, and they seem quite happy. My brother and I held not much interest for them when we were small, I think. We stayed in the nursery, but we often devised our own games there together. It's rather strange."

"Strange?"

"I had quite forgotten how much time Rob and I spent together then. We hardly see each other now he is so busy with his new career and with Amy."

"It's amazing how lonely one can be, in the midst of a family," Nicholas said.

Emily glanced at him in sharp surprise. "Surely not in your family, Nicholas! They wouldn't have the time to be lonely."

He gave her a strange smile. "Have you ever been to a party, where you thought you were having fun, and suddenly you just wanted to go home? Or at least go somewhere where you can really be seen, as yourself?"

"All the time," Emily said.

"Then you know. Even surrounded by people, people you love, it can be lonely. A duke is seldom alone, but he's also seldom a real part of other people."

"Yes, I see." And she did—and her heart ached for him, for all he was giving her the privilege of seeing now. She had thought she could help him by being perfect in her duty. But maybe they could help each other most by just sitting and listening. Learning each other so they need never be alone in a crowd again.

Was that even possible?

"Have you ever met someone like that? Someone who could see you?" she asked.

"My siblings, sometimes. And once—well, once there was a person. But that was a long time ago, when I was too young to appreciate what such an understanding was."

A woman, someone besides Valentina? Surely it must have been. But Nicholas said nothing else about it. Emily gathered all her courage and held out her hand to him. He took it in his, just holding it as they sat in silence.

Emily didn't know how it could be, after all they had done to each other's naked bodies in the bedchamber, but just sitting there holding hands with him felt like the most intimate thing she had ever done in her life. It felt just exactly right.

Chapter Seventeen

"Come along, I want to show you something!" Nicholas tugged Emily by the hand along a narrow, winding pathway that led around the furthest end of the lake. It was cool and shady here, a mossy shelter against the suddenly warm day, and the air smelled of sunlight and wildflowers.

Emily laughed. They had been at Welbourne only a fortnight, and yet she felt transformed. She had never had such a sense of being free and unbound before, untethered from the etiquette and cares of the earth and floating above it all as if in one of those terrifying hot air balloons.

Was it this place? Did Welbourne truly have some magic built into its stones? Or was it Nicholas, and the time they had spent together, alone? They did nothing extraordinary, just ate meals, played cards, read together. He taught her chess, or tried to, and over the carved board they told stories of their childhoods or tales they had heard of acquaintances in London. They made love at night, throwing aside all inhibitions in each other's arms—and he left her before dawn.

The one thing they never spoke of was the future, plans and hopes for it, what would happen when they left the cocoon of Welbourne.

Maybe that was why the days felt so enchanted. They weren't part of the real world at all.

And now she was traipsing about outdoors with Nicholas, clad only in a simple white-muslin round gown with her hair loose over her shoulders like a girl. What was more, she did not even feel in the least bit self-conscious about it. She hadn't had such moments since she was a child, back when she could run free with no worry of how she looked and what everyone was thinking of her.

Now she only cared what Nicholas thought. He was so much kinder than she had ever expected, more thoughtful. He took his tasks so seriously, showing her plans for new tenants' cottages on his estate and ideas for new, experimental crops, new breeds of sheep and ideas for irrigation techniques. When Emily tentatively suggested a school for the daughters of his servants and farmers, he had not dismissed her, but asked her questions about possible plans.

It was all a much better beginning than she could have hoped for.

Nicholas grinned at her over his shoulder. "Not far now."

Emily laughed. The path had taken a turn and spiralled downwards, toward a small hidden pool of the lake. It was cooler here, the tall trees growing close together for dense shade. There was even a small waterfall, a steely, musical flow of blue-grey water dancing over craggy rocks into the pool below.

"Where are you taking me?" Emily said. "To lock me away in some hidden grotto behind the waterfall?"

"I really should. Then no one could ever look at you but me! I would be the dark magician in one of my mother's old fairy tales, kidnapping the princess and holding her for my own pleasure alone."

She laughed even harder. "I think my nanny also told such a tale when I was a child. It did not end well, either for the princess or the magician."

"This tale would. We would just hide there, you and me, and no one could find us and interrupt us with messages and quarrels and dull things like that. We could sing and weave daisy chains, and lie in the sun all day long."

"You have never heard me sing, Nicholas, or you would not suggest such a thing," Emily warned. "My brother says I sound like a scalded cat."

"And I am sure he can't be correct." He took her other hand, holding them both tightly. "There's moss here on these rocks, it gets a bit slippery."

"What is this place?" she asked quietly. As the trees closed in around them, she felt like she should whisper, as if woodland creatures listened to them. The air was cool, filled with the rich scent of green leaves, the flowers under her feet, and sun on water.

"When we were children, we rather uncreatively called it the Hidden Pool. No one ever came here but us, it's too small for rowing and not much good for fishing. We thought no one knew about it but us."

"And what did you do here?"

"Swim. Dive from the waterfall. Found frogs to hide in the house. Mostly we lay around in the grass and talked about what we would do when we grew up."

He came to a flat, low boulder near a bent, leafy tree.

He spread the coat he had carried over his shoulder across its mossy surface and helped her sit down there. He propped his booted foot beside her, his elbow braced on his knee as he stared out at the swirling water.

"What did you want to do when you were grown?" she asked.

"I always knew I had no choice. Except for a brief plan concocted when I was nine, to run away to sea and fake my own death so poor Stephen would have to be duke, I had to be resigned to it. Stephen and Leo always wanted to work with horses—or be acrobats at Astley's. Annalise decided she would be one of the few females admitted to the Royal Academy, and she seems well on her way to that. Charlotte just wanted to write novels and plays, and raise dogs. One of which will soon be ours, alas."

"Unless we can devise a way out of it. That run-away-to-sea plan sounds quite good," Emily said, trying to match his lighthearted tone. Inside, though, she felt quite sad for the boy whose siblings could dream of being whatever they liked, while his life was sealed. "It can be so difficult to have no choices."

"There are always choices, Emily. My father chose to pretend he was not the duke, while still reaping its benefits. I choose to be useful, when I can." He grinned at her. "But that doesn't mean a duke can't have any fun."

He quickly kissed her cheek and dashed over to that bent, ancient-looking tree. As Emily watched, he grabbed on to one of the low-lying branches and pulled himself up. He climbed higher through the leaves until he came to a thick branch that twisted out over the water.

"What are you doing?" Emily cried. "You'll fall!"

"Oh, ye of little faith. I used to do this all the time."

"*Used* to?"

"I'm only a little out of practice." He stripped off his shirt and boots and tossed it to her. He looked like a primitive woodland god himself as he balanced there on the branch, bare-chested, tousle-haired. A mischievous, sensual spirit of the trees.

He reached up and unlooped a long, knotted rope from the branch above his head. A small wooden seat was attached to its end as a swing.

To Emily's wary eyes it looked rather old and precarious. Surely it had been there since his childhood days! But Nicholas stepped fearlessly on to the wooden seat, wrapped his fists around the rope, and launched himself into space.

"No!" Emily screamed.

"Watch me, Em!" he called back. As he swung past her head and back over the water again, his expression was one of such immense exhilaration and joy she couldn't scold, despite her terror. "It's easy, see?"

He swung past a couple more times, higher each time, before he dived into the pool. A great splash marked where he went in, but for a long moment he did not come out again.

Emily stood up as she pressed her hand to her mouth, waiting breathlessly. She remembered when he fell into the Serpentine with that poor child in his arms. This was much deeper than that river.

Then he plunged upwards with an echoing shout, his arms pounding at the water. "It's wonderful! So warm."

She laughed, her arms clutching at his shirt. "I will just take your word for it."

"No, you must try it yourself," he insisted. He swam towards shore, long, smooth strokes that cut through the water with barely a ripple. As he stepped on to the pebbled bank he shook himself, sending crystalline drops flying. He looked at her intently.

Emily's laughter faded as she took a step back. "I don't know how to swim."

"Not at all?"

"Not at all. My mother considered it an unladylike pastime."

"Well, my family does not think so. All my sisters can swim. Come, I'll teach you."

Emily remembered her un-coordinated dancing skills. Surely swimming was even harder. "What if I fall?"

"I wouldn't let you. I promise." He took his shirt from her tightly clenched hands and tossed it away, holding on to her as he looked steadily into her eyes. "Do you trust me?"

Did she? *Could* she? Feeling as if she was stepping off a great, steep precipice, she slowly nodded. "You did not let me shoot myself at archery, I suppose."

Nicholas laughed. "And you were very adept with the bow, just as you will be at swimming."

Before she could change her mind, Emily took off her shoes and stockings and gown, and waded into the water in her chemise.

"It *is* warm," she said in surprise. And soft, lapping around her legs and hips in gentle ripples.

Nicholas held her hands as they moved ever deeper. Before her feet dropped away beneath her, he grasped her by the waist and lifted her high. He twirled her around, the sun dappling their wet skin and turning the water to shimmering diamonds around them. She laughed and laughed, holding tightly to his shoulders as the whole world went mad and she did not care at all.

She stared down at him, at his elegant, chiselled face revealed by his slicked-back hair. He was laughing with her, his eyes alight with delight, as if her moment of sheer pleasure was his as well.

And in that one moment she knew, as a lightning bolt out of that blue sky. Being with him was no longer a duty, a compromise and escape from scandal. In only a few days with him, getting to know him, getting to know *herself*, it had become so much more.

She was in love with him. In love with her own husband.

That jolt of knowledge was so wonderful and so terrible at the same time. He did not love her.

Please, please, do not let me end up like his poor mother, she thought desperately. *Don't let him know how I really feel.*

Before she could scream those fateful words aloud— *I love you*—she ducked her head and kissed him. Into that kiss, she put everything she could not say, all that had to stay hidden. Maybe for ever.

His arms tightened around her waist, and she wrapped her legs about his hips. Their kiss deepened, desperately seeking *something* that seemed to hover just out of reach, shining and elusive. Some connection that she craved so very much.

Emily felt suddenly bold. She wasn't herself; desire, and that newfound force of love, made her into someone else, someone whose passionate longing could burst forth. She buried her fingers in his hair and opened her mouth under his, daring to touch her tongue to his, to taste him deeply. How delicious he was, like sunshine and clean water, and something dark and sweet that was only him. It made her head spin, as tipsy as if she had drunk too much frothy champagne.

She wanted more of him, more of this feeling, this wild sense of life and longing. She wanted more of *everything*.

"Emily, Emily," he gasped. His open mouth traced her cheek, her jaw, the taut line of her throat as she arched her head back. He bit at the soft curve of her shoulder, making her cry out at the rush of hot lust that shot through her. "You are making me insane."

"I don't even feel like myself any more," she whispered. Her fingers tightened in his hair as he kissed her shoulder, the swell of her breast above her wet chemise. "You make me feel like—like…"

"Like what?"

"I don't even know! So wild, so—free."

"I want you to be free, Em," he muttered. "I want to give you everything you want."

Emily very much feared that what she wanted more than anything, ever, was *him*. Their lips met again, in a wild kiss that held no thought or careful art, just a raw need that wouldn't be denied.

She felt the shift and movement of his body against hers, his mouth never leaving hers even as he carried them to the banks of the pool. He lowered her to the soft earth, on his discarded shirt, his body coming down atop hers. Emily slid her legs higher around him, pulling him even closer. She wanted nothing at all to come between them.

"Emily," he moaned. He kissed the curve of her ear, nipping gently at the soft lobe, his breath warm on her skin. It made her tremble, and she caressed the hard, damp muscles of his shoulders, the hollow of his spine. Her fingertips skimmed the edge of his breeches, unaccountably angry that the fabric kept her from what she wanted—to touch him, to touch his bare skin.

She threw her head back, opening her eyes to look up at him. He was outlined in the sunlight, which turned him all to gold. How handsome he was, her husband. She wanted to weep with it, with the overwhelming force of her desire for him. How had this ever happened to *her*?

He slid down her body to grasp the hem of her chemise, slowly drawing it up along her body. As he went, he kissed every inch of her newly bared skin, from the arch of her foot, the curve of her leg, that sensitive little spot just behind her knee, the soft flare of her hip. Soon he tossed the fabric away and she lay there naked before him.

Unlike in their candlelit ballroom, here there were no shadows to hide in. She couldn't escape from the light, and suddenly she felt shy. She tried to cover her bare breasts, but Nicholas wouldn't let her. He twined his fingers with hers, holding her hands to her sides as he kissed a heated ribbon along her throat, her shoulder.

"Nicholas," she whispered tightly, gasping as his open mouth slid over her left breast, wet, hot, teasing. "Please!"

"What is it you want, Emily?" he said teasingly, licking at the delicate hollow between her breasts. "This? Or—this?"

He nipped at the soft curve just underneath her breast, and soothed it with the tip of his tongue.

She arched up, pressing her body to his in silent longing, and at last he took her aching nipple deep into his mouth. He caressed her other breast gently on his palm until she moaned again. Through that hot cloud of desire, she felt him ease her legs even further apart.

He knelt between them, his kiss trailing away from her body, leaving her feeling bereft.

Her eyes fluttered open and she stared up at him. His eyes were narrowed, darkened with desire as he looked down at her bare body. She felt so heavy and damp, aching with a passion she was only beginning to understand.

He touched her there, one finger sliding inside her, rough and hot. He caressed that one tiny, sensitive spot, making her cry out.

"I'm sorry, Em," he groaned. "I can't wait any longer."

"I don't want you to," she whispered. And she didn't—she wanted him right that instant. Her whole body cried out for him.

How could everyone have been so very wrong about the marriage act? It was surely the most splendid thing ever!

"Hold on to me," he said, and as she wrapped her arms around his shoulders he slid carefully into her, inch by slow inch. She sighed at the delicious, hot feelings of fullness, of being joined with him in all ways.

He drew back and thrust forwards again, and then again, faster. She knew his body now, knew how to move with him, to find their own rhythm. Their cries, the warm rush of their breath, blended with the sun and the wind around them, and she felt like she was soaring up into the sky. They were part of the whole world even as they became part of each other.

The bubble of light and sensation built deep down inside, expanding, growing, until it suffused her whole body. She couldn't see or think—she could only feel. And that bubble burst in a brilliant shower of sparks.

"Emily!" he shouted, his head thrown back, his

neck taut. He thrust one last time, one long moment that seemed wondrously suspended for ever before he drew out of her. "Emily."

Then he collapsed to the ground beside her and Emily slowly, slowly, floated back to earth.

Her eyes closed and she caressed his shoulder, his damp hair, resting her head on his chest as a weakness closed over her. She felt the breeze over her skin, the heat of the sun on her closed eyelids and his kiss on her brow.

"I doubt anyone else has ever had quite such a honeymoon as this," she whispered, wishing they never had to leave Welbourne at all, just before the warm lure of sleep claimed her.

Nicholas watched Emily as she knelt by the pathway to examine some wildflowers. The dappled sunlight trickled over the loose fall of her hair, turning it into molten gold and gilding her fair, soft skin. She smiled as she touched the petals, suddenly looking so very young and free. The shy, slightly worried London lady was gone.

And he could feel his old, grief-saddened self melting away, too. Ever since he came home after losing Valentina, he had felt so solitary, distant from his family, bound only to his duty. The old Manning joy in life, the abandon, was gone from his heart and there was only that terrible numbness.

Until now. At first this marriage with Emily seemed yet another duty, but in spending this time with her it had sneaked up on him—this was becoming so much more than duty.

He enjoyed waking up each day, full of anticipation about what could happen in those hours he spent with her. He wanted to find ways to make her smile. He wanted—well, he just wanted to be with her. To learn more about her. He was finding his wife to be ever-surprising, so much more than she appeared. And he wasn't lonely any longer.

How had that happened? How was it he felt the warm touch of life on his heart again?

Nicholas shook his head hard, trying to clear it. He should be on guard against such feelings, they were dangerous. He had to remember Valentina, and what happened when he let the wild Manning emotions get the better of him. He had to be careful.

But that was almost impossible to do when Emily looked up at him and smiled.

"I've never seen a flower like this before," she said. "What is it called?"

Nicholas knelt beside her and pretended to examine the pink blossoms. All he could see was her, the light on her hair, the warm scent of her skin, roses and clean water.

"I'm not much of a botanist," he said.

Emily laughed. "I thought you knew about everything. Horses, stars, archery…"

"Not flowers, though." He plucked one of the delicate blossoms and tucked it into her hair.

"I love it here at Welbourne," she whispered. "I would never have thought it could be, but it has woven its spell on me. I wish we never had to leave."

It had woven its spell on him, too. He had to fight to break free of it.

"We should get back to the house," he said abruptly. "It grows late."

Her smile faded, and she nodded as he took her hand and helped her to her feet. They made their way back to the house in silence, the enchanted pool growing further and further behind them.

A man waited for them on the drive at the front of the house, pacing back and forth.

"Who is that?" Emily asked. "Are you expecting a caller?"

"It's my secretary from London," Nicholas said. "And, no, I wasn't expecting him. There must be some unexpected business that's come up."

"Business on your honeymoon?"

Nicholas laughed wryly. The reminder of the real world seemed to be a timely one. "The work of a duke never ends. Go on inside, Em. I won't be long."

"Yes, I'll just go write those letters I've been neglecting."

Emily started towards the house, her hand trailing out of Nicholas's clasp. Before she could leave him entirely, he pulled her towards him and kissed her one more time. She tasted of sunlight and faded laughter.

"I enjoyed our day," he said.

"So did I. Very much," she answered with a wary smile. "Now, your Grace, go and do your duty. I will see you at dinner."

His duty. Yes, he could never forget that. He watched Emily disappear into the house, and then turned towards the waiting secretary.

Chapter Eighteen

Emily drifted around the library aimlessly, humming a little tune as she picked up various little boxes and figurines from the tables and put them down again. She couldn't seem to settle to anything, despite the wealth of tempting novels and volumes of poetry on the shelves, all the letters that waited for her. Ever since she and Nicholas had finally roused themselves to dress and return to the house, she hadn't felt like herself at all.

She had never felt so restless before, as if she simply could not sit still. But it was a good kind of restless, a happy kind. She wanted to twirl around, to laugh aloud, to run and skip!

She did neither, of course. It would be most unbecoming for a duchess to be caught dancing alone in the library in the middle of the day! Instead, she drifted over to the half-open window to gaze out at the waning afternoon.

The breeze was growing cooler, the heat of the spring day dissipating, and it was soft through the damp braid of her hair and on her bare neck. The light was turning pale gold, almost pink at the edges. Soon it would be time to change for dinner, but Nicholas was still talking on the terrace with the secretary who had brought letters from London, and who had been waiting on their return from the lake.

Emily glanced toward the desk where she had left her own missives, letters from her mother and from Mrs Goddard, a short, chatty note from Jane lamenting the departure of everyone "interesting" from town. And yet Jane had somehow managed to attend two more parties since Emily's wedding, where she had encountered an "utterly heartbroken" Mr Rayburn, and promised to divulge "delicious secrets" as soon as she could write again.

She knew she should answer them, of course, right away. It was her duty to attend promptly to correspondence, no matter how much she would rather have a walk in the sunset! And she did rather want to know Jane's new secrets. She slowly turned away from the lovely evening outside, and from the view of her husband on the terrace, and went to sit down at the desk.

The desk, an ornate French affair of giltwork and enamel insets, was cluttered with books, little *objets*, and a cluster of odd rocks and feathers that seemed to be some of Stephen's good-luck charms. Emily pushed these to the side and reached for Nicholas's slope-topped travel desk to look for paper and ink. She should at least have time to write her mother before dinner.

Unlike the Welbourne desk, Nicholas's was surprisingly neat and tidy, with everything in their proper slots. A small account book sat on top of the blank stationery, marked with the ducal arms pressed into creamy paper.

"Mama should appreciate that," Emily murmured

as she reached for a piece of the fine paper. But as she pulled out a pile of sheets, she dislodged a small gold box. It fell on to the desk with a loud thunk, one of the little hinges knocked loose.

"Oh, blast!" She scooped it up in dismay. Surely breaking her husband's possessions was *not* the way to impress him! The tiny, intricately worked lid fell open, spilling out a miniature portrait framed in pearls.

Emily caught it on her palm. The gold edge was engraved "V. M. M." Behind a clear panel on the back coiled a dark curl of hair entwined with a finer blond strand.

She turned it over, and found herself staring down at a beautiful woman, possibly the most beautiful woman she had ever seen. Glossy, dark-brown curls fell over her shoulders and framed an oval face that was all high cheekbones, classical aquiline nose and melting dark eyes. She smiled up at Emily, her eyes sparkling as if at some hidden joke.

Emily felt as if the breath was knocked from her. This could only be Nicholas's first wife, his Valentina. She rubbed her thumb over the smooth ivory. The dark woman really was uncommonly beautiful, and she seemed to glow with some inner fire of life. A fire which Emily herself had only begun to understand when she came here to Welbourne. Here, she had felt the first hopeful stirrings of something real and vital deep down inside.

Now she only felt cold. How could she compete with a woman like this? A dark, vivid beauty who was gone and therefore perfect.

She carefully replaced the painting in its damaged box and hid it down deep in the desk. She closed the lid over it gently, but still it seemed to glow.

Her glance fell on Stephen's little pile of charms, and she began to think he must have the right idea. The title of Duchess of Manning seemed cursed. First Nicholas's mother; then Lady Linwall, who died of a fever in Naples as soon as she married her love; now foolish Emily Carroll. Did Stephen have a charm to fight off a curse like that? She rubbed her palm over the tiny horseshoe that hung around her neck with the precious emerald pendant that was Nicholas's wedding gift to her. Were they enough to ward off ill luck?

She heard a sudden noise in the corridor, voices and heavy footsteps on the marble floor. Quickly, she wiped her damp eyes and reached for the paper and a pen. She could not let anyone see that she had found that portrait! She couldn't cry to Nicholas, and demand to know why he kept Valentina's portrait so close. Like a jealous wife. Not when they were both trying so hard to make this ridiculous marriage work.

Nicholas opened the library door, letting in more of the dying daylight. It fell across his damp, curling hair, turning it as pale as the second curl in the portrait casing. "What are you doing so industriously, Em?"

She glanced up at him and forced herself to smile. She couldn't let him see that she had found the portrait. "I'm writing to my mother. She chided me in her letter for not sending word as soon as we arrived."

"Well, she can see you for herself soon enough."

"What do you mean? We're meant to be here a fortnight, then go on to Scarnlea Abbey."

Nicholas sat down in the chair across from the desk. He smiled at her, but his brow was lined with a tension that had not been there at the lake. "A slight change of plans, I fear. Some business has come up in town I must attend to at once."

Emily stared at him in shock. "Y-you're going back to London? Already?"

"I thought perhaps we both might go. Then you could see your parents before we travel to Scarnlea, and I dare say there might be a party or two to attend."

"But what sort of business…?" Emily remembered the letter he had received from Derrington. "Not your sister Charlotte?"

"No, no. In fact, Charlotte has given birth to a beautiful baby girl. Drew says that mother and daughter are recovering well, thank God."

"Then your niece Katherine will have a playmate!"

"She will indeed. No, my business is something dull to do with an unfortunate loan my brother Leo took out. It should not take long to solve."

Emily nodded, but she couldn't help but wonder if there was more to it all. Perhaps the dark-eyed lady needed him, or maybe he could not bear to be away from her so long. Whatever it was, she would have to find the strength to bear it. To be that perfect duchess she had resolved to be for him.

She laid aside the pen and smiled at him. "Well, the news from Derrington is certainly welcome. Hopefully we will soon add to all those little playmates."

To her surprise, he responded to her light words with a fierce frown, and leaned across the desk to grasp her hand. "Emily, are you…?"

His clasp was too tight, his reaction to her teasing not at all what she expected. Surely he *wanted* children— an heir—and very soon? It seemed to be what all men wanted.

"No," she said. "At least I don't think so. Surely it is too soon to know?"

He nodded, and raised her hand to his lips for a quick

kiss. "There is no hurry at all," he muttered. "There are so many Mannings running about, I don't think we need to add to them."

"Of course there isn't," she said, bewildered. Was he disappointed in her, that there was no child already? "We are young, and only just now married."

He pressed her hand to his cheek. "Emily, my dear, if you suspect anything you will let me know at once, won't you?"

"Yes, of course."

"I won't let anything happen to you, I promise. Nothing will ever hurt you, not while I am here."

"I know you will take care of me, Nicholas." She slowly reached up to rest her free hand on his head, the strands of hair like damp silk against her skin. "I will never let anything hurt you, either."

Emily kissed Nicholas, putting all her hidden feeling into it, all she couldn't say to him. Inside she felt cold and hollow. She had always longed to be a mother, to have her own children to love and care for, but Nicholas did not seem to share her desire. Would a baby just be one more tie to the wife he hadn't really wanted? And if that was so—how could she ever live with it?

Nicholas watched Emily across the dinner table as she told him the news from her mother's letter. The candlelight cast a soft amber glow around her, making her look like a gentle angel in some Renaissance painting, all golden and ethereal.

Here at Welbourne, she wore her hair in loose waves pinned atop her head rather than stylish ringlets, and her evening gown was simple pale-green muslin trimmed with gold ribbons, though she wore it with her emerald pendant and the pearl earrings Justine had given her.

In the last few days, she had laughed and smiled more than ever before, her expression taking on an open, curious aspect as she stepped into the magical world of Welbourne, explored their new life with him. Though she still seemed rather shy and careful, so much of that had melted away to show the laughing, tender-hearted girl beneath.

It was entrancing to watch her slowly blossom. It made him feel alive again, too, made him want to jump into the world in a way he never had since Valentina died. Tonight, though, it looked like her smile was strained, her chatter just a little too quick, too taut and bright.

What had made her change? The prospect of returning to London?

Or perhaps she had sensed his panic at the thought she might be pregnant. He had grabbed quickly on to his self-control again, but that fear had been too real, too raw. The force of it shocked even himself, that realisation of what it would be to lose Emily when he had just found her.

He had never dreamed he could feel that way about quiet, proper Emily Carroll. But then again, she was not always so very *proper*. And she had so many hidden, fascinating depths, like a summertime rose with its golden heart hidden away. His world would be dark without her. She had made him see the way to a new life, a new brightness. He had to protect her in return.

And yet he had not been as careful in bed as he should.

"…says we must give a ball as soon as the next Season begins," she was saying. She nodded to the footmen to bring in the next course, and they scurried to obey her. Even the servants of Welbourne, so stubbornly devoted to his family and wary of outsiders, had taken her to their hearts. Crusty Mrs Courtney made sure her linens were laid with rose sachets, and Signor Napoli made new titbits every evening to tempt her.

"Your parents are giving a ball?" he said.

Emily laughed. "Certainly not. They could scarcely fit twenty people into their town house. Mama says *we* must have a ball, and put Manning House to fine use again, as it was back when they were such friends with your father."

"You can have any sort of party you want next year, Em," he said as he reached for his wine glass. "It may take some time for the redecorating, though."

"That can be my excuse for putting a ball off until the next year, then!" She bit her lip uncertainly. "Unless you think people will expect one sooner?"

"They can expect whatever they like. We'll just have to be very lavish, and thus very slow, in our refurbishments. Maybe we could order a new painted ceiling from France? Silks from India? Plasterwork from Italy?"

"A hardwood dance floor from the West Indies, maybe?"

"You are the duchess. Whatever you want is what we shall have."

"I want something simple and pretty, and smaller than Manning House. But I also want you to be proud of your house. I have so many ideas for refurbishment, but I want to be sure it's just right."

Nicholas frowned as he studied her through the candlelight. Her eyes looked so worried, her thumbnail ragged as she reached for her glass. He had learned that when she bit her nail it was a sure sign of inner turmoil. His heart ached at the thought. He had vowed to make her life easy and happy, not cause her more worry! He hadn't yet learned how to be a husband; probably he never would.

"You could never do the wrong thing, Emily," he said gently. "Everyone is quite envious of me already for marrying the most beautiful lady in London. *They* will look to *you* to set the styles now, to tell them what is the right thing to do. If you wore a pineapple on your head, they would all do the same."

Emily laughed, and to his relief some of the clouds cleared from her eyes. "I doubt I should want to wear fruit on my head, but if I decide differently I will keep that in mind." She was becoming more confident of late, but perhaps not *that* confident. There had to be other fashions she could start that would not involve groceries!

"You're already a splendid duchess. Now, what else does your mother say in her letter?"

"She and Papa are packing to return to the country, and the noise of it all is giving her fainting fits. And she has caught a cold. And she tells me I must stay out of the sun or I will freckle. Advice that comes too late, I fear."

She told him the other news from town, and they laughed together over a card game after dinner. Yet still Nicholas couldn't quite shake away the dark cloud that had descended over their golden idyll. Even as he held her in his arms that night, listening to her soft, sleeping breath, she was drifting further and further out of his grasp.

Chapter Nineteen

"Emily, I was just..." Amy stopped abruptly in the doorway of Emily's Manning House bedchamber, one glove half off her hand. "Oh, Emily, are you ill?"

"Close the door, Amy, quickly," Emily croaked. She shut her eyes tightly and clung to the chamberpot where she had just lost her breakfast. The queasy dizziness still washed over her in clammy waves, but not as intensely.

Amy swiftly shut the door behind her and hurried over to the basin of water on the wash stand. She rang out a cloth and knelt beside Emily to gently wipe her brow. "Better now?"

Emily leaned towards her, grateful for her sister-in-law's brisk efficiency, her take-charge manner. She needed such sensible help now.

"Yes, thank you, Amy," she said.

"You are certainly doing your duty as duchess very quickly, Emily," Amy answered, a hint of satisfied amusement in her voice.

"My duty?"

"Yes. This is not just a food that didn't agree with you, is it? It's morning sickness. My mother always said she had it right away with me and my sisters."

Emily sat back hard on her heels, stunned. Underneath her shock, a bright spot of hope bloomed, flickering and tentative. "You mean—I might be *enceinte*? Already?"

Amy covered the pan with a wrinkle to her nose and put it away when it seemed Emily's sudden illness had passed. "I haven't been blessed with my own child yet, but I do know the signs. It must have happened on your wedding night, you clever girl."

Emily pressed her hands to her stomach. Under the soft muslin of her morning gown it felt as flat as ever. But she remembered that wedding night, or rather the morning after, and that wondrous pleasure she found in Nicholas's arms. Could they really have made a new life then? She smiled to think of it, a tiny child growing inside her. The start of a new family.

"When will I know for sure?" she said. She slowly got up and made her way to the *chaise* by the fireplace, feeling shaky.

"Not for a few weeks, I would think," said Amy. "But how do *you* feel? Do you sense it's true?"

"I certainly hope it's true, but I just don't know. Everything is just so new—being married, being a duchess." *Being in love*.

"Well, your parents will be terribly happy," Amy said. "Not to mention your husband! A little heir already."

"Even if it is true, it might be a little ladyship and not an heir." But even that thought made Emily's hope burn even brighter. A little lady swathed in lace, with her father's beautiful blue eyes. She had never imagined such a vast and burning joy.

Amy laughed. "Even better. Then Rob and I will have a son and one day they can marry!"

Emily laughed, too. "It might be rather early to sign the marriage contract. I'm not even sure there is a child yet, and Nicholas will have to be told. Oh!"

A sudden fear struck her, and she clutched tighter to her stomach. She remembered Nicholas's reaction at Welbourne, when he thought she might be pregnant. He looked horrified, as if having a child with *her* would be a terrible fate.

If she was truly with child now, would that horror be a hundredfold? What would she do? She couldn't bear it if he turned from her now, when she was beginning to see just how much she needed him. And she absolutely could not bear it if he turned from their child.

"Amy, you won't tell anyone, will you?" she said. She reached for Amy's hand and held it tightly.

"Certainly not. It's your place to announce the happy news."

"Not even Rob. Not yet. Promise me?"

Amy shook her head. "I promise, if you like. But surely this is happy news!"

"I just want to be sure first. I don't want anyone to be disappointed if it's not true." Or disappointed if it *was* true. Things were so new, so delicate between her and Nicholas now. She didn't want to disturb it just yet.

"I won't tell, Emily. But is something amiss? Is there something—not right between you and your husband?"

Emily shook her head. "It's just too soon."

"Then it can be our secret for now."

"Thank you."

"But in return you must promise me you will write

to me as soon as you know for certain! I will be aching to know."

Emily noticed suddenly that Amy wore a travelling pelisse and carriage dress. "Are you leaving town so soon?"

"Within the hour, I'm afraid. We're to spend the summer in Derbyshire at Rob's new estate, soliciting votes for the next election. It's terribly exciting! And Rob is so grateful for your husband's help in seeing us settled. We could never have expected it so soon."

"I'm glad you're looking forward to the summer. I just wish you didn't have to be so far away right now."

"You must come visit us. If you feel up to travelling, that is. But now I fear I must say goodbye, and beg a great favour from you."

"Of course I will help if I can."

Amy smiled. "Dear Emily, always so generous! But you may regret it when you hear what it is."

"I'll only regret it if you need someone to clean up after *your* illness!" Emily said with a laugh.

"Not at all! I was invited to a tea-and-cards party at Lady Arnold's house this afternoon. I'm afraid my backing out at the last moment will leave her card tables uneven. Can you go in my place?"

Emily remembered what happened the last time she was at Lady Arnold's—scandal and a forced betrothal. She laughed ruefully. "I will go if I must. I'll have to start going out in society again soon anyway. But are you sure Lady Arnold would accept me as a substitute, after what happened at her ball?"

"That was the social triumph of Lady Arnold's life. And she will be in alt to have the Duchess of Manning at her party. I will write to her immediately. If you are sure you're feeling well enough?"

Emily pressed her palms to her stomach. There was no hint of nausea now. "Yes," she said in surprise. "I feel wonderful now, quite energetic."

Amy smiled smugly. "It must be pregnancy, then. But do write to me when you're sure. And don't forget the tea party!"

"Oh, your Grace! I can't tell you how happy I am you could come to my little gathering today," said Lady Arnold, rushing forwards to greet Emily as she entered the drawing room. "It has not been the same in town since you and the duke left us."

Emily almost laughed as Lady Arnold kissed her cheeks in the French fashion of greeting. Surely Lady Arnold had not addressed more than a dozen words to her before that fateful scene at the ball! It hardly seemed to warrant such an effusive greeting now. Besides, she and Nicholas had only been gone for a short time. Surely the whole city had not changed.

And yet in a strange way it felt as if it *had* completely changed. Everyone she met looked at her differently, spoke to her differently. It felt strangely—good. But she didn't even want to consider what the consequences of that attention would be on her work at Mrs Goddard's. She had planned on slipping away to the school today, while Nicholas was away on his business, but then the invitation arrived to tea and cards at Lady Arnold's house, not to mention the unexpected illness.

"Oh, you must go, Emily dear!" her mother said when Emily dropped by her house on the way to Lady Arnold's and found her ill with a cold. "I know it is shockingly last minute, but it's your first engagement as a married lady. It's never too early to begin to claim your rightful place in society, my dear. I only wish I could go with you, but my cold is keeping me at home, I fear."

And Nicholas urged her to go as well. "I'll be gone until dinner, Em," he said. "Go and have fun. You can tell me all the new gossip this evening."

"I doubt there will be anything to tell, not from Lady Arnold's," Emily answered wryly. "Unless you are interested in the newest colours of bonnet ribbons."

Nicholas laughed. "One never knows what might prove useful. What if I wanted to buy my pretty wife some ribbons? I would hate to buy the wrong colour." And he kissed her cheek as her mother watched them, beaming.

That was how she found herself in Lady Arnold's drawing room now, her hostess leading her to a seat near the windows, by the tea table, while the assembled guests watched her avidly, as if she was a curious creature in a menagerie—duchess in captivity. At least she wore a new outfit from her trousseau, a stylish ensemble of a pale green muslin gown and darker green silk pelisse and feathered hat that gave her more confidence. She was learning this duchess business better than she expected!

The ladies gathered on the brocade chairs around the table, the sunlight glowing on their silks and feathers and making them look like a collection of parrots, hastily made room for her.

"Married life does seem to agree with you, your Grace. You look positively radiant," Mrs Smythe-Hawkins said. Her sharp gaze drifted over Emily's abdomen, as if she suggested a little heir was already nestled there. And she might be quite right.

Emily remembered Nicholas's strange reaction when news of his niece's birth had arrived. That black cloud had quickly passed that day, and he had not mentioned it again, instead staying light-hearted and teasing with her. But she could not quite forget. Was he disappointed she was not yet pregnant then? Or worse—was he glad of it?

Or was he shocked by the thought of a child with her?

Emily resisted the urge to press her arms over her stomach. "I am enjoying married life very much, thank you, Mrs Smythe-Hawkins," she said.

"I am sure you must be, your Grace, with such a handsome husband!" Amy's friend Lady Carter said with a giggle. "Every lady in London is quite envious of you."

Lady Arnold passed Emily a delicate china cup. "You seem to have started a fashion for betrothals, too."

"Have I?" Emily said weakly.

"Yes. Miss Swanson and Lord Linley are to be married next month, and Sir Walter Chase's younger daughter is engaged to an Italian count. Imagine that!" Mrs Smythe-Hawkins said.

"They also say your friend Miss Jane Thornton wished to be engaged," Lady Arnold whispered. "But she was disappointed in her hopes, and her parents whisked her away from town."

"Miss Thornton?" Emily gasped in surprise. So that was why there was no answer to the note she had sent around to Jane's house when they returned to town. And then there were Jane's words of some "surprise" in her letter. But who could she have been engaged to? She had said nothing to Emily, unless Mr Jameson came to the point at last.

"They say she was quite in love with Mr George Rayburn," Lady Carter whispered. The ladies all leaned closer, all wide-eyed with scandalised delight. "And he had been seen with her at the park after—well, after you married, your Grace."

"But then her parents took her away, and Mr Rayburn has been seen all about town again."

Poor Jane. Emily stared down into her tea, stunned. Here she had thought they were such good friends, that Jane was so open and confiding, and yet she was in love with Mr Rayburn of all men and had said not a word. It was so very odd.

Unless these ladies were making far more of one sighting in the park than there was. That would certainly not be the first time such a thing had happened.

She would have to write to Jane herself, at the earliest opportunity. And maybe find her another, more suitable beau. She was in a position to help people now, as Nicholas had with Rob and Amy, and it felt good.

"I do not blame her parents at all," Lady Arnold said. "I would not wish my daughter betrothed to Mr Rayburn."

"Quite so," said Mrs Smythe-Hawkins. "My husband says he loses terribly at cards…" She lowered her voice. "He does not pay his considerable debts in any timely manner. He owes so many people, I am sure the day will soon come when he does not dare show his face in town."

"Miss Thornton has had a lucky escape, as has her family," Lady Carter said. "They need her to make a good, solid match, with all those daughters to look after. Mr Rayburn, let us face it, is not good *ton*. And there are the rumors of all those women…"

Emily had thought she could not be shocked by anything now, not after her hurried marriage and all she had discovered since then. But she *was* surprised by this news of Mr Rayburn's debts and impecunious state. He had courted her once, rather ardently, and she had had no idea of his true circumstance! Such gossip was only imparted to her now, when she was a married woman, long after it could have proved useful.

She and Jane had had fortunate escapes. But Emily did not understand why a man in need of money would court *her* in the first place. The Carrolls had no fortune now. Unless he was also not in possession of useful gossip about people's real financial state...

Her head spun in confusion. She suddenly wished she was back at Welbourne, with only Nicholas. Things made sense there, and she felt she belonged with him there, belonged to her new place in the world. Here, she was not so very sure.

"Do tell us where you found that green silk, your Grace," said Lady Arnold. "Such an elegant shade! I have been thinking we don't see enough green in the draper's shops of late, and I hear it is so à la mode in Paris."

"You must have had it straight from France!" one of the other ladies said. "You always did have such exquisite taste, your Grace. We can all learn so much from you in our ensembles, I'm sure."

"I have heard this shade is called *vert à la duchesse*," Lady Carter said. "So appropriate."

Emily almost laughed. Amy, her mother, even Nicholas had said that as a duchess she would set the fashion, and she had not believed them in the least. But it seemed they were right. Everyone would show up in green now, all because her husband seemed to like her in green and bought her emeralds.

No, she understood *nothing* of this strange world. She was learning, though. She was finding her place as duchess. She had to—she had her baby to think of now as well as herself, and she was determined to be the best mother she could be to him or her. It was of vital importance.

"Back to Manning House, your Grace?" the coachman asked as Emily stepped out of Lady Arnold's, her head whirling with gossip and the challenge of fending off nosy questions intended to turn *her* into gossip.

She bit her lip. Going back to cold, echoing Manning House alone, especially if Nicholas was still out, held no appeal. Nor did she really want to go to her parents' house and be in their way as they packed to leave town—and as her mother peppered her with questions about Lady Arnold. And she could not go to Mrs Goddard's in such grand state. She didn't want to cause shameful gossip, as a duchess visiting former ladies of the night would surely do! Not with the new baby to think of.

"No, Smith, to Gunter's first," she said. A raspberry ice would be just the thing to clear her head, and perhaps she could buy some pastries to have for the pudding at home. It was very hard to do without Signor Napoli's delicious creations after becoming so used to them at Welbourne, and it seemed the baby craved sweets. Or that was as good an excuse as any to indulge!

The scents of warm sugar and ripe, sweet fruit greeted her as she stepped into the confectioner's shop, comforting scents that wrapped around her reassuringly. There were no long lines as there had been only weeks before, and few people seated at the little tables by the windows for tea and ices. London was indeed much quieter now, which was all for the best. Her duchess début had been relatively painless, and now she deserved a reward.

But as she ordered her ice and took it to a quiet seat in the corner, she could not quite forget the ladies' gossip about Mr Rayburn and Jane's hidden hopes of him. Emily had always thought herself somewhat observant; there was little else to do from behind potted palms and along walls at parties than watch and listen. Yet she had seen none of Mr Rayburn's financial difficulties, despite the scene in her mother's drawing room before her wedding, or of Jane's interest in him. Jane always seemed resigned to marrying her suitor Mr Jameson. It was all rather odd.

And it also made her wonder what else she had missed, what she did not know. She remembered the stunned look in Nicholas's eyes at Welbourne when he thought she might be pregnant. It was most worrisome.

The thought made the sweet-tart raspberry ice suddenly taste like ashes in her mouth. She had expected nothing of Nicholas when they married so suddenly, had expected nothing of herself except to be a good duchess. Those golden days at Welbourne, so fleeting and sweet, seemed to have changed so much. Or they had changed things in her own heart, anyway, so completely. Surely nothing had changed for Nicholas. She was still the wife he had to take, and now she bore a child he didn't seem to want.

She carefully placed her spoon on the half-consumed dish. She loved her husband. He did not love her, not yet, though he did seem to care about her. If she could learn to be that good duchess, surely she could learn to be a good wife, too? Nicholas could find deeper feelings for her—and forget Valentina. Or was that merely another silly dream?

The little bell over the door tinkled merrily as someone came into the shop, and Emily glanced up eagerly, hoping for some distraction from her own twisting, desperate thoughts. Her stomach sank sickeningly when she saw who the newcomer was.

George Rayburn, the man who was the new talk of London.

Emily slid to the back of her chair, hoping he would not see her there and she could slip away before she had to speak to him. She had no idea what to say to him, and her duchess acting skills were not yet as sharp as she would like. But she was not so fortunate. He gazed around the room with a supremely confident air, a little smile on his handsome face. It was as if the rumours had never happened. His searching stare landed on her, and that smile widened.

"Why, if it is not the new duchess!" he said, hurrying towards her. "Is the honeymoon at an end already? So sad."

"How do you do, Mr Rayburn," she said quietly, offering him her hand. She had removed her gloves to eat, and his grasp was too warm, too tight, to be strictly polite. He actually touched his lips to her knuckles rather than merely brushing the air above them, and she tugged her hand free.

"My husband has urgent business in London," she said. "We are here only for a few days."

"Just a few days? What a sad loss for those of us trapped in town. You've been missed here."

"Have I? It seems to me the world of London has gone on well enough while I've been away these few days."

"Then you have not been paying attention. Some of us have found these streets a desolate place without you."

Without being invited, he sat down across from her, his knees pressed close to hers under the tiny table. He leaned towards her, so near she could smell the spiciness of his French cologne, feel the unpleasant heat of his body. She remembered that day before her wedding, when he trapped her just so, and shivered with a rush of cold fear.

She glanced out the window to where her carriage waited, along with her coachman and footmen. There were also the serving maids at the counter and the few other customers. She was not alone, Mr Rayburn surely dared not grab her in such a public place.

She bit her lip to keep from calling out and creating a scene, and leaned as far away from him as she could. Her back bumped into the wall. "I am surprised to see you here, Mr Rayburn. I heard you had left town."

That confident smile twitched toward a frown. "Have your friends been prattling about me, then? Gossip does move fast, your Grace—like a poison."

Emily thought of Lady Arnold and her friends, their avid eyes as they told her all about Mr Rayburn's misfortunes and Jane's disappointments. "Not at all. It merely seems as if everyone has already departed for quieter environs. I would have thought you would do the same, you seem so—fashionable in all things."

"Well, like your illustrious husband, I, too, have business to conclude before I take my leave."

"And will you then travel to Thornton Park, Mr Rayburn?"

His eyes narrowed. "Thornton Park? Certainly not. It is in Cheshire, yes? Dull place, and I hardly know that family anyway. I shall be for Brighton, or perhaps even for the Continent. They say Baden-Baden is quite the place to restore one's spirits."

"You seem healthy enough, Mr Rayburn."

"Ah, my dear Duchess, I fear my illness is of the spirit entirely. A broken heart is not so apparent, but is painful none the less."

Much like a broken purse? Or perhaps he was in truth pining for Jane. "Then surely Cheshire would be more the place for you, if that is your ailment."

"Only if you were there, your Grace." He leaned close again, and Emily slid back until she found herself quite mashed up against that wall. The warm, sugary smells, so comforting earlier, now felt nauseatingly oppressive.

"Did you not realise how many hearts were wounded the day you married?" he said, quiet and intense.

"That is utter nonsense," Emily said. "My husband's was the only offer I received all Season. If hearts were 'aching' they were well hidden."

"Emily!" He grabbed for her hand again, but she pulled it away, that cold fear trickling over her. "You know I was going to speak to your father, I merely had certain matters to resolve first, before I could be worthy of you and your family name. Surely I made my interest most evident, even to you. Remember when I came to your house before your wedding?"

She remembered that all too well. But she shook her head. "No, Mr Rayburn, I was aware of no such interest before that day, when you so importuned me in my own house. By then I was committed to my husband." She yanked on her gloves, refusing to look at him. It was time for something quite extreme. She was going to have to be *rude*. "And even if I had not been, we would never have suited, you and I, we are much too different in our manners and our ambitions. I am sure you agree with me now. You will soon find a much more compatible match, I am certain."

"As you did? A match with a fine title?" he said harshly. "You will soon be sorry for such a tawdry bargain. You will wish you had listened to me, had given me a chance."

Emily had had quite enough from him. She did have a title now, and surely one of the advantages of a title was not having to listen to nonsense. She stood up, her chair scraping across the floor. "I must go now. Please say nothing further to me."

But he was not finished. He grabbed her arm, his bruising grip wrinkling her fine sleeve. "When you *do* rue your devil's bargain, Duchess, I will be here. Perhaps you would care for a visit to Baden-Baden as well? A time away from your oh-so-virtuous husband and his family of bedlamites. We could have a grand time together—I could show you things he never could. Things in the bedchamber…"

Emily stomped down hard on his foot, under cover of her hem. Her kid half-boot could not inflict much harm, but the surprise of her move drove him back from her. She pushed past him. "I will thank you never to speak to me again, Mr Rayburn, or to my friend Miss Thornton. Our acquaintance is quite at an end."

"I would not be so quick to dismiss me, your Grace," he said harshly. "You may have your lofty position now, but your husband's family is notoriously fickle. What will you do when you are alone in the world, and feel the chill of scorn and ridicule, as I have? When your husband will no longer protect you?"

Emily hurried out of the shop, not daring to breathe until she was safe in her carriage and rolling away from the square. Only then did she peer out the window, to find Mr Rayburn standing on the walkway watching her depart. His stare seemed to burn right through the thick glass.

She had not realised the depth of his feelings before, and they frightened her. He said his feelings were love of some sort, but she knew enough to see what they really were—a man denied the toy he wanted. Worse, that it had been snatched away by a man of greater status, and far greater worth in every way. But the crude way he would suggest an affair in some far-off watering place...

Emily's hands were shaking. She twisted them together in her lap, fighting the urge to chew her thumbnail. She knew very well she should not feel that way. He was nothing, a denied suitor who could not hurt her. But still she could not push away her dark feelings.

What will you do when you are alone in the world?

The carriage drew to a halt outside Manning House, and for once that cold edifice looked positively welcoming, a haven. She hurried up the stone steps and into the foyer, leaving her gloves and hat with the butler, who informed her the duke was in the drawing room.

Emily walked slowly up the grand staircase, trying not to run, not to slam the doors behind her and lock them. But when she saw Nicholas there by the fireplace, his bright hair rumpled, she could not help herself. She dashed into his arms, holding on to him as tight as she could. Only when his embrace closed around her did she feel finally safe.

But for how long?

Nicholas laughed, and lifted her off her feet to spin her around until she laughed, too.

"What a grand welcome," he said. "I venture to guess

it was a very good tea party—or a very horrid one, and even I look good in comparison."

"It was somewhere in between, I would say. Tea and gossip, the usual sort of thing. And I think you will *always* look better than that."

"High praise, my dear. And I dare say you are in need of some sherry, your cheeks look rather pale." He set her down on a *chaise* and poured out a generous measure of the amber liquid from the sideboard.

Emily usually didn't care for the sweetness of sherry, but today she needed its bracing warmth. It felt even better when Nicholas sat beside her and rested his arm lightly around her shoulders. Mr Rayburn was surely wrong—she was not alone in the cold world. Nicholas was her husband, and this was her home. Not George Rayburn, or beautiful ladies in hidden portraits, or even herself could change that.

"Did you hear anything interesting at the party?" he asked, idly toying with a loose curl at her temple, the pearl earring in her ear.

Emily could hardly remember anything at all when he did that. She laughed and playfully swatted his hand away. "Not at all. Broken engagements, elopements, card debts. How was your own business?"

"Equally dull. But we should be able to leave in a few days." He leaned over and kissed her deeply, his arms going around her waist to carry her down to the *chaise*. Emily giggled, her empty glass falling from her hand to roll away across the carpet. How delicious he smelled, her husband, of clean air and soap and lemony cologne, how strong and warm he felt in her arms. She wrapped her legs around his hips, drawing him even closer to her.

"Nicholas…" she said, and gasped as he nibbled at her earlobe. "My parents are coming for dinner later."

"Mmm, much later, I hope," he muttered against her neck. "There's plenty of time until then. I missed you today."

Plenty of time indeed. He kissed her again, his tongue sliding over hers, and Emily forgot everything but the two of them and their own precious, fragile world.

Chapter Twenty

"Oh, Miss Carroll—that is, your Grace! Mrs Goddard asks if you can come to the school as soon as may be."

Emily glanced up from the menus she was perusing to see Sally in the doorway of her little sitting room. The butler hovered there, too, a disapproving look on his face that such a caller had come dashing in so improperly at Manning House.

But Emily felt a little thrill of happiness to see her. It had been days since they returned to London, and she had only been able to make one short visit to the school amid all her new duties. She missed it so much.

But then Sally's words sank in, as well as the strained look on her pretty face, the way she had so forgotten her carefully learned manners. Mrs Goddard asked her to come quickly—and Mrs Goddard never sent for her. Emily pushed back her chair and hurried across the room to take Sally's hands. She dismissed the butler and closed the door behind him.

"Sally, my dear, please sit down," Emily said, leading

her to the sofa by the window. "You look quite flushed. You must have dashed all the way here."

"Oh, yes, your Grace. I got lost, I'm afraid, and had to hunt around for a bit to find this place. I'm not sure how I could miss it, though!"

Emily laughed. "It is quite the behemoth, isn't it? Here, have a bit of tea—I think it's still warm. And tell me what is amiss."

"Mrs Goddard is ill."

"Ill!"

"Oh, not dreadfully ill, your Grace. It's a cold that won't go away because she refuses to rest as she should. But the doctor came this morning and insists she take a tisane and stay in bed for a few days."

"Days? I doubt she will be able to do that even on doctor's orders."

"No, miss—your Grace. But the other teachers are standing guard at her door. If she doesn't rest it could turn into pneumonia. She's fussing about the school, though."

"Poor Mrs Goddard. What can I do to help? I fear I would be no good at making her rest. I never could argue with her."

"She wants you to come and talk with her, your Grace, to see if you can organise the school for a few days while she rests. She says you're the only one who can do it."

Emily felt a sudden touch of pride at Mrs Goddard's confidence in her. She was overjoyed to be of help—as long as it wasn't in the mornings. "I will come right away. Just let me fetch my bonnet."

They set out into the sunny day a few moments later, making their way through the crowded streets. Once they left Mayfair and the fashionable houses and shops behind, the walkways were quieter and they were able to slow down a bit.

"Mrs Goddard told me you've been working very hard on your lessons lately, Sally," Emily said, linking her arm with Sally's. "Soon you'll be able to find a good position, I'm sure."

"If anyone will hire me, your Grace!"

"Certainly they will. With everything you have learned at Mrs Goddard's, and the letter of recommendation I will give you, you will have a suitable place in no time." A letter from a duchess could go far indeed. Emily had to admit she very much liked all she could do for her friends now. "Maybe one day you'll have a school of your own."

Sally smiled happily. "A school of my own! That would be splendid." But then her smile faded as she glanced across the street. "I fear it will have to be some place far from London."

"What do you mean?"

"If I stay here, I will just keep seeing people who knew me—before. Like that man across the street who is staring at us."

Emily looked, and to her shock saw it was Mr Rayburn who watched them. She glimpsed him between the flash of passing vehicles, just standing there smiling. Had he been following her all this time? He caught her eyes and mockingly tipped his hat to her.

"Mr Rayburn," she whispered.

"You know him?"

"He once was something of a suitor, though it was never a serious thing. Not on my part, anyway, and I thought not on his until recently. He used to—visit you?"

Sally's lips tightened. "He visited the house quite

often, sometimes to see me, but not always. He was not choosy about which girl he saw. And he was also a man of, um, interesting tastes. You're lucky you didn't marry him, miss. Very lucky."

"I'm seeing that more every day," Emily murmured. And thank goodness Sally and Jane were both well away from him!

But now he had seen her with Sally, a woman whose past he knew all too well. Surely just one gossipy word about the new Duchess of Manning's "friends" would not go well for her new family, for her reputation and her husband.

She looked out across the street again. He was gone, but she was sure he would not be far.

"Should we go, miss?" Sally said worriedly.

Emily shook her head. "We must not allow such an annoyance to ruin our day. He is gone now. Come, we need to get on and see Mrs Goddard."

Nicholas heard Emily's light footsteps as she hurried past the library door. It barely seemed like a breeze over the parquet floor, a faint rustle of her skirts, yet he knew it was her. After only a few weeks of married life, he knew her step, sensed that she was in his house. *Their* house. It had become shockingly normal.

And he had let his guard down, just as he had vowed he would not. Emily, with her shy laughter, her bright green eyes, her sweet passion, had slipped in close to him before he even realised it.

He knew he should back away now, keep his distance for her own sake, but he could not stop the way the day suddenly grew lighter and brighter when she was there. He pushed away the dull account books and swung open the door.

She was already far down the corridor, her pale muslin dress a ghostly blur in the gathering twilight. Her head was down, as if she was lost somewhere in her own world.

"Emily," he called softly, but she didn't hear, still lost. "Emily!"

A tremble went through her shoulders and she spun around to face him. "Nicholas! I didn't see you there."

"I heard you walk past the door. What have you been doing today?"

"Oh. Just—shopping. Seeing friends. The usual sort of London thing." She sounded oddly out of breath, and she would not quite meet his gaze. The laughing woman who had kissed him on the drawing-room *chaise* was nowhere to be seen.

What had happened today? Surely more than shopping or visiting. But Emily clearly did not want to say, and he didn't know how to draw it from her. In his family, no emotion or experience went unexpressed.

He crossed his arms over his chest and leaned back against the doorjamb. "Are we dining out tonight?"

Suddenly, a hoarse sob escaped Emily's lips. She ran back along the corridor and flung her arms around his neck, burying her face in his shoulder.

"Em! Is something amiss?" he asked in shock. He held her against him. "Did something happen to you today?"

"No, nothing happened, I just—I suppose I missed you. That's all."

"After one afternoon? If this is going to be my greeting every time we part, I must go away more often."

"No." She peered up at him solemnly, her eyes wide. "Do you remember on our wedding night when I promised I would always do my best and never make you ashamed of me?"

"Yes, I remember."

"I still promise you that. Don't forget."

"Em, I would never be ashamed of you. How could I?"

"Please, Nicholas. Just don't forget."

Then she dropped her forehead to his shoulder again, hiding her gaze from him, and said nothing else. But Nicholas could feel the way she trembled against him, and he knew something was very wrong with his wife. He had made his own vow on that wedding night, to do whatever he could to make Emily happy. And now something was making her very miserable, just when she had brought him such joy.

He was going to find what that was and put a stop to it—whatever he had to do.

Chapter Twenty-One

"You have a visitor, your Grace."

Emily glanced up from her book to find the butler standing in the morning room doorway, silver tray in hand. A tingling shiver seemed to tremble up her spine, and even before she took up the card she knew.

It was George Rayburn. Ever since he had seen her with Sally two days ago she had been sure this moment would come. Several times she started to tell Nicholas, to confess all about her work and the way Mr Rayburn had caught her out. Nicholas knew how to deal with scandal; he and his family had been doing it all their lives. He would surely know how to fix this, too, or he would tell her to ignore it, it did not matter.

But then he would smile at her, or take her hand and kiss it, and her resolve to confess and pay the price would falter. Her marriage seemed off to such a fine start, which she had never dared dream would happen. But it was still young, and so fragile.

She loved Nicholas, but he did not yet love her. She so much wanted him to, wanted them to have a *real* marriage. It was too early to bring such trouble to him. And she had to protect the new baby above all else. No one could be allowed to harm that precious little life.

She would just have to solve this business herself. And she had to begin by confronting Mr Rayburn.

"Please show him in," she said.

"Very good, your Grace. Shall I have refreshments sent in?"

"That will not be necessary. Mr Rayburn will not be staying long."

As the butler left, Emily carefully set aside her book and sat up very straight on the settee, her hands folded protectively over her stomach. On the wall across from her hung a painting by Nicholas's sister Annalise, a sunny scene of the lake at Welbourne. The sight of it, and the happy memories it evoked, gave her a jolt of courage.

She had so much to protect now. She would fight anyone who dared threaten it.

George Rayburn swept into the morning room and gave her an elegant bow, smiling his charming smile as if this was the most pleasant of social occasions. Emily refused to be lulled, or even to smile in return.

"Your Grace," he said. "How lovely you look today. Marriage certainly agrees with you."

"It is not the usual hour for calls, Mr Rayburn," Emily answered shortly. "To what do I owe this honour?"

"I am wounded. Even if you are a duchess now, surely you still have time for old friends? You certainly seemed to at Gunter's—and at the worthy Mrs Goddard's school. She does have the most interesting collection of pupils, as I discovered when I looked into the matter."

Emily's eyes narrowed as she studied the odious smirk on his face. "Mrs Goddard is quite respectable, and a lady in my position is often called upon to work for charity."

"Very true. But what will people say of an *unmarried* young lady—or even a married one of such high title—associating with women like the fair Sally? An earl's daughter gallivanting around town with a common prostitute? Think of the things she could have told the innocent young lady, or the places she might have taken her. Terribly shocking, if a sweet new wife learned such naughty things in all sorts of vile places. Perhaps that was how she captured such a marital prize. Perhaps she was practising whorehouse wiles on him at the Arnold ball when they were caught."

His eyes widened with feigned shock. "So appalling. One more scandal on the Manning title, and surely the worst one to date. Who knows what kind of children such a duchess would produce?"

Emily's stomach tightened with a sick spasm. *This* was the sort of man Sally warned her about when she cautioned her about the wedding night. Selfish, greedy men with no thought to anyone else. He stood right before her, this former suitor, and for an instant she glimpsed the appalling life that might have been hers, if not for Nicholas and her own doubts.

"What is it you want?" she said quietly.

"You need not speak to me so unkindly, your Grace. I merely ask the help of an old friend in my time of need. I wish to go abroad, to make a new life in Italy or Switzerland. To mend my broken heart. Sadly, I must settle some debts first, and find a way to buy a proper home once I am settled."

Emily nodded. Blackmail—of course that was his game. "I did hear you had found yourself in some rather dire straits, Mr Rayburn. Gambling debts, I believe?"

A muscle ticked along his jaw, his eyes hard as he looked at her. "You see how gossip spreads so quickly."

"If you are in such need of money, why did you ever court *me*? I had only a small dowry."

"Oh, my dear duchess," he said with a sad laugh. "You do underestimate your charms. You are quite beautiful, if sadly stubborn, and an earl's title opens many doors to the right person. We could have built something together, you and I. Built a much more refined life than could be had with some vulgar cit's rich daughter."

Built a life of lies and con games, always dodging creditors? Coming up with blackmail schemes? The mere thought of it made Emily shudder. "And a rich cit would surely urge his daughter to aim higher than a penniless gambler with no title."

His hands curled into fists, his face darkening with fury. Emily half-rose, ready to run for the bell if she had to, but he leaned away from her, forcing his hands to loosen.

"I no longer have even that option, unpleasant as it is, because of you," he said tightly. "So I must throw myself on your mercy—your Grace. If you cannot help me, I must regretfully tell your husband of your unsavoury friendships with women of the night. What will he think of his lovely new wife then?"

"I have no ready money," Emily said.

"Oh, but you have so many resources now, Duchess." He gestured to her emerald pendant, Nicholas's special wedding gift to her. "I am sure you can find it in your heart to help me. I will expect your answer by this evening."

He gave her another bow and an infuriating smile, and then he departed just before her anger bubbled over inside her and she could throw a vase at his head. She ran to the window and watched the street below until she saw him walk away and knew he was gone.

The villain. How *dare* he threaten her? Threaten her marriage, her new life, her child?

Emily kicked at the wall in fury. She had done nothing wrong, yet she could see how easily her association with Sally and the others at Mrs Goddard's could be twisted and made into something ugly. She knew how quickly the flames of gossip could spread out of control.

She had promised Nicholas she would never make him ashamed of his wife. How could she keep that promise without giving in to blackmail?

She closed her fist around her emerald necklace, the gift Nicholas had given her on their betrothal. She wouldn't give it up. She wouldn't give up anything, least of all her marriage.

And she knew just who to turn to for advice. Who would know how to deal with such a man on his own underhanded terms. She had to go back to Mrs Goddard's.

She snatched up her bonnet and shawl and hurried down the stairs to the foyer. She had hoped to slip out before anyone could see her, but of course that was too much to hope for in such a vast, crowded house. The butler was in the foyer, scolding a housemaid who had insufficiently dusted the banister.

"You're going out, your Grace?" he said in surprise. "Shall I call the carriage?"

That was the last thing she needed, for everyone to see the ducal carriage at Mrs Goddard's door! "I am only going a short way, thank you. I will not be gone long."

Before he could say anything else, she rushed out the front door and down to the street. Once she was safely around the corner, out of sight, she hailed a hackney. She would just find a way to deal with this matter herself, before Nicholas could even find out.

No matter what it took.

"Is the duchess at home?" Nicholas asked the butler, wearily stripping off his gloves. It had been a long, dull day of business. Now it was absurd how happy he was to be back at draughty old Manning House—how much he wanted to see Emily. The thought of her smile, of hearing about her day and just being with her, was a bright prospect indeed. Blast it all, it even made him feel better just to ask after his duchess!

"Her Grace went out a few hours ago, your Grace," the butler said, taking his hat. "She has not yet returned."

"Went out?" Nicholas was rather disappointed, which was absurd. He had seen her only that morning, kissing her in the dawn light before he slipped out of her bed. And he would see her again at dinner, across their table. Yet still there it was.

He would never have thought he could feel that way back on his wedding day. But Emily was not at all what he expected. She was turning everything around him upside-down.

"Did she say where she was going?" he asked.

"No, your Grace. She did seem rather in a hurry."

"A hurry?"

The butler hesitated before adding quietly, "I should not say this, your Grace, but I was rather concerned about the duchess. I wondered if she might be ill. She looked very pale, and she did rush out so abruptly. She did not want the carriage called."

"She seemed ill?" Nicholas asked in rising alarm. Could she be with child after all? He had been careful, but nothing was certain. Or perhaps she had bad news from her family, or had heard some disturbing bit of gossip from Lady Arnold and her flock. She had not yet learned to shrug such things away, as he and his siblings did. As they had to.

He remembered how she had run to him yesterday, holding on to him so tightly. He should have pressed her then to tell him her worries. He hadn't wanted to frighten her, to press her before she was ready to confide in him. Before she really trusted him. Their marriage had a surprisingly promising beginning, but he had to take it carefully, day by day. He had to be careful with her, to curb his usual impatience.

Now he regretted that caution. Emily had run away somewhere.

"Did she have a message of some sort before she left?" he asked urgently. "Or give any indication at all where she was going?"

"She did have a caller. A Mr George Rayburn. Her Grace left very soon after he departed."

Rayburn. Why did that damnable man always seem to be appearing in their lives? What was his strange effect on Emily?

Nicholas was done being patient. Emily was *his* wife, and he needed the truth from her. He would not allow Rayburn to help her. And he would not hurt her himself, if she was in love with Rayburn.

He took his hat back and dashed out the door to the crowded street. He had to find Emily, right now, and discover what was amiss with her. He wasn't sure where she would go in the wide city—to her parents' house, to track down Rayburn's lodgings—he would go any place to find her.

As he hailed a hackney, he remembered the day of their betrothal, when he followed her to that quiet brick town house. Whatever that place was, could she have gone there again? Even if she hadn't, surely they would know something about his mysterious wife. They could give him one more piece of the puzzle that was his Emily.

Chapter Twenty-Two

"Yes, sir? Can I help you?"

Whatever Nicholas had expected from Emily's mysterious house, it wasn't this. A perfectly ordinary housemaid in a crisp white apron and cap opened the dark-painted door at the top of the immaculately swept front steps. Curtains were drawn closed over the windows, and the only things that set it apart from its neighbours was a small brass plaque by the door: *Mrs Goddard's School for Disadvantaged Females*.

The maid's face was polite, but wary. She looked as if she would shut the door in his face at the least sign that he meant mischief.

"I am very sorry to disturb you," he said, holding out his card. "But I am searching for my wife, and I wondered if she might have called here today."

The maid gaped down at the card. "We haven't had any duchesses here today, your Grace, I'm sure."

Nicholas glanced again, carefully, along the row of narrow houses. He was quite certain this was the dwelling Emily went to that day. "Perhaps you know her as Lady Emily Carroll?"

"Miss Carroll? She's a *duchess*?"

"She hasn't been for very long. We are newlyweds." And he had never felt that newness quite so acutely as at that moment. He felt as if Emily had tugged him down into some new, topsy-turvy world.

There was nothing a Manning liked better than an intriguing mystery to solve. And he had the feeling his whole future happiness rested on this one particular mystery.

"Won't you come in, your Grace?" the maid said, opening the door wider. "I'll send for Mrs Goddard to see you. She hasn't been well, but I'm sure she would want to meet with you."

He was left in a small sitting room, sparsely but comfortably furnished with simple dark-upholstered chairs, seascapes on the walls, a piano under the windows and improving books on the shelves. Occasionally from above came a burst of female laughter, a rush of light steps across the floor. Once he thought he heard the door open a crack, a soft giggle, but when he turned it was gone.

He wasn't alone for long. Soon a tall, respectably dressed and capped older lady swept into the room. A small bunch of keys dangled from the sash of her grey silk gown, and she assessed him with calm, careful eyes. She seemed pale and red-eyed, as if she was recovering from a cold, but she was impeccably dressed and coolly polite.

"So you are Emily's husband," she said. "We did not know she had made such a grand marriage, or at least she did not tell us herself. I saw the notice in the papers."

Nicholas gave her a bow. "I'm afraid you have the advantage of me, ma'am."

"I am Mrs Goddard, of course. I own this school."

"And may I ask what your school has to do with Emily?"

For the first time a hint of doubt crept across Mrs Goddard's handsome face. "She has not told you about us?"

"I fear my wife speaks little about herself," Nicholas said ruefully. "I want so much to make her happy, and I don't have the slightest idea how to do that! She won't think of herself. And now I know something is amiss with her, but I can't help her fix it if I don't know what it is."

Mrs Goddard gave a little laugh. "Oh, your Grace. I am not surprised Emily won't speak much of herself to you. She has always wanted to make others happy first. I fear she is not here at the moment, though."

"How do you know her so well, Mrs Goddard?"

"I was her governess. Please, your Grace, sit with me for a moment."

"I must find her…"

"And I think I can help you with that. But you must listen to me first."

Nicholas was aching to run out in search of Emily again, but he knew that would be futile. He would be more likely to learn of her whereabouts if he listened to Mrs Goddard now. She ushered him to a *chaise* by the empty fireplace and settled herself across from him. She clutched a handkerchief in her palm.

"I will confess," she said, "I was worried when I saw Emily was to marry you."

"Worried? Because of my family's reputation?"

"No, because—well, because of her own nature. You

see, your Grace, by the time I came to work for Emily's family I had been governess to many young ladies of high rank. I could see right away Emily was different. She was so quiet and shy, but so very eager to please, to be of use to everyone around her. She worked so hard at her lessons. I must confess I came to love her as I would my own daughter. I wanted to help her see her own worth."

"That is what I want, too, Mrs Goddard," Nicholas said eagerly. "I have never known anyone as sweet and serious as my Emily."

"Your Emily?" Mrs Goddard said with a smile. "Surely you have seen this eagerness she has to please, to always do the right thing?"

"Yes. She has often told me she wants to be the perfect duchess. I try to tell her a duchess is always perfect just as she is, that others will be eager to follow her lead and she need only be herself."

"I doubt she would believe you. I was worried that just this sort of thing would happen when I saw she had married a duke. That she would try to change herself rather than find who she really is. The fact that she could not tell you about her work here only confirms my fears."

"What is this place, exactly, Mrs Goddard? Why would she not tell me she came here?"

Mrs Goddard hesitated. "This is a school, and Emily teaches here whenever she has a chance, usually every Tuesday. But our pupils are not the usual young ladies. They once worked in brothels or walked the streets of Covent Garden. When they wish to make a change in their lives, we train them to be milliners or ladies' maids. Emily works hard to help them, and they care about her very much. It is worthy work."

"But it's not hard to see that someone could persuade her otherwise," Nicholas said tightly.

"Yes," said Mrs Goddard. "They could have told her a perfect duchess would never associate with such people, even in a charitable way, and poor Emily would probably believe them."

"Blast it all! I don't care who she associates with. I don't *want* her to be perfect, I just want her to be Emily," he said, furious with whoever had made Emily feel so unsure of herself. Furious with himself, and whatever it was he had done to make her believe she could not come to him.

"You do care about her," said Mrs Goddard.

"I love her," Nicholas said, startled by the stark truth of those words that spilled out of him without thought. He loved her, his sweet, selfless, serious, beautiful wife. And he would kill whoever had hurt her.

"I see that you do." Mrs Goddard rose to her feet, her keys rattling. "Emily was here earlier. She spoke with one of our pupils, Sally. They are friends. Perhaps she could tell us where Emily has gone."

"Sally?" Nicholas remembered the Sally Emily spoke of on their wedding night, the friend who advised her so disastrously on the marriage act. "Are they *good* friends?"

"They seem close. Emily has been teaching her French, in the hope that she can find a better position than most. They were together a few days ago. I am sure she can help us."

Mrs Goddard summoned the maid who had answered the door and sent her to fetch Sally. When she arrived, she seemed most reluctant to say anything about Emily. But Mrs Goddard's quiet urging, and Nicholas's pleas about how worried he was for his wife, softened her. Her pretty face turned uncertain and she twisted her hands in her apron.

"I'm not sure where she was going when she left here, your Grace, I swear it," she said, tears in her eyes. "I told her to tell you what had happened, to not pay off that bast—that man. I told her worms like him would never go away, but she was so worried you would be angry."

"What bast—man?" Nicholas said, a fury growing inside him.

Sally let out a ragged sob. "Mr Rayburn! He saw her with me on the street, and I knew he would pester her with it, just from the way he looked at her. He ain't— isn't a gentleman."

"Rayburn," Nicholas growled. "Of course. He black-mailed her about this place?"

Sally nodded. "He said he wanted money to go abroad. That's what she said. But I bet that's not all he wanted from her. He wanted to marry her once, your Grace, until you snatched her away from him. And he doesn't like to lose, he'll want revenge."

Revenge. Nicholas would like some of that himself, taken right out of Rayburn's cowardly hide. "And she did not say where she was going from here?"

"I don't know for sure. But she did ask me if I knew a pawnbroker. I gave her the name of someone who wouldn't cheat her, but I did tell her she should go home instead. Miss Emily is sweet, but she's also the most stubborn lady I have ever seen."

"So she is. And where might this pawnbroker be?"

Only moments later, Nicholas was on his way to the establishment of a certain Mr Green, and there he found Emily's emerald pendant, his wedding gift to her which she always wore, and the pearl earrings Justine had given her as a wedding present. He redeemed them, and set out in search of Emily once again. Mr Green had said he was worried about the lady, who seemed to have been crying, and his apprentice had followed her to Hyde Park to make sure she was quite well and did not do anything like throw herself into the river.

And that was where Nicholas found his wife, sitting on a bench in the spot by the Serpentine where he had saved that child on that long-ago day. It was quiet there today, all the fashionable crowds dispersed. Only a few children played on the pathways with their nursemaids, a few couples walking along together as they talked quietly. It now seemed a place to hide, to think, to not be seen.

At least Emily seemed to think so. She stared silently at the water, her hands twisted in her lap, her face white and expressionless. She didn't notice anything around her, and the wondrous laughter he loved was nowhere to be found. He found himself terribly sad, and angry, too—angry that she had lied to him, had not trusted him after everything they had been through in their short marriage.

But he would not just turn and walk away, leave her to her worries. He couldn't go back to Manning House, and greet her as if he knew nothing, as if her secret was safe. He could easily dispatch Rayburn on his own without her knowing, and they could go on for ever living on parallel planes that never quite intersected. Two lives joined, but never meeting in truth. So many people did that, married for convenience or family or property, and they rubbed along contentedly enough—as long as they didn't have to see each other too often.

That was what his own parents had done—until it all exploded in their faces. But most people with such marriages did not fall apart as the duke and duchess did. Most people kept up their façade and got on with it.

At first, he thought that was all he could hope for with Emily Carroll. A proper society marriage, maybe a partnership of sorts. The love matches his siblings had made could not be for him. That had all changed as he came to see Emily, the real Emily, the hidden heart of her. The shyness, the fear, melted away and her laughter glowed—only for him. It changed his whole world.

She was a passionate woman with a good, kind heart. Seeing the school where she worked, meeting the people there who loved her, whose lives she had touched and changed, showed him that even clearer. The fact that some brute would dare to hurt her, to use her tender heart against her—it made him burn with a raw fury he had never known before. He was angry that she felt like she had to lie to him.

He forced that anger down, erased it from his expression and relaxed his curled, hard fists before he said gently, "So here you are, Em."

A startled tremor went through her, and he thought she might not respond, would not turn and look at him. But then she slowly stood up and spun around to face him.

"How did you find me?" she said softly. Her whole body seemed tense, as if she was poised to flee like one of Stephen's more skittish horses.

Nicholas remembered how his brothers treated such creatures, with slow movements and a quiet, reassuring tone. He didn't want her to run from him, not now. It felt as if this moment was so important for them, as if their whole future together depended on their connecting now.

He took one slow step towards her, then another. "It

was a lucky guess. And also you were not in the other places I looked."

"Where did you look?"

"Well, Manning House, of course. Your parents' house. And then I went to Mrs Goddard's school." He held out her jewellery boxes. "I wanted to return these to you."

She stared at the boxes, her face turning even whiter under the brim of her bonnet. "You know, then."

"About your teaching work, and that piece of dirt, Rayburn? Yes, I know. I wish you had told me yourself." He forced himself to speak quietly, gently, to not frighten her with his own anger and confusion. He wanted to be a good husband to her, but how could he if he did not even really know her? If she didn't know him well enough to see that she could trust him?

Emily sank down on the bench. "I didn't want you to worry. I just wanted to take care of it myself, to—to make it all go away."

"Emily, why?" he demanded. He sat down beside her, very close, but not quite touching. She felt so tense he feared if he touched her she would snap. "I am your husband. Why would you think you could not tell me, come to me for help? I thought maybe you were in love with Rayburn, that our marriage separated you from the man you truly wanted."

Emily gave a bitter laugh. "Quite the opposite. I never wanted to marry him, even when it seemed he was my only possible suitor. But I never imagined he felt as he did, that he would do what he did. And as for why I did not tell you, Nicholas—I had promised you and your family I would always do my best, that I would work hard to be your perfect duchess. Being blackmailed for associating with former courtesans didn't seem the way to keep that promise."

"Oh, Emily." *You precious, silly girl*, he thought. She thought she was protecting *him*. That anger faded away, leaving only a bitter sadness. "You know my family. We have come through far worse scrapes than this intact."

"But I did not want to be one more 'scrape' for you! You have enough to worry about, without a scandalous new wife. I want to help you, not be a burden, even after the way we had to marry. I never want to be a burden."

"Oh, Em." Nicholas set down the boxes and gently took her hand in his. "How could you ever think you are a burden? You are the furthest thing from that to me."

"You mean—you are not angry?" she said doubtfully, staring down at their joined hands.

"Oh, no, I am certainly angry. But not with you."

"Oh." She frowned, turning to look out at the river as if she was trying to fathom something totally new and unexpected.

He knew the feeling very well. He had been trying to do the same ever since they married and he found this unexpected gift in his life.

"You are not angry about my work, about the way I kept it secret even from my parents?" she said. "Or that I tried to sell the jewellery you and your sister gave me?"

"It was wrong of Rayburn to take advantage of your kindness, Em," he said. "I am only angry you did not think you could tell me about it. I am your husband. We're together in this now, in all things." And to his surprise he realised just how true that was. They had begun with much against them, and they were working hard to build a life together. But they had to learn to trust from now on.

She nodded, but he could tell from the shadows in her eyes that something was still bothering her. If he had learned one thing about his wife, it was that she could not be pushed. She was as stubborn as the rest of his family.

"You must continue to work anywhere you like, and associate with anyone you like," he said firmly. "You are the Duchess of Manning. These cursed titles are mostly a lot of hard work and a complete nuisance, but at least it gives us that freedom. Gossip can't hurt us, not you and me, my dear. Do you see?"

She looked him right in the eye and smiled. "I am beginning to think I do. And I'm glad you don't want me to give up Mrs Goddard's. She was my governess, you see, and one of my dearest friends. She's been doing such good work with her school, and made such a difference in those women's lives. I haven't been able to help her very much, but I do what I can, to repay her for what she gave me."

"Now you can help her as much as you like. Maybe she'd like a bigger school, in the country somewhere? More teachers?"

Emily laughed, a wonderful, open, free, delighted sound Nicholas had never heard from her before. It was like the brilliant sun bursting forth on a cold, grey day. He wanted to hear more and more of it. He would do absolutely anything to make her laugh like that again.

"Oh, Nicholas," she cried, and threw her arms around his neck in the way he loved so much. "What a great fool I was not to tell you. Sally said so, but I did not believe her, and here she was quite right. I should have known you would understand—but I was afraid."

"Don't be afraid," he said, holding her close. He buried his face in her neck, breathing in her sweet scent. "Never be afraid of me. There is just one more thing I need to know now, my dear."

"And what is that?" she asked. Her voice was muffled against his shoulder as she clung to him.

"Where are you supposed to meet Rayburn to give him his blood money?"

Chapter Twenty-Three

"I'm surprised you haven't decamped to France already, Rayburn," Nicholas said from the shadows. He had been waiting there at the top of the stairs in that shabby lodging house for hours, his anger slowly simmering. Now that anger was so cold it fairly burned. "You're rather late for your appointment."

Rayburn spun around, his fists clenched. Even in that half-light Nicholas could see the wild shock in the man's eyes, the flash of panic. *Good*—he should be terrified for daring to threaten Emily. The fact that he told her to come here, to his lodgings, told Nicholas that Rayburn wanted more than money from her, even though Emily had not seen it. The man was lower than the low.

Nicholas crossed his arms over his chest. "Surprised to see me, are you?"

Rayburn quickly regained his equilibrium and gave Nicholas a humourless, taunting smile. "So, the little mouse went and tattled on me, did she? She's braver than I thought."

"And you're even more foolish than *I* thought.

Surely you'd know better than to insult my wife even further?"

"What else can you do to me, Manning? My life is ruined, my place in society gone, my fortune vanished, the lady I wanted to marry stolen by you. Not even a duke could make things worse for me now."

"I wouldn't place a bet on that if I were you, Rayburn. An infuriated husband is surely worse than any duke."

"Oh, so now you care about her, do you?" Rayburn sneered. "Everyone knows you were forced to marry, and just one more disgrace for your family. But now you come to her aid, when someone else seems to have feelings for her? Forgive me if I am not convinced—your Grace."

"I do not care whether you are convinced or not," Nicholas growled. "I only care that you leave my wife alone from now on. Do not even so much as look in her direction, or we will be having a very different sort of conversation."

Disgusted and fed up with having to even look at the villain, Nicholas half-turned toward the door to take his leave. He had to get back to what really mattered—Emily. But Rayburn suddenly lunged at him, catching him on the jaw with an unexpected blow that sent Nicholas reeling back against the wall. All his raw, burning fury was released and he let it all fly free, grabbing Rayburn and slamming him into the door. He curled his fists in the man's coat, holding him pinned there.

"You call blackmailing a lady, frightening her half to death, having *feelings* for her?" Nicholas said, tightening his fists as Rayburn tried to twist away. "I call it being a damnable villain. Emily had a lucky escape when she did not marry you, you would have bled her sweet heart until she was crushed."

"And she's so much better off with you, is she? A brawler with an insane family?" Rayburn kicked out at Nicholas, driving him back, but only for an instant. Nicholas remembered all his lessons at Gerard's Saloon, and came back with a sharp right uppercut that sent Rayburn crashing to the floor.

All that fury came pouring out of him as the small room rang with curses, shouts and the dull thud of blows. All his passion for Emily, his struggle to be a good husband, that raw anger when he learned she was being threatened, was released in the primitive thrill of the fight.

This man would never hurt Emily again. As Nicholas drove his bare fist into Rayburn's face, he doubted any lady need fear from him ever again. This was over, for good.

"Wot's all this?" a woman suddenly screamed. "You're tearing up my house, you bastards!"

Through that red haze of fight-fury, Nicholas felt tiny, sharp fists rain blows on his head. He tossed Rayburn aside and slumped back against the wall as a small, thin, grey-haired lady pummelled at him. Her wrinkled face under a grubby mob cap was contorted in a fury that surely surpassed even his own.

She kicked at Rayburn, who tried to crawl away from her even though he couldn't see where he was going through his swollen-shut eye.

"I knew it was a mistake to rent to the likes of you!" the woman shrieked. "You never paid your rent on time, and now you're bleeding all over my floor!"

Nicholas started to laugh, but winced as his lip gave a twinge. He held his hand to the blood dripping there, and saw he was contributing to the mess on the woman's floor. His knuckles were bruised and bleeding, his ribs on fire and his face aching, but Rayburn was in a worse state.

And certainly, Nicholas reflected as he watched the landlady finish the job he himself had begun on Rayburn's battered self, the man would never harass a female again. It was a good day's work.

The woman left off Rayburn, who finally lay still, and spun around to face Nicholas. His laughter faded.

"And you, sirrah!" she cried. "I don't know who you are, but you're no gentleman to be brawling in a lady's house like that."

"You are quite right, madam," he said, as best as he could through his split lip. "My deepest apologies."

"He must owe you money, too," she said. "People are pounding on this door day and night, demanding their coin."

"I'm sure they are. But he'll be gone soon enough, I assure you." Nicholas dug a handful of coins from inside his torn coat and pressed them in her hand. "Pay to have the room cleaned before you rent it out again, madam, with my deepest apologies."

A smile lit up her face. "I will, sir, thank you." She cast a baleful glance at Rayburn, who was slowly sitting up on the floor. "And what about *him*?"

"I'll take care of him."

The woman gave a cackling laugh. "I'm sure you will at that!" She hurried out of the room without a backward look, clutching at the coins.

"Get out of England, Rayburn, as fast as you can," Nicholas said. "And pray no one in my family ever sees you again, or this afternoon will seem like the merest trifle."

And he turned on his heel and followed the woman out of that cursed room. She was nowhere to be seen as he left the house, but Rayburn's incoherent curses followed him out the door.

His carriage waited at the end of the narrow street, and he collapsed on the seat with a groan. Only now could he feel the aches of nearly every blow, every cut, but it was certainly all worth it. A brawl was surely not as gentlemanly as a duel, but it was far more satisfying.

And Emily, his sweet Emily, was safe now. That was the most important thing of all.

Chapter Twenty-Four

"You ridiculous, wonderful fool." Emily slowly soaked a cloth in cold water and rang it out, pressing it gently to the bruise on Nicholas's cheek as he lay stretched out on the *chaise* in her bedchamber. That bruise was turning purple and yellow at the edges, a vivid reminder of the violence and noise of the afternoon.

She had to admit it gave her a strange sort of satisfaction. Not that Nicholas was hurt, never that. But that he had defended her, like a knight of old with his damsel. She had never imagined anyone would do such a thing for her. She wasn't the sort of woman men fought over, were passionate about. It was rather—thrilling.

As long as it never happened again.

"Why do you smile like that?" he said hoarsely. "Are you making fun of the ruin of my pretty face?"

Emily laughed, and he smiled up at her, only to wince at the movement. She pressed the cloth closer. "It is certainly very colourful. Does it hurt terribly?"

"Truthfully, it hardly hurts at all. But I'm very willing

to swear it's absolutely excruciating if it means you will stay close to me."

"I won't go anywhere, whether it hurts or not." She smoothed his rumpled hair back from his brow. Despite the circumstances, she loved this moment with him, just the two of them in her quiet room, bound together by all that had happened. Even the woman in the portrait, who had haunted Emily ever since she saw her, seemed far away now. "Wherever did you learn to fight like that?"

He shrugged. "When you grow up with brothers like mine you learn to defend yourself. And I go to Gerard's Saloon. They will beat the daylights out of anyone who pays them enough, and they've taught me well."

"Indeed they have. You were certainly not the one who had the, er, daylight beaten out of them today. I'm sure Mr Rayburn will be fortunate if he can even walk tomorrow."

Nicholas gave a smugly satisfied laugh. "It was rather well done, I think. I can be fearsome when I wish."

"Oh, yes. I doubt he will ever try to blackmail a lady again."

"He won't be allowed into any drawing room in London again, either," Nicholas said grimly. "He will go abroad and stay there if he has any sense of self-preservation at all. Or perhaps he should go to Canada or India, if he truly wants to stay out of our way."

"I don't think we need to worry about it. He won't come around here again, I'm sure." Emily rinsed out the cloth again, trying to collect all her scattered thoughts. She knew truly what she owed Nicholas now; she knew what she had to say to him. She simply didn't know the words. How exactly did a woman set free a man she loved so desperately?

"You are a good friend to me, Nicholas," she said. "I can never repay you for all you have given me."

He frowned up at her. "I am your husband, Em. There is no question of repaying."

"Of course there is. You have given me so much: a home, a family, a position in society where I can do my work. You've even come to fisticuffs over me! My Galahad. Our marriage has, I fear, never been as open and honest as marriage should be. Even the beginning of our betrothal was based on a scandalous lie. But I will not do that any longer. I care about you too much."

I love you. Those words hovered on her tongue, longing to be said. She forced them away. This was the moment to let him go, not hold him to her, no matter how much she wanted to. No matter how bleak she feared her life would be without him.

"I can find my own residence," she said. "Or move to another apartment here at Manning House—this place is so vast. No one ever needs to know the truth, I won't bring more gossip on to you."

"Em, please." He grabbed her hand, forcing her to look at him again. Raw sorrow was written on his face, more vivid than that bruise. Worse, it seemed to be a bruise from the inside, a wound from his very heart. "What is the meaning of this? Is there something else you aren't telling me?"

"Only that I saw that miniature, the portrait of your Valentina that you kept in the desk at Welbourne. I did not mean to pry, but the hinge came loose and I saw her there. I know how much you miss her, and that I can never replace her in your heart. I don't want you to feel obligated to me any more…"

"Obligated? Is that what you think? That I can't let her go? That I can't move into the future with you?"

"I fear I don't know what to think. When it comes to you, Nicholas, and to our life together, I can only—feel."

"Emily." Nicholas kissed the top of her head. The tender touch made her want to cry. "I do love her memory, and I always will. I never knew love like that before her. Now I keep her portrait close to remember all she taught me."

"What did she teach you?" Emily thought surely Valentina had taught him what Nicholas himself had taught *her*—how to love, how to truly care and thus to put another person first. It was a truly wonderful thing.

"She taught me to be careful with the ones we love, to never take a moment with them for granted. To never put them in any danger. Yet I fear I forget that last lesson all too often."

"What do you mean? I have never seen anyone take such care with the people around them as you do," Emily protested. "You take such care of me and of all your brothers and sisters..."

Nicholas gave her a sad smile. "I fear I did not take care of Valentina. She died in childbirth, you see, and the poor baby with her."

"Oh. Oh, Nicholas, I am so very sorry," Emily whispered. How he must have suffered, losing the woman he loved so much and their child, too. Being suddenly alone in the world after knowing that love for such a short time. Her heart ached for him. She wrapped her arms around him and rested her head on his shoulder, wishing she could take that pain away from him.

"My darling Emily," he said, kissing her on her brow. "I am sorry I forgot that lesson, that I put you in danger."

"That is nonsense! You *saved* me from danger, you

went after Mr Rayburn. What do you even mean, you put me in danger?" Then she realised what he must truly mean. She drew back, staring at him in shock. "Nicholas. You think I will die in childbirth, too."

He just looked back at her, all that pain written starkly on his face. She felt tears prickle at her eyes and she dashed them away. He feared to lose the same things she did—their marriage, and the happiness they had somehow found against all the odds. She had never thought this could happen, not to her. It was all too glorious, and she was going to fight for it with everything she had.

"I can't lose you, my sweetest Emily," he said. "I've only just found you. I never thought I could love anyone again after Valentina, not until you came into my life. You are the kindest, dearest woman I have ever known, and I—need you. That's all. I need you."

Tears spilled from her eyes at his words. "You can't possibly need me half as much as I need you, my Galahad," she said. She rested her head on his shoulder again, closing her eyes to listen to his heartbeat, his breath, to revel in the heat and strength of him. She wanted nothing but to stay there close to him for ever, revelling in the joyous knowledge that he loved her. He was *hers*—they belonged to each other.

"I only felt half-alive until I found you," she said. "Now I see everything so much more vividly, I see the colour in everything, the whole world. I want to dance and laugh all the time, and I am a terrible dancer! Most of all, I want everyone to feel just as I do, just as happy."

Nicholas laughed and kissed her temple. "Everyone?"

"Well—maybe not Mr Rayburn." Emily drew back

to look up at him. She felt so urgently that she had to make him understand all he had done with her. All she felt for him. "You are the one who has given me that joy, Nicholas. I'm so proud and happy to be your wife. I could not bear it if being with me has taken away *your* joy. I only want you to be happy."

"I am happy with you." He gently took her face in his hands, as if she was a most precious jewel. He kissed her forehead, the tip of her nose, her lips. "I want to protect you, to keep you safe."

"And you do. Who else would have thrashed a man like that, simply for trying to get a little money from me?" She covered his hands with hers, holding him to her. "But none of us can be completely safe in life. I want to have children—*your* children. You would be the most wonderful father, and this house needs some life in it. It scares me, too. But I am stronger than I look, I'm ridiculously healthy, and I have you to help me."

"I will always help you, Emily, in anything you want."

"And do you want a family with me?"

His jaw tightened, but he nodded. "I do. I want us to have everything life can give us, together."

"And we will." Emily smiled up at him, her wonderful, handsome, strong-hearted husband, full of wild joy and bright hope. "Oh, Nicholas. With you by me, I feel I can do anything at all!"

"With you, I know I can." Nicholas kissed her, warm and lingering, all his heart in that embrace, all their burning hope for a glorious future together. "I love you, Emily. My wife, my perfect duchess."

"And I love you," she whispered. She gathered all her courage around her for what she had to say now.

"With all my heart. But there is something I must tell you now."

Nicholas laughed. "More revelations, my dear? I'm not sure I can take it."

Emily watched him steadily. He wouldn't like what she had to say, at least not at first. She had to persuade him all would be well. "You are not the only one to carry secrets, I fear. And now I must tell you mine."

She took his hand and pressed it flat over her stomach. For a moment, he looked puzzled—but then his eyes widened and she could see that he knew.

"Truly, Em?" he whispered, his voice thick with emotion. Was he happy—or angry?

"I have not yet seen the doctor, but I believe it is true," she said. "It must have happened the morning after our wedding."

He didn't answer, but his arms came around her very tightly, pulling her close against him. "We're going to have a baby?"

"Yes. And you needn't worry, my darling. I am very strong, much stronger than I look, and I will have you to help me. All will be well, I am very sure," she said quickly, trying her hardest to reassure him—and herself.

He stopped her words with a fierce kiss. She felt all his emotions in that kiss, all the feelings she shared with him, all the joy, hope and fear.

"You will have all the best doctors in the country, nurses, midwives, everything," he said, kissing her again.

Emily laughed. "All I need is good fresh air, *one* midwife—and you. All will be well, with me and the baby, too, I promise."

"That is a promise I insist you keep. I can't do without you, Em. You are everything to me."

"As you are to me." Emily rested her head on his chest, closing her eyes as she listened to his heartbeat. "We have everything together, Nicholas. I won't lose it."

And she would not be parted from him ever again. They were her family now, Nicholas and the new baby, her whole wonderful world. She would protect them with all her strength, for ever.

Epilogue

Eight months later

Nicholas paced the length of the library at Scarnlea Abbey, all the way from the carved marble fireplace to the windows, open to the warm spring day. The painted eyes of his ancestors in their portraits along the panelled walls watched him with faint disapproval, but he didn't notice them at all. Nor did he notice the soft, flower-scented breeze from the gardens, or hear the happy shrieks of his nieces as they toddled along the pathways.

He could only think of that bedchamber high above his head, where Emily laboured to bring their child into the world. He could hear nothing from up there, no screams or shouts, but his imagination conjured all sorts of terrible scenes. All sorts of mysterious things that could be happening to his darling wife in that room of women.

"Nick, do sit down," Stephen said from his seat by the bookshelf. He held up his decanter of brandy. "You're going to wear a hole in that carpet with your infernal pacing. Have a drink."

Nicholas shook his head. "I can't sit down."

"Well, you won't help Emily that way. She has Justine and Charlotte and her sister-in-law with her, as well as the midwife and who knows how many servants. She would have her mother, too, if the lady hadn't fainted and been carried out of the room. She will be quite well."

"Surely it should be over now," Nicholas muttered. He paused by the window to watch Katherine and little Anna stumble past on their tiny toddler legs, their nurse-maids running behind them. Their golden hair and white dresses gleamed in the sunlight, their laughter ringing out like music.

The sight of his sister's children, so robust and healthy, did reassure him. But still—why was there no word?

"You said she felt the first pains this morning. Justine said it could be hours yet," Stephen said, infuriatingly reasonable. He held up the brandy again. "A drink will help, Brother, I am sure."

Nicholas finally gave in. He sank heavily into the chair across from Stephen and accepted a large snifter of the amber liquid. He took a long, bracing gulp. "This is the best bottle in my cellar, I think."

"Only the best for such a momentous occasion!" Stephen said cheerfully, draining his own glass. "Besides, I have nothing so fine at Fincote. I have to take every advantage of a visit to Scarnlea."

Just then, Emily's maid Mary hurried past the open door with a basin full of bloodied rags in her hands. Nicholas leaped up and ran to the doorway, but she was already gone. The house was still quiet.

"Damn it all," he muttered. "Why will no one tell me what is happening with my own wife?"

"Probably because nothing *is* happening yet, Nick," Stephen said. "You need to sit down and forget about this for a while."

"That is easy for you to say now. Wait until it is your child being born, your wife in danger. You will not be so sanguine then."

"You sound like our sisters, always pestering me to marry since they have you safely paired off." Stephen poured himself another brandy. "If this is what marriage does to a person, then I am better without it."

Nicholas leaned against the doorjamb, his arms crossed over his chest. "Well, what is this I hear from Charlotte about her friend Mae Halford? She tells me that you—"

But he was interrupted when Justine appeared in the corridor. Her hair was tousled, falling from its pins, her gown spotted with water and what looked horribly like blood. But she was smiling.

"Oh, Nicholas," she said softly. "You have a son!"

"I have a…" A son? A child who lived? "And Emily? Is she safe?"

"Yes, perfectly. Tired, of course, but quite well. The birth was very easy, especially for a first child."

"I must go to her," he said, already running down the corridor and taking the stairs two at a time. Emily was safe. But he had to see her for himself, to be absolutely sure.

"Nick, you can't go yet!" Justine called after him. "She is still abed."

"There is no stopping a man so desperately in love, Jussy," Stephen said. "Come, have a drink with me. We have a new heir to celebrate, God bless him. I'm saved from heirdom!"

Nicholas burst into Emily's chamber. It was crowded with women: his sister Charlotte, Amy Carroll, the plump, efficient midwife Emily insisted on over the London doctor, and Lady Moreby, who was recovered from her faint and beaming. The windows were closed and a fire blazed in the grate, making the palatial room warm and stuffy, thick with smoke and blood and lavender water.

Yet he could see only the bed, with its curtains and blankets pushed back, pillows piled high. Emily lay there, but unlike in the nightmares he had since she told him she was pregnant, she was not pale and still. Her cheeks were bright red and damp, her hair clinging to her damp brow. A tender, tired smile curved her lips as she stared down at the bundle in her arms.

A bundle that was shrieking like a tiny banshee.

Emily glanced up to find him standing there, and she held out her hand to him. Her green eyes glowed. "Oh, Nick, my darling. Come and look at him."

He went to her, his heart bursting with relief and hope, with a fierce happiness he had never known before. He clasped her hand in his, her blessedly warm hand, and kissed it before he looked down at the baby nestled in the crook of her arm.

He was red and wrinkled, his tiny face creased with terrible discontent at finding himself suddenly in this bright world. A tuft of blond hair covered the very top of his head, and when he looked up at them Nicholas could swear he saw a hint of emerald green in his eyes, just like his mother. He waved his fists furiously, a true Manning spirit.

"Isn't he beautiful?" Emily whispered.

"He looks a bit like an angry radish now," Nicholas said. "But I can see he is going to be heartbreakingly beautiful, like his mother."

"No, he looks like you, especially when you get angry about something." She smoothed her finger over the soft baby cheek and he immediately ceased his wailing. He went still and stared up at his parents with wide eyes. "See, he knows us. Probably from all those hours we spent talking and singing to him these last months."

"So he does," Nicholas said, fascinated by his son's face, his little fingers and the tiny button of his nose. He was alive, this baby, alive and well.

"I think we could name him Stephen," she said. "Your brother's gift to me of that horseshoe was a very thoughtful one. See what luck it has brought us? We have each other, and a child. We have so much love."

"Oh, Em. That wasn't luck. It was you, my beautiful wife. Only you." He gently kissed her lips, his heart bursting with all he had now. His wife and family, a life full of joy and love ahead. "You are all the luck I need."

Emily smiled up at him radiantly. "I hope so, Nick. Because we're going to need lots of luck indeed if we're going to have what I hope for now."

"And what is that?" he said, knowing that, whatever it was, he would go to the ends of the earth to get it for her.

"A daughter next year."

* * * * *

COMING NEXT MONTH FROM

HARLEQUIN®
HISTORICAL

Available March 29, 2011

- **THE BRIDE RAFFLE**
  by **Lisa Plumley**
  (Western)

- **DELECTABLY UNDONE!**
  by **Elizabeth Rolls, Michelle Willingham, Marguerite Kaye, Ashley Radcliff, Bronwyn Scott**
  (Anthology: Various time periods)
  Five sensual short stories specially selected from Harlequin Historical Undone! digital program.

- **WANTED: MAIL-ORDER MISTRESS**
  by **Deborah Hale**
  (Regency)
  Gentlemen of Fortune

- **HIGHLAND HEIRESS**
  by **Margaret Moore**
  (Regency)

HHCNM0311R

REQUEST YOUR FREE BOOKS!

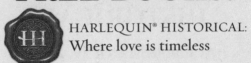

HARLEQUIN® HISTORICAL:
Where love is timeless

2 FREE NOVELS PLUS 2 **FREE GIFTS!**

YES! Please send me 2 FREE Harlequin® Historical novels and my 2 FREE gifts (gifts are worth about $10). After receiving them, if I don't wish to receive any more books, I can return the shipping statement marked "cancel." If I don't cancel, I will receive 6 brand-new novels every month and be billed just $4.94 per book in the U.S. or $5.49 per book in Canada. That's a savings of at least 18% off the cover price! It's quite a bargain! Shipping and handling is just 50¢ per book in the U.S. and 75¢ per book in Canada.* I understand that accepting the 2 free books and gifts places me under no obligation to buy anything. I can always return a shipment and cancel at any time. Even if I never buy another book from the Reader Service, the two free books and gifts are mine to keep forever.

246/349 HDN FC45

Name	(PLEASE PRINT)	
Address		Apt. #
City	State/Prov.	Zip/Postal Code

Signature (if under 18, a parent or guardian must sign)

Mail to the **Reader Service:**
IN U.S.A.: P.O. Box 1867, Buffalo, NY 14240-1867
IN CANADA: P.O. Box 609, Fort Erie, Ontario L2A 5X3

Not valid for current subscribers to Harlequin Historical books.

Want to try two free books from another line?
Call 1-800-873-8635 or visit www.ReaderService.com.

* Terms and prices subject to change without notice. Prices do not include applicable taxes. N.Y. residents add applicable sales tax. Canadian residents will be charged applicable taxes. Offer not valid in Quebec. This offer is limited to one order per household. All orders subject to credit approval. Credit or debit balances in a customer's account(s) may be offset by any other outstanding balance owed by or to the customer. Please allow 4 to 6 weeks for delivery. Offer available while quantities last.

Your Privacy—The Reader Service is committed to protecting your privacy. Our Privacy Policy is available online at www.ReaderService.com or upon request from the Reader Service.

We make a portion of our mailing list available to reputable third parties that offer products we believe may interest you. If you prefer that we not exchange your name with third parties, or if you wish to clarify or modify your communication preferences, please visit us at www.ReaderService.com/consumerschoice or write to us at Reader Service Preference Service, P.O. Box 9062, Buffalo, NY 14269. Include your complete name and address.

HH11

Selene wanted nothing to do with the father of her son, Alex; but Aristedes had other plans...that included them.

Read on for an sneak peek from
THE SARANTOS SECRET BABY by Olivia Gates,
available April 2011, only from Harlequin Desire.

"You were right to turn my marriage offer down," Aristedes said.

And Selene found her voice at last, found the words that would not betray the blow he'd dealt her. "Thanks for letting me know. You didn't have to come all the way here, though. You could have just let it go. I left yesterday with the understanding that this case is closed."

Before the hot needles behind her eyes could dissolve into an unforgivable display of stupidity and weakness, she began to close the door.

The door stopped against an immovable object. His flat palm.

"I can't accept that." His voice was low, leashed.

What did her tormentor mean now? Was he ending one game only to start another?

She raised eyes as bruised as her self-respect to his, found nothing there but solemnity and determination.

Before she could voice her confusion, he elaborated. "I never let anything go unless I'm certain it's unworkable. I realize I made you an unworkable offer, and that's why I'm withdrawing it. I'm here to offer something else. A workability study."

She leaned against the door, thankful for its support and partial shield. "Your son and I are not a business venture you can test for feasibility."

His gaze grew deeper, made her feel as if he was trying to delve into her mind, take control of it. "It's actually the other way around. I'm the one who would be tested."

She shook her head. "Why bother? I know—and *you* know—you're not workable. Not with me."

His spectacular eyebrows lowered over eyes she felt were emitting silver hypnosis. "You're right again. Neither you nor I have any reason to believe that isn't the truth. The only truth. It might be best for both you and Alex to never hear from me again, to forget I exist. But then again, maybe not. I'm only asking for the chance for both of us to find out for certain. You believe I'm unworkable in any personal relationship. I've lived my life based on that belief about myself. I never really had reason to question it. But I have one now. In fact, I have two."

Find out what happens in
THE SARANTOS SECRET BABY by Olivia Gates,
available April 2011, only from Harlequin Desire.

HARLEQUIN® HISTORICAL:
Where love is timeless

USA TODAY
BESTSELLING AUTHOR
MARGARET MOORE
INTRODUCES
Highland Heiress

SUED FOR BREACH OF PROMISE!

No sooner does Lady Moira MacMurdaugh breathe a sigh
of relief for avoiding a disastrous marriage to Dunbrachie's
answer to Casanova than she is served with a lawsuit! By
the very man who saved her from a vicious dog attack, no
less: solicitor Gordon McHeath. Torn between loyalty for a
friend and this beautiful woman who stirs him to ridiculous
distraction, Gordon knows he can't have it both ways....

But when sinister forces threaten to upend Lady Moira's world,
Gordon simply can't stand idly by and watch her fall!

**Available from Harlequin Historical
April 2011**

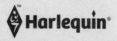

A *Romance* FOR EVERY MOOD™

www.eHarlequin.com

HH29638

Harlequin® *Blaze*™

red-hot reads

Sunny, sensual Hawaiian spring break…again!

Three best girlfriends are recapturing an amazing spring-break vacation they had a decade ago.

First on the beach is former attorney and all-around good girl Mia Butterfield. Meeting up with her boyfriend of old is a bust, so she's shocked when her hero turns out to be someone she'd never have expected…

Find out who it is in

SECOND TIME LUCKY

by acclaimed author

Debbi Rawlins

Available from Harlequin Blaze® April 2011

Part of the sensual miniseries,

Spring Break

Part 2: Delicious Do-Over (May)

Harlequin®

A Romance FOR EVERY MOOD™

www.eHarlequin.com

HB79607

MARGARET WAY

In the Australian Billionaire's Arms

Handsome billionaire David Wainwright isn't about to let his favorite uncle be taken for all he's worth by mysterious and undeniably attractive florist Sonya Erickson.

But David soon discovers that Sonya's no greedy gold digger. And as sparks sizzle between them, will the rugged Australian embrace the secrets of her past so they can have a chance at a future together?

***Don't miss this incredible new tale,
available in April 2011
wherever books are sold!***

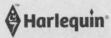